“Wha ... g to be all right.’

It wasn’ ... all right. She was the twisted minion of an evil god. What comfort could a mortal man like Ray really offer her? And yet his arms were the only safe place that she’d ever known. “You have no idea who I am or what I’ve done.”

“I know what you’ve done. I was there, remember?”

“I’m nothing, nothing but what he made me!”

“Don’t say that,” Ray murmured against her lips. “It’s not true.”

But it was true. And yet, as Ray rocked her, it wasn’t fear that surged through her.

She kissed him. Because it might be the last time she could.

She’d never thought that Ray was hers to keep, but she hadn’t realized before now that she wasn’t even her own to give.

Books by Stephanie Draven

* *Poisoned Kisses* #98
* *Mythica*

STEPHANIE DRAVEN

is currently a denizen of Baltimore, that city of ravens and purple night skies. She lives there with her favorite nocturnal creatures—three scheming cats and a deliciously wicked husband. And when she is not busy with dark domestic rituals, she writes her books.

A longtime lover of ancient lore, Stephanie enjoys reimagining myths for the modern age. She doesn't believe that true love is ever simple or without struggle, so her work tends to explore the sacred within the profane, the light under the loss and the virtue hidden in vice. She counts it amongst her greatest pleasures when, from her books, her readers learn something new about the world or about themselves.

DARK SINS AND DESERT SANDS

STEPHANIE DRAVEN

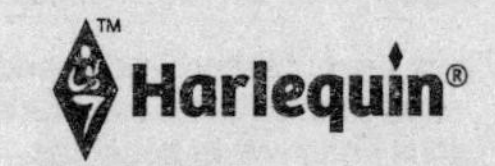

TORONTO NEW YORK LONDON
AMSTERDAM PARIS SYDNEY HAMBURG
STOCKHOLM ATHENS TOKYO MILAN MADRID
PRAGUE WARSAW BUDAPEST AUCKLAND

Recycling programs
for this product may
not exist in your area.

ISBN-13: 978-0-373-61871-2

DARK SINS AND DESERT SANDS

This edition published by arrangement with Harlequin Books S.A.

For questions and comments about the quality of this book please contact us at Customer_eCare@Harlequin.ca.

www.Harlequin.com

Printed in U.S.A.

Dear Reader,

The Minotaur was a bastard child born to a cursed queen. His mother rejected him as a monster and the cuckolded king locked him in a labyrinth, giving him sacrificial children to eat. In the end, it was the Minotaur's own half sister, Ariadne, who helped to engineer his demise.

For me, the symbolism of the story seems obvious. Our darkest secrets can never truly be locked away, and always come with a price—whether it's a sacrifice of our innocents or our innocence. In this novel, I've envisioned a much happier ending for my Minotaur, but I hope that, like the heroine of this book, you ask the crucial questions that need to be asked.

I love hearing from readers, so please stop by www.stephaniedraven.com.

Yours,

Stephanie Draven

ACKNOWLEDGMENTS

I'm indebted to my friend Ibrahim C. for shedding light on the various beliefs and practices of American Muslims, but any misunderstanding or cultural insensitivity in this book is my fault, not his. Thanks also to my agent, Jennifer Schober, and my editor, Tara Gavin. To the Romance Divas. To Sheila Accongio, Leah Barber, Lisa Christie, Sabrina Darby, Inez Kelley, Kai Lawson and Christine Rovet. To my husband, who made this—and every other book I write—possible. To my sister, for her inventive support. And to Neil Gaiman for *American Gods*. Though I invented most of the riddles in this book with the help of Inez Kelley and Adam Dray, I'm also indebted to Phil Cousineau's collection, *A World Treasury of Riddles*.

DEDICATION

To my brother-in-law and sister-in-law for their service. And to my parents, who gave me a moral compass with which to navigate the world.

Prologue

The eyes are the windows to the soul.

The old proverb was wrong, Ray thought. Eyes aren't windows to the soul; they're doorways. And through those doorways, Ray Stavrakis could cross into another person's mind. Into memories. Into dreams. Into fears. Into the darkest corners of the human soul.

Unfortunately, Ray had never seen the eyes of the man he was trailing, and, in the dark, he could only glimpse the back of his victim's head.

The old Syrian neighborhood in Aleppo was a confusing labyrinth of twisting cobblestone streets and covered bazaars, but even without light from the occasional hanging lamp, Ray knew his way as if it were mapped in his blood. After all, Aleppo was part Greek and part Arab—just like him. His ancestors had settled in Aleppo after leaving Crete; he should've been comfortable here, but so soon escaped from his dungeon, every sensation stung.

The faraway horns of taxis in the distant marketplace pained him like trumpets blaring directly into his ears. Someone in one of the apartments above was smoking a hookah pipe and the smoke floated down from an open kitchen window, mixing with the heady scent of oregano. The smell sickened him; it was as if, having spent two years in a box where the stink of sweat and blood and urine were his only companions, he couldn't bear any other odor now.

Swallowing his bile, he stalked his prey through the narrow, shadowed streets, his long leather coat snapping at his heels with every step. The man he followed walked faster, slipping a little on the cobblestones. The street was slick with the evening's dew, which mixed with moss to form a primordial ooze. Still, Ray's footsteps kept pace, clopping steadily behind, closing in.

Bathed in the faint yellow light of a street lamp, the man turned to look over his shoulder. Ray saw the furious whites of the Syrian's eyes—the threshold—and those dark pupils beckoned. Ray leaned forward, ready to seize the man's mind, but something made him hesitate. Maybe he wasn't yet the monster they tried to make of him. He wanted to give the man a chance. Just one.

As his prey opened his mouth to shout for help, Ray shoved him beneath the stone archway, his broad forearm at his victim's throat. The Syrian struggled, barely choking out in Arabic, "Who are you? What do you want?"

The Syrian's voice was the sound of petty tyranny, the sound Ray had learned to obey for his survival. It was almost enough to make him quake. But Ray reminded himself that he was free now. He wasn't the one trying to run away. "Don't you recognize me?" he snarled at his former prison guard. "Then again, you did put a bag over my head."

The first hint of recognition showed in the man's eyes. "I know you...Rayhan Stavrakis."

It was good to hear his name. A name gave him back a little of his humanity. After all, in the dungeon, he'd had no name. They'd only ever called him by number. He watched his former guard struggle, trying to catch his breath. Ray saw the man's fingers twitch, inching for the pistol in his pocket. So much for trying to do things the nice way.

The guard shuddered. "How did you escape?"

Just like this, Ray thought. Focusing his powers, he reached into the periphery of the Syrian's mind and seized control. Ray had escaped by turning his captors into his puppets. Now he'd stay alive the same way. "Drop the gun," Ray commanded, feeling the slightly dizzying rush of his power. "And give me your wallet."

To the guard's obvious astonishment, he obeyed Ray's commands. The pistol hit the stone and skittered away as the man reached for his wallet and thrust it into Ray's hand. All the while, his eyes were wide. "How are you doing this?"

Ray couldn't have answered that question even if he wanted to. "Where are you keeping my family? Tell me, or I swear I'll end you right here."

The guard's astonishment turned to fear. Even in the pale light, Ray could see that the blood was draining from the man's face. "We don't have them!" the Syrian cried. "They're back in your country. Safe. We only told you we captured them to make you talk." It was what the others had said, too. "I'm telling you the truth," the guard insisted. "What else do you want from me?"

At this question, Ray heard himself snort into the dark, low and bestial. There were so many things he wanted. He wanted the past two years of his life back. He wanted to clear his name. He wanted to know who had accused him of working with the enemy. But the Syrians didn't know why his own government had wanted him tortured, nor had they cared.

"I want the woman," Ray finally said. Every day he'd spent in the dungeon, he'd held her face in his mind, obsessed. He remembered her questions and her cool-eyed stare. He hadn't had these powers then; he'd been at her mercy and he remembered how her questions inexplicably, impossibly, were *worse* than torture. Most of all, he remembered the way she'd toyed with his emotions. "The psychologist. The one who interrogated me. I want her name. Her *real* name."

The guard's mouth tightened into a thin, infuriating line of silence.

Ray had already given the man one chance. He wouldn't give him another. As the anger welled, Ray's scalp felt as if it were being pierced by some outgrowth of bone. His feet seemed to harden into iron hoofs. He never knew if it was an actual transformation, or just the sensation that accompanied his power. He only knew that when he bucked forward, he was able to ram through the pathetic psychological bulwark his guard threw up against the invasion.

Then neither man was simply standing on the street; they were both inside the Syrian's mind.

"Get *out!*" the Syrian shrieked, but Ray was unmoved. The maze of the man's mindscape wasn't complicated. To the left, a shadowy upbringing of poverty. To the right, his secret fondness for pornography and his fear of scorpions. It shouldn't be difficult to find the information Ray was looking for.

"Wh-what are you? Just a bull. Just a creature," the guard stammered, as if to reassure himself. He wasn't the first to mistake Ray for an animal. Perhaps he wasn't mistaken at all. Lowering his head so that his sharpened horns twisted like glinting daggers toward the man's heart, Ray chased the panting and terrified guard through his memories, ramming open another door, and then another. At last, he cornered the Syrian in the memory of the room with the steel floor.

The air puffed out of Ray's nostrils in an angry cloud of rage. Here, in the guard's memory, Ray's torture lived vividly. Ray saw himself on the table, blindfolded and strapped down, his hardened muscles bracing and twitching as the guard swung a set of bloody cables in a hissing arc through the air until they broke with a snap on the bleeding palms of his shackled hands. The well-aimed blows had felt like a jolt of electricity. Agony had jumped up his arms and exploded in his temples. Ray remembered. This torture made the toughest men scream and he'd been no exception. He watched now as his memory-self twisted and writhed, rattling the chains against the table in torment.

He'd always wondered if his tormentor felt any guilt or regret. Now that he saw it through the guard's eyes, he knew the answer. No guilt, no remorse. Not even the coldness of duty. Instead, he felt the man's sadistic pleasure at the memory, sickly sweet, almost sexual in nature, and it stoked his rage.

"What do you want?" the guard pleaded again. "What more do you want?"

"I told you," Ray said. "I want the woman."

"She was a civilian contractor working with the Americans. I don't know her name!"

But he did. The memory was filed away in the cluttered recesses of the Syrian's mind and Ray was able to find it. Ah, there she was. *Dr. Layla Bahset.* How could someone so exquisitely beautiful have taken any part in such ugliness? He'd have to find her and ask her himself. Ray would be the interrogator this time, and she'd help him clear his name if it was the last thing she did. *The very last thing.*

The Syrian lingered in the torture room, obviously enjoying the memory. Inside the mindscape, Ray could make the Syrian feel anything. Ray could make him gasp for air and think he was dying, so he grabbed him by the throat and the man stopped breathing. But unlike the Syrian guard, Ray didn't enjoy the pain of others, so he relaxed his mental hold.

The man came up gasping, without any apparent gratitude. "I'm not sorry for what we did to you, Rayhan," the guard rasped. "I liked how you screamed. And why shouldn't I have enjoyed it? For once, they gave me a real traitor to punish. A man who cannot decide if he's one of *us,* or one of *them.*"

It was a common, but foolish taunt. As if Ray couldn't be both an American and a Muslim—not that he believed in God anymore. "You enjoyed my screams?"

The guard wheezed. "So much. And when they

catch you and throw you back in that box, I'll make you scream again. You'll beg—"

"Shut up!" Ray's teeth clenched, his temper a haze of red blood. This same man had burned his inner thighs with cigarettes and had locked him in a coffin for days on end. Now Ray shoved him against the blood-spattered wall of the imaginary torture room and growled.

The guard laughed, an edge of fear in it. "When they catch you, I'll break each bone in your hands and feet and make you thank me like the dog you are."

Ray felt himself snap, pulling the Syrian forward by the neck.

The guard gasped over the fingers clamped around his imagined windpipe. "Where are you taking me?"

Ray didn't answer; he just dragged the man like the carcass of a hunted animal. The guard began to scream even before he realized it was the room with the scorpions. Ray had glimpsed it, the memory of a boy playing in the sand, stung again and again by the creature's venomous stinger. Perhaps it was a real memory or only a childhood nightmare. It didn't matter either way. Hauling the man to the door, Ray threw him inside.

There, in anticipation of his fear, the scrambling scorpions multiplied and swarmed over the guard's face and hands. The man struggled to escape them, his mouth open in silent horror. He tried to pull himself up from the depthless sandpit of his own terror, but before he could, Ray slammed and locked the door.

On the dark streets of Aleppo, one man slumped under a lamplight, clutching desperately at his face. His eyes rolled back and his lips went blue with fear as he screamed incoherently about scorpions. The other man—the one in the dark leather coat—dabbed at the rivulet of blood that dripped from his nose. "*Dr. Layla Bahset,*" he murmured, then turned and walked away.

Chapter 1

Questions to try, answer or die, what am I?

Layla Bahset had a secret; she didn't know who she was.

Oh, she knew her name, but standing here with her feet in the timeless sand, staring up at the persimmon sunrise over the Mojave Desert, she remembered nothing of herself before she'd come here. Beyond the past two years of her life, Layla's mind was bare—every glimpse of memory bounced like tumbleweed out of her grasp. She remembered no family. She remembered no friends. She didn't even remember where she'd lived before moving to Nevada.

The certificates on the walls of her office told her that she was a licensed therapist; her diplomas boasted the finest schools. But she couldn't remember attending them. She was a riddle with no answer—a complete mystery to herself—and the one rare puzzle she didn't want to solve.

As the dry morning winds whipped hair into her face, it prickled like the needles of a cactus, but Layla didn't mind. For in spite of all the things she didn't know about herself, there was one thing of which she was absolutely certain: she belonged to the desert.

It wasn't just that her skin was the color of golden sand and that her hair was as black and glossy as a scorpion's shell. It wasn't even that her eyes had been described as a lush green oasis. It was that when she looked into the desert, she felt as if the desert looked back.

Even out here, alone in the dunes, she knew that someone was watching her. She didn't know who he was or what he wanted. She only knew that he was closing in on her like a storm, getting darker, and closer, every day.

"Tell me how you felt the last time it happened," Layla prompted and her patient twitched like a frightened warhorse, about to rear up. Some people might be surprised at how shy the eighteen-year-old art student was, given that his gregarious father was a Pulitzer Prize–winning war reporter, but Layla's heart went out to him. "Tell me, Carson. I want to help you."

The young man just shoved his hands down into his pockets like he was totally lost in the world. "You're gonna laugh at me."

"No. I only want to help you," Layla said in her most soothing voice, just as everything about her office was meant to soothe. The neutral colors, the soft rug and the nondescript lamps had all been chosen carefully. "I promise, I won't laugh."

Carson stared out the office window and Layla followed his gaze. Her office had a spectacular view of Las Vegas and the mammoth mountain ridges that encircled the city like a fortress, cutting it off from the ordinary world. By daylight, the flat expanse of Vegas seemed almost commonplace with its craggy maze of middling skyscrapers and tired tourists stumbling out of the casinos like bleary-eyed vagrants. But at night, Las Vegas would be different. The lights would sparkle even before darkness chased away dusk. Then the tourists and the gamblers would be gods again, their eyes clear but for the avarice. At night, the visitors and the city's residents would mingle on the streets together to party. There would be an atmosphere of festival, the magic stuff of life. But unless she could help young Carson Tremblay, he would never get to experience anything like that.

"My dad thinks I'm on drugs or just doing it for attention," he said.

"Are you?" Layla asked.

Carson shook his head. "I guess I thought I was just some kind of moody artist who gets off on destroying shit. You know, like those rockers who smash up their guitars? I even wondered if maybe I was allergic to paint. But it doesn't just happen to me in galleries or studios. The last time it happened, I was visiting the Grand Canyon with my family and my girlfriend. Well, she's my ex-girlfriend now. I scared her off with what I did."

"What triggered it?" Layla asked.

Carson's lower lip wobbled. "It wasn't fear of heights

or fear of falling down the cliffside, if that's what you're thinking. It's just that when I looked at the enormity of the canyon—the jagged rocks and the water-carved curves—I picked up the tire iron and started swinging it blindly."

It was hard to imagine a gentle soul like Carson Tremblay wielding a tire iron. The young man hadn't hurt anyone, but he'd destroyed his father's car, upset his family, and scared away the girl he loved. "Were you angry, Carson? Did something make you so angry at your father that you'd want to smash his windshield and the headlights?"

"Yeah. No. I dunno. My dad wanted us all to look at it, you know? He's gotta know everything. He's gotta uncover everything. I guess that's his job as a reporter. But I was just staring at the rocks and the scrub. The wildlife and the barrenness. It was everything right and wrong with the world, and my heart started pounding."

Layla's heart started pounding, too. Thinking of the desert. Thinking of the yearning.

"I heard this rush in my ears and I went weak with a cold sweat," Carson said. "I tried to close my eyes, like I couldn't bear to look. It was just too..." He struggled to find the word.

"Beautiful," Layla breathed, finishing for him.

At last, Carson met her eyes. "Yeah. Exactly. Too beautiful. Can things really be too beautiful?"

Layla was sure of it. Things could be too beautiful. Too delicious. Too pleasurable. Desires were dangerous. Passion unlocked things in a person that might otherwise be best left undisturbed and unexamined.

Layla cursed herself. She shouldn't have let her mind go there. Without any real memories of her own, she seldom brought her own issues into therapy. It was one of the reasons she was very good at this, she told herself. One of the reasons she justified keeping her memory loss a secret. This way, it could be all about her clients. She could help people. *Heal* people. "Carson, you may be suffering from an unusual case of Stendhal Syndrome."

"I looked that up on Google," Carson said, meandering around her office as if he couldn't make himself sit still. He stopped by her bookshelves, running his fingers over the spines of her neatly organized books. "It's where tourists faint or freak out after seeing great works of art, right? But I told you, it doesn't just happen in a studio, and even if it did, I'm an artist. I can't avoid art. I've got an exhibit this week. There's got to be a cure."

Some therapists would recommend a psychiatrist who would almost assuredly prescribe antidepressants, Layla thought. But that would treat his symptoms, not the underlying cause. Besides, she worried about deadening his emotions. She didn't want to turn Carson into someone like her. Someone numb to everything but the fear. Someone who couldn't even remember herself and didn't want to.

"Carson, I think we're going to try something called trauma-focused cognitive-behavioral therapy, which is a fancy way of saying that we're going to slowly expose you to the trauma until you have a more balanced perception."

"I don't know what any of that means," Carson said. "But I guess you know what you're talking about. I mean, you must get some real crazies who come in here."

Layla glanced up to see that he'd plucked a piece of paper off of her shelf. Carson handed it to her. "I like to think I'd never really hurt anybody, but if I ever get like the guy who wrote this, I hope you have me locked up."

Layla didn't recognize the note or the handwriting, which spelled out the words in bold strokes upon a slip of paper that was crisp and textured like papyrus. But she recognized a threat when she saw one: *I'm always watching you, Layla, and when I come for you, there will be a reckoning.*

As she crumpled the note in her hand, her heart hammered so loudly in her chest that she worried her patient would hear it. All this time, she'd been half-convinced that her nighttime rituals of checking her locks were simply what any sensible woman who lived alone would do. But now she knew her dread wasn't imagined. It was all real, scrawled in bold black ink.

He'd been here. He'd slipped past her vigilant assistant and her locked doors. Whoever he was, he'd been in this very office. And he was coming for her.

It took Layla several long minutes to regain her composure. If she let her mask slip, her patient might see how terrified she was, and it might ruin all the progress they'd made together. "You'll never become like that, Carson, and no one is going to lock you up."

Fortunately, they were interrupted by Layla's efficient—and officious—assistant Isabel who tapped lightly on the door to let them know that the session was over. While Layla tried to hide her shaking hands, Isabel marshaled Carson out of the office, then returned with a cup of tea and the newspaper, folded over to the crossword puzzle.

It was a nice gesture, but Isabel wasn't normally the kind of assistant who catered to her, which meant that Layla must not be hiding her emotions as well as she hoped. "What's the occasion?"

"Feliz cumpleaños!" Isabel crowed, and just like magic, she produced a lone muffin with a lopsided birthday candle on top. "Happy birthday, Dr. Bahset!"

Was it her birthday? Layla fought the urge to check her driver's license, which was the only way she could have known for sure. Layla hadn't celebrated her birthday last year and her confusion must have been obvious, because Isabel added, "And don't fuss at me that you don't like sweets. It's a low-fat bran muffin. Bland and tasteless, just how you like it!"

Layla *did* prefer bland. Food was just fuel, after all. "Thank you, Isabel. It was so nice of you to remember."

Isabel clucked as she lit the candle atop Layla's bran muffin. "Who else would remember?"

That wasn't quite fair. Over the past two years—the only two years of her life she could remember—Layla had made friends. Well, colleagues really. And she occasionally dated. There were other people in her life, but admittedly, probably none of them knew whether or not it was her birthday. After all, she'd become a master at deflection, always turning conversations away from herself and away from her past.

"Let's celebrate tonight!" Isabel said. "Come out with me and the girls."

Layla was tempted. After reading that threatening note, she didn't want to be alone tonight. But Isabel was the very definition of a social butterfly with a swarm of adoring fans always in her wake. Layla wasn't sure she could handle quite so much company. "I'm really tired lately."

"Don't be loco. Come with us to amateur hour. I'll teach you to dance up on stage." Isabel, who was studying to be a sex therapist, managed to say this as if it weren't scandalous at all.

"No, thank you. I prefer not to be paid for my skills in dollar bills."

"Ha! I think you got other plans. Is Dr. Jaffe taking you out tonight?"

"Boundaries, Isabel. Boundaries," Layla warned, picking up her pen. She always did crosswords in pen.

"*Chica,* you'd have more fun if you didn't have all those boundaries."

Layla didn't dare reprimand Isabel for her sass. After all, Isabel not only helped Layla keep track of her day-to-day life, but stood as a living reminder of all the lies she'd spun to cover the things she didn't know. Isabel was the first person Layla had fooled into thinking that she wasn't an amnesiac, and because of Isabel, it was easier to fool the rest. On the other hand, sometimes it seemed as if Isabel wasn't fooled at all. "You're sure not dressed for a hot date tonight, Dr. Bahset..."

Layla wouldn't have the first idea how to dress for a hot date. She owned a closet full of dark skirts and high-necked blouses. Isabel, by contrast, was *always* dressed as if she had a hot date. Today Isabel was wearing a curve-hugging suit and leopard print heels that weren't entirely office-appropriate but made her look like some kind of sex goddess.

Isabel handed Layla a lovely box from a fashionable

Las Vegas boutique. "Here. A present for you. Open it, then I'm gonna sing."

"You didn't have to get me anything," Layla started to say.

But Isabel held up her hand. "Trust me, I did. You need somebody to put a little sexy in your step!"

Neatly folded beneath sparkling tissue paper was a siren-red dress. Layla pulled it out, laying it over her knees. "It's lovely, thank you." And it was. Given Isabel's own taste in clothing, it was a remarkably restrained choice: a knee-length, sleeveless sheath with delicate shirring at the neckline. Layla didn't own anything like it.

Isabel grinned. "Wear that on your date with Dr. Jaffe and he'll want to give you birthday spankings."

"Isabel!"

Isabel laughed and in spite of everything, Layla couldn't help but laugh with her. Her incorrigible assistant had that effect on everyone, so as far as Layla was concerned, Isabel could say, do and *wear* whatever she wanted.

"Happy birthday to you…" Isabel sang, her voice a Spanish purr. But when Layla leaned over to blow out the candle on her bran muffin, Isabel stopped her. "Wait. What are you gonna wish for?"

That was a good question. Layla already had plenty of money, though she had no idea where it came from. She had a successful practice, but not successful enough to justify her fat bank account. So, what *should* she wish for? Did she dare wish for her memories back?

"You're thinking too hard," Isabel scolded. Then she

leaned forward, pursed her ruby-red lips, and blew out the candle. "There, I made a wish for you!"

Layla put the dress back in the box and tried to make her desk as neat as it was before Hurricane Isabel arrived. "I'm afraid to even ask what you wished for me."

"Just because *I* can't find a man who can keep up with me doesn't mean *you* have to settle," Isabel said, sashaying toward the waiting room. "All I'm saying is that you shouldn't be surprised if a new man comes walking into your life. And unlike Dr. Jaffe, this one will actually be your type!"

"I'm pretty sure I don't have a *type,*" Layla assured her. But did she?

She couldn't remember anything from her past. No husbands, lovers, boyfriends. She was only dating Dr. Nate Jaffe because healthy adult women had relationships. The aging psychiatrist was interested in her and it'd seemed easier to go to bed with him than to say no. She was fond of him, but not more than that. She couldn't let it be more because whatever lurked in Layla's past, she knew it was dangerous, and she didn't want anyone else to have to pay the price.

Ray was home. Well, he was stateside anyway. For the past two years, he'd imagined himself climbing up the steps of his mother's front porch—the one she swept clean and adorned with pink petunias. He'd imagined his nephews throwing open the front door and running into his arms to welcome him. Instead, he'd had to sneak back into the country under an assumed identity, greeted only by the bells and whistles of the slot machines in McCarran International Airport.

Las Vegas was where he'd find Dr. Layla Bahset, so here he was.

The first thing Ray did was rent a cheap motel room that accepted payment in cash. Now he stood before the grimy bathroom mirror, which was steamy from his shower. Staring at his reflection, he tried to recognize himself. As a soldier, he'd always been fit, but the musculature of his hulking shoulders was something entirely new. He'd wasted away in a dungeon for two years; he should've been gaunt and frail. Instead, his biceps bulged and his muscles strained over the broadness of his chest.

But not everything about him had changed. He still had the marks of his captivity. The burns, the cuts, the lashes. Some parts of his body were a gnarled web of scar tissue that made him shudder to look at. Ever since he'd escaped, he'd been going on pure adrenaline. Now that was subsiding in favor of exhaustion, and his limbs felt heavy and sluggish. He thought about sleeping, but then he'd be at the mercy of his nightmares. If he wasn't dreaming about being locked in a box, then he was dreaming about his brother's suicide or he was dreaming about Afghanistan. The hail of bullets. Screaming at his buddy to stop shooting. All the blood…

Best to stay awake. At least for a little longer.

He had a palpable need to hear his family's voices and make sure they were okay. He'd never thought he'd miss his mother's nagging or his father's sardonic comments, but he did. He only hoped they'd be happy to hear from him even though he was a fugitive. No. He couldn't even call them. The last thing he wanted was to incriminate or shame his family, which meant there was only one person in the world that Ray could contact.

Jack Bouchier answered on the third ring. "Howdy!"

"It's me," Ray said.

There was a shocked pause on the other end of the line until his old war buddy finally said, "Naw…it can't be. Ray?"

It was almost too much to hear his name spoken by someone who knew him when he was a soldier, when he was still a man and not some kind of monster. Emotion welled up in Ray's throat until he wasn't sure he'd be able to speak over it. He had to squeeze his eyes shut. "Yeah. It's me."

Jack's slow and lazy Southern drawl suddenly snapped to stiff attention. "Where the hell are you, brother?"

They *had* been brothers. Brothers-in-arms and more than that, too. There was no one Ray trusted more. But even though Jack was a good ol' boy from Virginia with ancestors he could trace back to the Jamestown settlers, that didn't mean Homeland Security wouldn't pick up the call. "Not on the phone," Ray said.

Jack breathed heavy into the phone. "They wouldn't tell us what happened to you. You just didn't show up for muster one mornin' and when we asked, they told us to mind our own business."

Ray's knees wobbled, so he sat on the edge of his motel room bed. "Just tell me about my family. Are they okay?"

"They're fine, Ray. I ain't gonna tell you they're right as rain, but they're fine as they could be under the circumstances. When I came back stateside, I helped

’em hire a lawyer for you, but you done disappeared. They’re scared outta their wits for you.”

Ray bet they were. His parents were immigrants. They’d fled from Syria and even though they’d always taught Ray that America was different—that America was a place of laws and tolerance—he wasn’t sure they ever truly felt safe. “Tell my family that I’m innocent and I’m alive. I’ll owe you one.”

“You don’t owe me shit,” Jack said. “Not after what you done for me.”

Ray didn’t like to think about what he’d done for Jack, so he didn’t say anything.

“I owe you big, Ray, and you know it, so what else do you need?”

“I need you to believe that whatever anybody says about me, I never worked with the enemy. You’ve gotta tell my family that and don’t do it on the phone.”

“You got it. Then I’ll come get you. Just give me an address and I’ll jump in the pickup.”

“Can’t.” Ray rubbed his neck, the image of beautiful but cold green eyes dancing mockingly in his mind. “There’s someone I need to take care of first.”

It wasn’t difficult for Ray to find Layla Bahset’s office. She hadn’t gone to any trouble to hide her identity. She was listed right there in the Las Vegas phone book like she was just an ordinary woman and not evil incarnate. This had probably been a mistake—to come directly to his interrogator’s office in the middle of the day. They’d have him on the security cameras and someone might be able to identify him. But unless he planned to stalk Layla Bahset down the street, like he'd done with the guard in Aleppo, this was the easiest way to handle things.

"Hola," the woman at the desk purred, eyeing him with unabashed interest while her fingers arranged a vase of flowers. "My name is Isabel. And aren't you just trouble in a tight black T-shirt..."

She was a glamazon with cinnamon-brown eyes, Latin curves in all the right places, and a smile that could cause a war or two. Ray felt himself flush under her magnetic charm. She was sexy as hell and it'd been a long time, but Ray couldn't let himself be distracted by flirtation. He'd come here for Layla Bahset. He'd come here for justice. He'd come here to clear his name. Nothing less would satisfy.

"So, will the doc see me, or not?" Ray asked.

"Lucky for you, Dr. Bahset's a workaholic. I'm sure she'll squeeze you in, *Papi.*"

Were they already to the nickname stage? "Thanks, *Cha-cha,*" Ray returned, swiping a piece of candy from her desk. He popped it in his mouth hoping the sugar would steady him, but the intense sweetness put him even further on edge.

Dr. Bahset's office door was half-open, and he took a moment to watch her. Was it just Ray's imagination, or had he been in prison so long that every woman looked like a goddess today? Layla Bahset was as flawless as he remembered her, and Ray found that comforting. If a wisp of her black hair had escaped the confines of her severely upswept coiffure, it might've given him pause. If her lips had been slightly chapped instead of delicately glossed, he might've hesitated. But she was perfect. Beneath the demure white blouse and dark skirt, there wasn't a single crack in the facade through which her humanity might have shone through.

Yet here she was, in the flesh.

It all happened in slow motion—fractional increments of time. He stepped into her office and locked the door, hearing the satisfying sound of the bolt sliding into place. Layla Bahset looked up, her emerald eyes disarmingly and deceptively warm. He remembered those eyes, as green as the Nile and as timeless as the pyramids. Eyes so penetrating and pitiless that his throat had constricted with every question she'd asked. Now he made himself just as hard and pitiless. His boots rapidly closed the distance between them and her smile faded. His coat caught the edge of a low end table and overturned it just as she rose to her feet to call for help.

Then he had her.

Kicking her chair out of the way, he slammed her against the bookshelf and felt her go boneless with fear. Rage blinded him as he wrapped his hands around her throat and he struggled not to let the beast in him take over. He reminded himself that he wasn't here to choke her; he just needed to keep her from screaming. He let her exhale and felt the heat of her breath on his face. Her palms flattened against his chest to fend him off but the rest of her was surprisingly warm and yielding. He could actually feel the heat of her through his shirt. She smelled like something sweet and fragile, like a desert blossom. Like something he could trample and destroy.

Damn. It had been a mistake to touch her. More than two years had passed since he'd touched anything so soft, and the intimacy of skin against skin might be his undoing. Her eyes were closed, lips trembling. He could almost taste the salt of her fear-induced perspiration. It should've given him a feeling of satisfaction or mastery, but it only made him hungry for her. Urges he no longer knew he had clawed their way to the surface. With his blood running hot and his knee between hers, he nearly forgot what he'd come here for.

"Look at me, damn it," he growled close to her ear until her pulse quickened beneath his fingertips and her eyelashes fluttered open. "I bet you thought you'd never see me again, did you? Take a good look and hope it's not your last."

Her eyes frantically searched his face as if for something she might recognize, and it infuriated him. *Her* face was burned into his memory. Her questions were branded into his flesh. That she could have forgotten him was unthinkable. He let his eyes blaze a path to the edge of her mind, but he was so angry he could barely focus on controlling her. The top button of her white blouse had come undone, baring her collarbone, and he wanted to press his mouth into the hollow of it. After everything she'd done to him, she was finally at his mercy. He could have her. He could show her his strength and power now that he wasn't in chains. The desire to *take* her was so strong that it actually shook him out of his stupor.

He wasn't *that* kind of monster, after all.

He let his grip relax, fingers splayed over her shoulder as she took a desperate breath. "You're not going to scream, okay?" She nodded and in spite of his admittedly tenuous hold over her mind, she didn't scream. She didn't claw at him either. Instead, she did the most astonishing thing. Her delicate hand slipped over the taut sinews of his forearm in a caress. "Let me help you," she whispered.

He couldn't remember the last time another human being had touched him in gentleness, and the intensity of it was unbearable. *Unbearable.* He was an escaped creature of the black dungeon. Perhaps he wasn't meant for the sounds, scents, or gentle sensations of the world anymore. Perhaps he knew only pain now. Her touch left him unbalanced. Unsteady. He had to pull away. "Sit down at your desk," he commanded, but he wasn't sure if it was his power that compelled her or just the fear.

"I want to help you," she repeated, settling into her chair.

"You didn't help me when I was in Syria," he snarled. "You just asked me all those questions, and they'd swirl in my head like you were some kind of sorceress. Like you'd bewitched me. And when I wouldn't answer, you'd send me back to have my hands and feet beaten until they bled. Of course, that was before you tried to make me think you actually cared about me..."

She shook her head as if she didn't know what he was talking about and it made him even angrier. "Oh, give it a second and you'll remember me. You see, everything has a price, sweetheart, and your bill has just come due."

Chapter 2

What can you hold without using your hands?

Layla couldn't seem to catch her breath. The stranger had told her not to scream, and she hadn't. He told her to sit down, and she'd done as he bid, like a marionette. He seemed to have some *power* over her. Something that she couldn't explain. Even now, it was as if he could silence her and keep her from calling out for help.

That wasn't possible, she told herself. It was her job to help the mentally ill, not become one of them. Was it just the fear or the lack of oxygen that had her thinking this way? The situation was so volatile, so unpredictable, so outrageous, that her mind must be suggestible. Hypnotists took advantage of such suggestibility all the time. She just had to calm down and analyze this situation rationally.

The stranger obviously felt persecuted. It was a

classic symptom of schizophrenia, but was it possible that she *did* know him? Was *this* was the man who had been stalking her?

Layla studied him more carefully. He was dark like an Arab or maybe a Greek, with full and familiar lips peeking out from beneath the stubble on his face. Surely if she knew this man, she couldn't forget those features. He looked like some desert warrior, some Far East prince, but he spoke like an American, without even a hint of an accent. He was also large, with overly broad shoulders and big hands, but it was his eyes that Layla fixated on. Surely she would remember eyes like those, dark and burning like coal.

"Ray, is that your name?" Layla began. "My assistant said—"

"Remember me, damn you!" His shout reverberated throughout the room like a clap of thunder. It vibrated through her as he stared into her eyes. Too late, she tried to throw up a defense against the invasion of her mind.

And then he was inside her.

Sand. In all the minds Ray had explored, in all the labyrinths in which he'd hunted down his prey, he'd never encountered a mindscape like this. Layla Bahset's was nothing but silence and sand. It had to be some kind of facade, a mirage. Where were her memories? Trudging through the dunes, Ray struggled to find the sights and sounds to tell him what she knew.

She must be blocking him, somehow. It couldn't be possible for a woman with a life, with a past, to have an empty inner world. Up ahead, he noticed a darkened shape on the horizon, sand-swept and half-submerged.

He squinted into the imaginary sunlight and pushed forward. What the hell was it? A triangle? No. A *pyramid.* Was that where she'd locked everything away?

Ray scrambled through the sand, focused on finding an entrance, when he felt the ground go soft beneath him. She'd buried all her secrets beneath this arid desert, and now she was trying to bury him along with them. The desert swallowed his legs, yanking down. Startled, Ray fumbled his way back, trying to follow the thread of consciousness back into waking reality. She was still fighting him. He sank deeper and deeper into the sand. But Ray had come too far—been through too much—to give up now. Did she think she could stop him? She could just forget it!

Forget it!

Those were the words echoing in Layla's mind when she was wrenched out of some kind of hypnotic state. It was Isabel's insistent knock from the other side of the door that jarred her back into the present. "Dr. Bahset?" Isabel called, her voice shrill. "*Que pasa?* Everything all right?"

Layla startled to realize that she was sitting across from a very attractive man and in the tension of the moment, she felt her cheeks burn. What had just happened? The stranger took great gulps of air, as if he'd been drowning. Blood dripped from his nose and she noticed that an end table had been overturned. Had he tripped over it?

The pounding on her office door became louder. "Dr. Bahset, I have a key, you know!"

The bleeding stranger stood, staggering a little as he

did so. "This isn't the end of it," he told her, accusation in his eyes. "I'll be back for you."

So it must be *him*. The man who had broken into her office and left her a threatening note. The man she'd feared for two years now. So why didn't she run from him? Instead, all she wanted to do was help him.

"You're bleeding," she whispered, pulling a tissue from the box on her desk.

He took it, their fingers touching softly, just as Isabel threw open the door. Then the three of them stood there awkwardly until the stranger brushed past Isabel and walked away without a word.

"Hay Dios!" Isabel said, eyeing the overturned end table. "What happened?"

"I—I have no idea," Layla croaked. Her throat felt raw and sore, but she had no idea why.

This had never happened before. It was true that she didn't remember her past, but she remembered everything since the day she first arrived in Vegas. There'd been no gaps. No blackouts. At least not until now.

Isabel came to her side. "Did he do something to you? I'll call the *policia…*"

Layla straightened the collar of her blouse, her fingers hovering over the top button. "No police." If she let Isabel call the authorities, the life she'd struggled to build for herself here would all come tumbling down. All the lies she'd told to cover up her memory loss would be exposed. Her patients would be hurt. What's more, she was certain to her very bones that her stalker was no ordinary man and that the police couldn't help her.

Maybe no one could.

* * *

It had taken at least five hours for the roaring pain in Ray's head to settle into a dull ache. Since his escape, he'd never come up against a mind that could physically resist him. But Layla Bahset had. Not only had she fought him, she'd nearly buried him right along with her memories. He'd trapped others in a state of madness, but he'd never come close to being trapped himself. If the assistant hadn't knocked at just the right moment, Ray wasn't sure he'd have made it back out with his own mind intact.

He was afraid to try it again without someone to shake him out of it, but the teenaged prostitute's expression hovered somewhere between curiosity and disgust, her lips making a perfectly cherry-round circle of surprise. "You some kind of freak?"

"Look, kiddo, it's easy money," Ray said, setting the alarm clock by the bed. He wondered if motel-rooms-by-the-hour came with a wake-up call service. Probably not.

"Easy money," she mimicked, shaking out her blond hair and pointing at him with the stained end of her Popsicle stick. "Easy money is how girls like me end up missing."

He didn't have time for this. "Just sit down, Missy. That's your name, right?"

"It's Artemisia, but yeah, you can call me Missy. Most everybody does." The hooker looked at him in lurid appraisal for a moment, as if considering whether or not his dark looks and hard body were enough to make her stay. Then some wiser instinct took hold of her. "Never mind. I'm outtie."

Ray sighed. Nobody ever wanted to do things the

easy way. Before she broke eye contact, Ray seized her mind. "Sit down, Missy."

She fell back into the chair as if pushed. He was relieved to find that it wasn't a struggle. Except when it came to Layla Bahset, Ray was able to use this power whenever he needed people to look the other way at an airport, or give him money from their wallets. Most times, people didn't realize what had happened, and shook it off. Unfortunately, Missy seemed acutely aware. "H-how did you do that?" The girl's garishly painted fingernails clawed at the chair as she stammered, "You're in my head. You forced me..."

"Look, I promise I won't hurt you," Ray said. "I won't touch you. I just need you to wake me up if I haven't come back to myself in an hour."

"You just want me to wake you up in an hour?"

"That's right," Ray said. "One hour."

The call girl bit her lower lip, shaken but wary. "Anybody could do that for you. Why me?"

"Three reasons," Ray said, ticking them off. "First, because it keeps a kid like you off the streets for an hour. Second, because hiring a hooker isn't exactly suspicious behavior in this town. And third, because underage girls like you don't talk to the police."

"Why are you afraid of the police?" Missy was way too curious for her own good. "Are you, like, a drug dealer?"

Ray removed his coat and threw it over the back of a chair. It was too damned hot for a coat in Vegas anyway. "No."

"Then you're an addict," she decided, eyeing the scars on his wrists. "You're going to shoot up, and you want me to make sure you come out of it."

"No drugs," he said, holding up a bottle of bourbon. "Just booze."

And he'd save that for later, when he was sure he'd need it.

Missy was still staring at him, giving careful consideration to his black hair and dark complexion. "You're a terrorist?"

"No, *goddammit,*" he snapped. In the army, everybody was supposed to be one color. Green. So he'd laughed it off when war buddies called him *Captain A-Rab* or teased him about being a *Muj.* But the assumptions people made about him now were no laughing matter. "I'm just going to sleep for an hour."

"No you're not," she said shrewdly, narrowing her eyes. "You're going into someone else's head, like you just went into mine. Aren't you?"

Clever girl, Ray thought. But he hadn't any use for clever girls right now. "Will you shut up, so I can close my eyes?"

"How do you know I'm not just going to take your wallet and walk out the door once you're asleep?"

"Because I peeked into your memories and I know you're not a thief," Ray replied. "Now, look, I'll pay you another hundred bucks to just shut up and let me close my eyes."

With the promise of cold hard cash, she went silent and Ray tried not to think about how nervous he really was. When his victims were in the same room, it was easy enough to enter their minds, but he'd blown it today with Layla Bahset. She'd nearly swallowed him up in the sands of her mindscape. Now he knew to be wary.

Flopping onto the hotel bed, Ray took a picture of

Layla Bahset from his pocket. It wasn't a glamorous photo; it was from a directory of mental health professionals, and showed her with her hair swept back and a pair of glasses precariously balanced on the bridge of her nose. Ray just needed the photo to help him focus. To help him remember that she had no power over him now. And if he could channel all his strength, she couldn't hide from him. He'd have to enter the maze of her mind from afar, with just the memory of her cat-green eyes as his guide. He'd stared into those eyes enough times to remember them—he'd pleaded with her to believe him when he said that they had the wrong guy. It was a thin thread of shared memory with which they were joined, but now, hopefully, he could follow it back to her.

Once, he'd been at her mercy, but tonight Layla's fate would be in his hands.

She'd taken sleeping pills to calm her nerves, so when Layla was half awakened by the rush of air by her ear, she told herself it was nothing. Just an all-too-vivid dream. Then she heard the sound again. A pant, bestial and strange. A breath not her own. A shadow fell across her, as if the darkness was a physical weight pressing down on her.

She wasn't alone.

Even though she'd locked the bolts on her door, even though she'd checked every window latch as part of her nightly routine, and set her alarms, someone was here with her. The certainty of it froze her heart in her chest and shot a liquid chill through her veins.

Layla opened her eyes slowly, an eternity passing as she lifted her lids by creeping degrees. It was dark, but the casino lights of the Vegas skyline flashed garish in the night and briefly lit his silhouette in slashes of green and magenta. The stranger stared at her, his breathing heavier now that he knew she was awake. She couldn't see the whole of him, only sense the strain of bone and sinew beneath his powerful muscles. Layla stifled a groan of terror, all but paralyzed.

He was an enormous man. Or was he something else? His chest was a mass of muscle. There was froth upon his…snout? It was as if she could see lust trembling upon his sleek haunches and it made her acutely aware of her body beneath the Egyptian cotton sheets. The way he stared at her made her feel vulnerable, obscene. Yet there must have been a time when it pleased her to have men admire her body, because a primal and utterly foreign rush of pleasure ran through her blood right alongside the fear. And she felt suddenly quite unlike herself, filled with some carnal delight that a man would seek her out in her own lair, that any man would dare.

Questions to try, answer or die, what am I?

As the little rhyme echoed in her mind, Layla slammed back into herself. The pleasure was gone and she pulled the sheet over her body. "Who are you?" she asked, her voice a low, terrified whisper. "I don't know you."

His answer was a snort of taurine rage that echoed through the bedroom. "You're still so pretty when you lie…."

Layla hissed, pushing herself up so that her back was against the silken headboard of the bed. "I want answers," he said, coming closer. "I want my life back. I want justice for what you did to me."

What had she done to him? Was he real, or some figment of her imagination, one of her lost memories come hauntingly to life? In desperation, she whispered the only words she could think to utter. “Are you the man from the desert?”

The words fell from her lips before she could stop them, and in response, she thought she saw furious flared nostrils. She thought she heard the thunder of hooves on her floor as he shouted, “You know who I am!”

“I don’t,” Layla said, shaking her head so violently that it dizzied her. “I can’t remember.”

“Then I’ll remember for you,” he said, his weight settling on the bed as he crawled overtop of her. “Let me in. Let me inside you.”

Was he a rapist? She’d be overtaken by his bulk, helpless against his size and strength. Layla shrank back, the sheet bunching up to expose one long bronzed leg all the way to the thigh. She saw the glint of sharp horns, as if he were intent upon goring her. Intent upon slashing through the sheets. Intent upon impaling her. She threw her hands in front of her as a defense, then heard herself scream.

This time, Ray expected the barren landscape of her mind. But there were subtle changes. The pyramid was more prominent, and he saw an entrance made of rotted old wood and iron. Maybe he could charge it—break it open and lay her memories bare. Inside the mind-scape he was as strong as a bull. Ray threw himself against the entrance, his massive shoulder rolling into his charge. Wood splintered and he heard the groan of hinges. He charged again, and again, smashing and bashing for what felt like hours. He ached with the effort, his throat parched with thirst, but all at once, the entrance gave way and he found himself standing in the labyrinth of an ancient Egyptian tomb.

He found only one torch burning, and he carried it through the sand-filled passage until he heard a low growl. He didn't see Layla's memories. Instead, amidst the glittering gold and carnelian pillars, a lioness appeared and said, "You shouldn't be here. Men who come near me die. They die. Choking, gasping…"

Shit! It was no lion, it was *her*. It was Layla Bahset. The same cat-green eyes. This was the way his cool, clinical interrogator envisioned herself in her own mind. Or maybe she was just trying to scare him off. "Don't threaten me."

"He'll hurt me if he finds you here," she said. "More importantly, he'll hurt *you*. He's watching…"

"Who?" Ray asked. "The guards? The sick bastards who got off on watching me bleed? I've already taken care of them. They aren't ever going to hurt me again, and neither are you."

"I'm different now," the lioness said. "I help people now. I *heal* them."

"I don't care what you do," Ray growled, though that wasn't strictly true. "I want to know why I was pulled out of my unit in Afghanistan. I want to know why I was arrested. I want a name. I want to know who it was that accused me of treason."

"My memories are locked away from me in the antechamber," she said. "And even if I could give you a name, what good would it do?"

What good would it do? The question made crimson fury pass like a taunting veil before his eyes. If he had a name, he could confront his accuser. He could prove his innocence. He wouldn't have to live as a fugitive anymore. He could be a free man.

"I can't free you unless you free me," she said, with a look of anguish. "Save me."

Had she read *his* mind now? Ray was getting confused. "How can I save you?"

"Make me feel something," she said.

He could have blinked only once, but when he did, he no longer saw a lioness on the ground, but a woman on her hands and knees, staring up at him with a needy gaze. Naked. *Completely* naked. He couldn't look away, unable to tear his eyes from the way her hair flowed like a dark river over her bare shoulders and the elegantly arched curve of her back.

Layla seemed to luxuriate in his openmouthed fascination. She let him look at her glistening body in vivid color. The taut nipples, dark as berries. The thatch of dark hair between her thighs. She let him stare. She was enticing him, daring him to come closer and touch her. "Make me want something. Make my pulse quicken with excitement. Make me sigh with longing. Make my body weak with pleasure. Make me, make me, make me."

Oh, the things he wanted to make her do…

But it had to be another trap. Just as she'd tried to bury him in sand this afternoon, now she was trying to make him lose himself in lust. He had no intention of becoming a desiccated carcass in the ruin of her mindscape. And yet, the heat of her wanton invitation was so strong that Ray felt himself harden in response.

If she understood the monster he was now, if she knew the mixed-up milieu of desire and hatred for her that swirled inside him, she'd run. Instead, she beckoned and Ray was atop her before he knew it, his body crushing down on hers. She didn't recoil, not even when she must see him for the horned monster that he was. She stretched her hands up as he lowered his head. Together, they rent the sand, with…his horns or her claws, he couldn't tell.

He was angry with himself, and angry with her. With his blood running hot, he'd nearly forgot what he'd come here for. He'd come here for answers, for justice. Nothing less would satisfy.

And then she asked, "Will you save me?"

Chapter 3

What lives without a body, and speaks without a tongue? Everyone can hear it, but it's seen by none.

Her plea was an echo and it tore something inside him, making him thrash. Another sound followed, shrill as a siren, and he thrashed again. Something shredded as a cacophony of beeps exploded in his brain. Someone was shaking him, pulling him out of Layla Bahset's mind and back into his own body.

It was the teenaged hooker that woke him up. A good thing, too. The alarm clock was ringing and probably had been for some time. What he'd seen inside Layla's dream had nearly unraveled his sanity and now a headache roared behind his eyes with renewed vengeance.

"What's the matter with you?" Missy asked, eyeing the shreds of fabric in his hands. He looked down to see that he'd torn the bedsheets, ripped them with such violence that lint floated in the air around them like fairy dust. What's more, he was burning up, and the motel room was fetid with his sweat. Then there was the blood, freely flowing from *both* his nostrils.

Missy took a few steps back. "Dude, are you sick? Are you trippin'?"

What *was* wrong with him? Ray used the ruined sheet to soak up the blood. He felt as chapped and dehydrated as if he'd been trekking a real desert. "Get me something to drink," he barked, and tried to get his shaking under control while she padded across his room and returned with a cloudy glass of his bourbon. He drank it down in three swallows and it burned all the way.

Squinting his eyes back into focus, Ray saw that his bag was open, his papers all over the floor. There it all was; all the clues and clippings, the file folders and photographs. "You went through my things?"

"I'm not a thief," the hooker said. "But I *am* a snoop…or didn't you see that when you were snooping in *my* head?"

A group of hooting partiers crowed about their winnings in the parking lot outside and Ray winced at the noise. The motel room door did little to block the sound and it bothered him. *Everything* bothered him. The colors, the smells, the sounds.

"So who is she?" Missy asked.

"I don't want to talk about it. In fact, I'll pay you double to just shut up."

"Double! No shit, big spenda!" the hooker gasped in feigned astonishment as she waved Layla Bahset's picture around. "Seriously, who is she?"

Layla Bahset was his tormentor, the cool-eyed bitch who had tried to win his trust—tried to convince him that there was something between them. But it had only been a trick to get him to confess to crimes he didn't commit. She'd abandoned him in that hellhole. She was a fiend. But now he'd seen inside her mind and… *What had he seen?*

He should know. He'd destroyed enough minds since he'd been cursed with these powers. He'd left his jailers and torturers trapped and ruined, afraid and devastated. But he wasn't sure that even he could have taken all her memories and buried them in sand. And he *hadn't* done it. Someone else had. Someone else, someone more powerful, had gotten to her first. The realization rocked his world. There might be others, just like him…

"You should really keep all your notes on a laptop or something," Missy was saying. "Otherwise you just seem like a paranoid nut job."

He wasn't paranoid. They'd taken his dog tags from him and put a black bag over his head. They'd bound him with a plastic zip cord that cut into his wrists. His protestations of innocence had made no difference at all. These were just the times.

Ray's nose seemed to have stopped bleeding, so he threw the bloody rags onto the floor. Then, with a shaking hand, he reached for the glass and the bourbon and filled it. "You can go now."

Missy didn't move. "I don't think you should be alone right now."

"Will you just get the hell out?"

Missy snorted. "Are you going to *make* me?"

He couldn't make her do anything in this state. He

could barely hold his drink. "Fine, stay or go, I don't care, but if you stay, put some clothes on."

"I *am* wearing clothes," Missy objected, straightening her miniskirt so that it covered more of her legs. "Besides, you were all hot and bothered in your sleep. So what's the matter now? Don't you want me?"

He realized she was actually propositioning him. "Not gonna happen, Jailbait."

"Why? I don't charge much. Don't you like me? I'm not your type?"

"Ask me again in ten years," Ray said, too weak to get up and gather his things, and still thinking about the woman who was very much his type, all naked in the sand.

Missy arranged some of Ray's notes in a new pattern on the floor. "Maybe I can help you find the guy who ratted you out. That's who you're looking for in all these little pieces of paper, isn't it?"

"Nobody ratted me out." Ray took another swallow of liquor. It soothed his nerves. "Somebody flat-out lied about me."

"And you think this woman in the picture knows who it was?"

Ray nodded. But a fat lot of good it was going to do him now, with her mind wiped clean. He'd hit a dead end and now Missy was laughing at him. "What the hell is so funny, Missy?"

"This chick is a shrink but *you* were trying to get into *her* head."

"Hilarious." Ray smiled wanly, throwing her a wad of cash. He guessed she'd earned it.

He'll hurt me if he finds you here, the lioness had said. *He's watching.* Was it just the crazy talk of a woman who'd had her mindscape destroyed by some-one like Ray? Possibly. But she'd asked him for help and he'd sensed that she was actually in danger.

He shouldn't give a damn. But he did.

"Hey, Jailbait," he said to Missy, who was on her way out the door. "Maybe you *can* help out… I want you to follow Layla Bahset."

Layla gasped fully awake. The horned monster had only been a dream. She was safe and alone in her own bed. The only thing she had to fear was the syrupy sweetness running through her veins, a dull but inces-sant throb between her legs. She still remembered the feel of the monster that had crawled into the cradle of her thighs and she didn't have to be Dr. Freud to un-derstand the symbolism. Could there be a more potent icon of masculinity than a well-endowed bull?

She thought she wasn't the kind of woman who re-sponded to things like that, but now the sensual tension streaked across the canvas of her body and trailed off, leaving her…unfinished. Incomplete. Wanting. It was better when she didn't want things, when she didn't need things, when she didn't feel like some kind of flower bud that wouldn't blossom.

A swath of morning sun made its way up the stark white bed and she watched it move over the pillows. Dear God, how long had she slept?

It wasn't until she slipped out of bed that she saw the jagged rips in the beige silk headboard. The fabric was slashed, like some horned animal had pierced it in the midst of angry passion, and Layla's heart seized. Throwing on a robe, she ran to check the bolts on her front door. All the locks were still in place. The alarm was set. There was no sign that anyone had been here. No sign at all—except for her torn headboard.

Layla returned to the bedroom and stepped out onto the balcony. The whole expanse of Las Vegas spread out beneath her at a comforting distance. Unless the man in her dreams could fly, there was no way he was actually in her high-rise bedroom last night. It was a dream. A nightmare. She must have slashed the headboard herself. Her stalker had terrorized her so thoroughly that she could no longer tell what was real.

She knew the old saying. *Physician, Heal Thyself.* It wasn't going to cut it anymore. She'd built her life on a shaky foundation and now it all seemed ready to come falling down. Reluctantly, she admitted to herself that it was time to ask for help.

She should've invited Nate Jaffe to her condo, but it was Layla's compulsion to pretend everything was fine that made her agree to meet Nate for dinner. She donned her lovely new red dress, the gift from Isabel. Pearls might have been a nice touch, but the only jewelry she ever wore was a sixpence coin on a long chain around her neck. Her first memory was finding that coin in her hand, and now she was afraid to be without it. Once she was dressed for dinner, she put on her happy face and hailed a cab. And why not? In this city, everyone wore a mask. From the feathered showgirls at the Rio to the gondoliers at the Venetian. In Las Vegas, how was anyone to know what was real?

A young blonde teenager in a miniskirt was standing by the street, sucking on a red Popsicle, probably in some vain hope it would cool her off. Technically, prostitution wasn't legal in Vegas, but it was a technicality barely observed and it was clear to Layla that the young girl was working. Another lost soul in need of saving…

The cab ride to the casino was brief. Stepping from the taxi onto the curb, Layla was hit with an oppressive wall of heat. It made her dark hair wilt, her knees soften, and little beads of perspiration gather on the back of her neck. The Egyptian motif of the Luxor had always bothered her. She told herself it was because the decor was a callow mockery of her ethnic heritage, but it was more than that. Layla couldn't bear to look upon the statuary outside, and having to actually pass under the sphinx at the entrance of the casino made her shudder. What's more, the inside of the pyramid was a claustrophobic maze of confusion. Balconies hung out over the floor, elevators moved along diagonal paths, and the lighting seemed low and eerie.

It shouldn't be so stark, she thought to herself. *Ancient Egypt was a riot of paint and color.* Why these thoughts crowded her mind, she couldn't say and, already upset, Layla wasn't sure how she was going to get through this night.

At the restaurant inside, Dr. Jaffe had already ordered for her, and now smiled expectantly from across the table. Layla gave him what she hoped was her fondest smile. They ate. They talked. He complimented her dress. It was all very pleasant. After all, Nate Jaffe was a very nice man. More importantly, he was a psychiatrist and she needed his help.

As she dragged her fork over a nest of green asparagus sprouts in a hollandaise sauce, Layla thought about what she should say. *I can't remember who I am.* No, if she started with that, he'd realize how long she'd been pretending, and feel betrayed. *Someone is stalking me.*

That would certainly get his attention, but he'd insist on calling the police. *I think someone can hunt me down inside my own mind.* If she told him that, he'd worry about her sanity. Which, admittedly, he should.

"Don't you like your filet?" Dr. Jaffe asked, peering over his spectacles.

"You know I'm indifferent to food," Layla said, then dared to glance up at him. People weren't meant to be indifferent, were they? They were meant to enjoy the pleasure of taste. They were meant to inhale beautiful scents that made them sigh. People were built to feel strong emotions other than fear, weren't they? It was something hardwired, right down to the lizard core of the brain. *She* was meant to feel things, to taste things, to take pleasure in things, even if she couldn't remember who she really was. "Would you kiss me?" Layla asked.

Nate Jaffe stopped midsentence. She had no idea what he'd been saying, and from the look on his face, neither did he. She'd kissed him before. She'd gone to bed with him, too. She knew he wouldn't hurt her. But in the past, she'd never felt more than the faintly soothing sensation of skin upon skin. Last night, in her dream with the monster, she'd felt something more. Now she wanted the man she was dating to take the spark inside her and coax it into a flame.

Dr. Jaffe didn't make any sudden moves and when he leaned forward to kiss her, Layla closed her eyes. It was a very proper kiss, one borne of sincere affection, but it didn't make her feel like she had last night. Nothing had changed, and even the decorative hieroglyphs on the wall, stolen from some ancient tomb, mocked her with their message of doom.

It was the hieroglyphs—not the kiss—that made the blood drain from her face.

"Layla?" Nate Jaffe was staring at her, but she couldn't reply. "What's wrong?"

I can read hieroglyphics, she thought. *That's what's wrong.* Among so very many other things. The symbols swam before her eyes, taunting her. There had to be a simple explanation for it. Maybe she'd been an archeology student in college. Maybe her parents had been curators of a museum. If she remembered her past, it would somehow make sense. "I have to tell you something," Layla began.

Dr. Jaffe's face reddened and he spread his palms on the table. "You don't have to say it, Layla. I've known for some time that your heart isn't in this relationship."

Layla's mouth fell slightly open. "Nate—"

"Are you going to deny it?"

Layla brought her lips back together, unable to tell even one more lie. A fatal moment of silence passed between them before he looked away. "We're both adults," he said, motioning to the waiter for the bill. "Let's just end things while we can still be friends."

She hadn't come here to break up with him. She'd come here for his help, but given the hurt in his eyes, she didn't dare ask him for anything right now. She'd call him tomorrow. Things would be better in the morning. They'd have to be.

He paid the bill and escorted her out of the hotel like the gentleman that he was. As they passed out of the lobby onto the street outside, he even gave her fingers an affectionate squeeze. "I'm sorry things didn't work out," he said, and then, because he looked so forlorn, Layla pressed a very soft kiss to his cheek.

* * *

After four tours of duty, scouting missions were a thing of second nature to Ray. What amazed him about Vegas was the ease with which he could hide in plain sight. Poised near the Luxor entrance with a disposable camera in hand, pretending to take photos of the sphinx, he knew the precise moment that Layla Bahset stepped out of the casino wearing that smoking-hot red dress.

He snapped a quick shot of her giving her date the polite brush-off. Ray didn't recognize the guy with her. He was older, with silver hair and gave off a well-mannered vibe. Totally not the type he would've envisioned for her, but whatever. Ray didn't think the guy was a threat. Even so, as she walked away from her date, Layla looked upset. She started down the drive toward the strip, rubbing her bare arms against the cooler night air.

Keeping his head down, Ray followed her, but he wasn't the only one. Maybe it was his training. Maybe it was a preternatural instinct. Maybe it was because he couldn't figure out why a cabbie would be wearing sunglasses at night. Whatever it was, he turned his head at just the right moment to see the driver lift a radio to his mouth, his attention riveted on Layla's retreating form.

Son of a bitch, Ray thought. So she *was* in some kind of danger. And not just from him.

Ray didn't like the crowds, didn't like the noise and the neon lights of the strip, but he kept his eyes on her. As he followed her, he noticed that she had a catlike grace. Maybe it wasn't just a fluke that she envisioned herself as a lioness. Still, she didn't seem comfortable in the night and she sure didn't have the focus of a predator. She didn't even look up to see the dark sedan that pulled around the corner, creeping behind her. Seemingly oblivious to her peril, she crossed the street, her sensible black pumps clicking against the pavement.

Ray followed her. So did the sedan.

Layla paused on the sidewalk outside the Golden Calf Casino. It was a crappy little hotel, nestled amongst the bigger, more glamorous ones. Hawkers and hobos gathered beneath the gilded statue of a steer, upon which was fastened a sign announcing the nightly pancake special. Layla stared, as if she were lost.

It was at that moment two big, beefy guys stepped out of the dark sedan.

Ray could have let it happen. He could have let them—what, arrest her? Attack her? Kill her? It'd be the least she deserved. But he *couldn't* let it happen. She was still the only chance he had at proving his innocence, he reminded himself. The information he needed was buried inside her ruined memory, and as long as he kept her alive, he still had a chance of digging it up.

Ray strode toward her and she turned. He saw just the corner of her eyes, the green glint of surprise. It was enough. He slipped into the depths of those eyes and grabbed onto the edge of her thoughts. "Put your hand in mine and keep walking," he said.

Forcing her to obey should've been easy, but with her, nothing ever was. He slammed into the same wall of resistance, and not wanting to wait for his powers to take full effect, he grabbed her hand and yanked her forward.

Chapter 4

He follows you wherever you go, but when you turn to meet him his face doesn't show.

It was the man of her dreams—*literally,* the man of her dreams—but he was no shadow monster now. No snout, no hooves, no glinting horns. Still, he clutched her hand like he could break it. He'd come out of nowhere and she'd been taken completely by surprise. "Wh-what are you doing?"

His close-cropped goatee scratched her cheek when he leaned in to whisper, "Someone's following you, so shut up and keep walking."

She took a few steps with him before she could stop herself. It was as if she wasn't moving her own legs; he was. But that was impossible. As they threaded their way through the crowd into the casino, the sirens of a winning slot machine screamed at them. The scent was beer mingled with sweat, and a thumping music played static behind the roar of voices.

"Who's following you?" he asked, and she started to turn her head to look. "Don't let them see you looking! Glance over there, at the glass doors. See the reflection?"

She saw them. Two clean-cut guys in suits pushing through the revelers. She tried to get her wits about her. For all she knew, the men could be chasing *him,* not *her*. She shouldn't let him guide her to the stairway behind the bar, but her hand felt small and somehow secure in his calloused palm. His presence, dark and brutish as it was, made her more…alive. She was actually *feeling,* and though it might be the death of her, she didn't want it to stop!

Still, she found the presence of mind to ask, "Who are you and where are you taking me?"

The question seemed to infuriate him. "You really don't fucking remember me, do you? My name is Ray. You probably remember me better as Prisoner Twenty-Four." The harshness of his words carried even over the hustle and bustle of the casino, and effectively silenced her until Ray skidded to a stop just outside of a bank of elevators. They nearly mowed down an elderly man who had just come down from a higher floor with his bags in hand, obviously ready to check out.

"What's your room number, gramps?" Ray barked.

"Five-thirteen," the elderly man answered, his jaw going lax and jowly as he stared into Ray's eyes.

"Give me your hotel key," Ray said, and Layla watched in astonishment as the old man did as he was bid. "Now go for the pancake special and forget to check out."

With that, Ray yanked Layla into the elevator. Until that moment—until the elevator doors shut—she'd thought that the stranger was in command of himself and in command of her. He'd been unbelievably strong, aggressive and self-assured. But the moment the two slabs of metal slammed together, shutting out the brighter light and noise, she watched her captor's face go ashen. The look that passed over his eyes was something desperate and feral.

She heard the deepening of his breathing as he backed up against the wall. She could've asked him a thousand questions in that moment. She could've asked why he'd grabbed her off the street. She could've asked where he was taking her, and why. But watching the blazing intensity of his dark eyes lose focus and turn glassy, her instincts as a mental health professional kicked in. "Are you going to faint?"

"I don't faint," Ray said, punching the button for the fifth floor and every one after it. His voice was filled with pain and contempt and sweat broke out over his face as he stumbled.

It'd been the closed doors that had triggered him. She'd seen it with her own eyes. And now his heart was beating so hard she could actually hear it. "Take a deep breath and focus on my voice," she said quietly. "If you can calm down, the feeling will pass."

"What the hell would you know about it?" he growled.

Layla wasn't surprised that he lashed out at her. "I know a panic attack when I see one."

In answer, Ray turned and pounded his fist into the door, as if he could batter his way out. Given the force of the blows, maybe he could. "Why is this elevator so goddamned slow?"

He looked like a trapped animal—one who might be willing to gnaw off his own arm to escape. He stumbled again, and this time she steadied him. "Close your eyes and imagine the desert, wide and open to the horizon."

He sagged against her, the bulk of his weight pinning her to the wall. She couldn't tell if he was even conscious anymore. He was a big man. He wasn't just tall; his shoulders were also very wide. His coat had fallen open so that the outlines of his muscles were clear beneath his black T-shirt. Something pressed hard into her side, and she looked down to see that he was wearing a holstered gun. It should have terrified her, but the proximity of his masculinity, so raw and powerful, also awakened the same yearning she'd felt in her dream.

"It's going to be all right," she said, softly stroking his arm.

Back in Syria, every time they'd thrown Ray in the coffin, he'd wondered if he'd seen light for the last time. The elevator brought back that sensation, and the terror had crawled up inside him until he was ready to claw the doors open with his bare hands.

Beautiful. As an army translator, he'd lived through firefights and hostage situations. As a prisoner, he'd been beaten and left for dead. But what frightened him now? A goddamned elevator. And to make matters worse, *she* was on hand to witness his weakness. Like she needed another weapon in the arsenal of tricks she'd used to chip away at his psyche and find the cracks.

As soon as the elevator doors opened, he flung

himself out into the hallway, crashing into the opposite wall.

"Count your breaths and breathe slow," she said, offering her voice as an anchor against the rising tide of panic. But they were being followed; he didn't have time for slow. Through sheer force of will, Ray straightened up and herded her down the hallway to the old man's room and pushed her inside. He shut the door and peered out the peephole.

He didn't see anybody coming, but that didn't mean they weren't out there. Ray ran a hand through his sweat-soaked hair, then checked his gun. It made him feel more secure somehow, to touch it. "Unless those guys are determined to search every room and alert casino security, we've probably given your entourage the slip for now." The panic was subsiding, but he was still unsteady. If she wanted to scream, or push past him and run away, he wasn't entirely sure he'd have the power to stop her.

She didn't try. Instead she said, "I'll get you a glass of water. It might help."

It was surreal to watch her return from the bathroom, carrying a drink for him, like she was Florence Fucking Nightingale. *I heal people now,* she'd told him in the shifting sands of her mindscape. *Right.*

He took the water and drank it down, then sat down on the bed, hard.

Layla was relieved to see that the stranger seemed to be coming back to himself now, getting it under control. But his eyes were still on her, pinning her in place like a red butterfly against a mat. "So now what? Are you going to shoot me?"

He snorted. "Is that why you think I brought you up here? To shoot you? Seriously?"

"The only thing I know is that you've taken me hostage."

"Lady, I just *rescued* you," Ray said.

"Is that why you have a gun?"

"I have a gun because people are after me. Let's both hope I won't have to use it."

"Why would you need to use it?" she asked, her voice rising an octave. "People seem to do whatever you say...."

"It's my animal charm," he said, but his acid tone was anything but charming. He slammed the empty glass down on the bedside table. "So let's see if I have this straight. You don't know who I am. You also don't know who is following you. What the hell *do* you know, Doc?"

Layla had held the secret inside her for so long, it seemed impossible that she was going to admit it to a complete stranger. But when the words left her lips, they came out in an exhilarating rush. "I don't know anything! I don't remember anything but the past two years of my life. I woke up in the desert, in my car, holding an old sixpence coin in my hand—this sixpence," she said, pulling the necklace out of her neckline so he could see it. "I thought maybe I was from England, but my wallet was filled with dollars and I had an American driver's license."

"And that didn't jog your memory?" he asked, examining the coin.

"No. I didn't recognize myself and I don't recognize you either. When was the last time we saw one another?"

"Twenty-four months, thirteen days and six hours ago… I got in the habit of counting when I was locked in a box."

Twenty-four months, Layla thought. Two years ago. Before she lost her memory. "And how did we know each other? Were we…" In spite of herself, her eyes drifted to the bed.

"Screwing?"

Her cheeks suddenly burned, both because of his crass word choice and because of the way her insides flip-flopped at the mere suggestion. *Were* they lovers? It was the only way she could explain her physical reaction to him. Or why he was stalking her and leaving threatening notes in her office.

"We never went to bed together, no," Ray finally said, but not before letting his gaze travel up and down her body. It made her go hot all over. "I was arrested because some anonymous informant accused me of colluding with the enemy in Afghanistan. You were my interrogator. I was innocent. I *am* innocent. But you let them torture me anyway."

The heat in Layla's body went to sudden chill. She had to sit down on the hotel room wing chair to keep her knees from buckling. "You must be mistaken."

Ray took off his coat and threw it at her. Now that his arms were exposed, she saw the crisscrossing lines of scars near his wrists. "Does this look like a mistake?"

"You could've made those marks yourself," she said, slowly.

He yanked off his holster—gun and all—throwing it onto the bed. Then off came his T-shirt. She watched the pure artistry of his torso in motion, his bare stomach coming into sharp focus. He was beautiful. Like some bronzed statue of an ancient athlete. But she wasn't the type of woman to wilt at the sight of a man's rippling muscles. She wasn't like Isabel, all open and sensual, so the feelings that rose in her weren't because of his raw physicality. It was the way he was staring at her, predatory and intense, compelling her to look at him. *Really* look at him.

As she stared, he turned so that his broad back was exposed to her, and now her breath caught in her throat. Scars knotted across his spine. The pale marks twisted together, snaking across his flesh like serpents coiling for a strike.

Layla's hand went over her mouth to stifle a gasp.

"You still think I did this to myself?" he asked.

For a moment—just a moment—she could envision his wounds, bleeding and raw. She thought she heard his throaty cry of pain and shook her head to dislodge the terrible sound. Was it possible that he was telling the truth? Could she be responsible in some way for the agony written large upon his flesh? Layla shook her head. No, it wasn't possible. She may not have all her memories, but it wasn't in her to hurt anyone. She was a healer. A *healer.*

"Convinced that I'm telling the truth yet, or do you need to see more?" His hands went to the front of his jeans, and he snapped the button open. "'Cause I've got plenty to show you."

"Don't," Layla said, reaching out to stop him. Their fingers tangled, right there at the front of his pants. Embarrassment flared even hotter at her cheeks and she tried to yank back. He pressed her fingers against the fabric, so that the rough teeth of the zipper scratched her skin. He was close to her now, and the scent of him filled her nostrils. The potent evidence of his masculinity at eye level was overwhelming and the reality of her situation hit her all at once. She'd been abducted by a stranger off the street and was now holed up with him inside a hotel room. Worse, he was looking down at her like some *djinn* about to devour her.

"Unzip me," he said.

Her mouth went dry. She couldn't say what made her do it. Maybe he was in her head, compelling her obedience. Maybe she was too afraid of him to refuse. Or maybe it was the heated sensation that curled in her belly. She pressed the flat of one palm against his thigh, French manicured nails splayed over the denim. Then she tugged gingerly on his zipper with the other hand. It was obscene to watch herself do this. Curiosity mingled with humiliation.

For one brief and wildly insane moment, she wondered what it would be like to touch him. Both shame and titillation shook her to her core as he slipped the waistband over his hips and exposed his boxer briefs and, just below the hem...the marred flesh of his thighs. A row of puckered burn marks trailed down his leg. Someone had taken a hot poker, or a cigarette, and pressed the burning end into his skin, over and over again. The sight seared into her, as if she'd been the one burned. "I did this to you?"

"No," he said, his voice low. "But you worked with the people who did."

It couldn't be true. If it *was* true, it made her sick. It made her even more of a stranger to herself than she already was. So how could it be that she was also feeling something warm, something petal-soft and exquisite?

Something like she imagined arousal was supposed to feel. No sooner did it begin to blossom inside her than it was crushed under the weight of recollection. "You're Rayhan Stavrakis."

"That's right."

She couldn't make sense of her memories, but she was astounded to be remembering anything. "Greek… Arab…Syrian?"

"American," Ray growled. "Not that it matters."

"I'm sorry," Layla whispered, staring at his scars. The words were so completely inadequate that she nearly choked on them. "I don't remember much, but I'm so sorry."

"Yeah? Well, now you're gonna make it up to me."

Well, wasn't Layla Bahset just full of surprises? Ray watched the blush intensify on her upturned cheeks, and though she'd completely misread his intentions, her reaction made him hard. Very hard. He remembered what she'd said to him when he'd entered her sleeping mind. *"Make me want something,"* she had pleaded. *"Make my pulse quicken with excitement. Make me sigh with longing. Make my body weak with pleasure. Make me, make me, make me…"*

Now she was poised at the edge of her chair in that red dress, nearly on her knees. Those glossy lips of hers were near enough to his cock to kiss it, but his desire was squelched by the humiliation he saw in her eyes. She'd once insisted he was a terrorist; now she apparently believed he was the kind of man who'd force her to trade in sexual favors. He wasn't sure which assumption was worse.

Tugging his jeans up, he fastened them again.

Deciding it might be easier to control himself if she were at eye level, he said, “Stand up.”

She rose, and he realized she was trembling. She stood there in front of him, hugging herself. He’d taken the calm and composed lady shrink and rattled her to the bone. It didn’t make him feel good about himself. The fact that she didn’t remember what she’d done didn’t make her innocent, but there wasn’t any satisfaction to be had from terrorizing someone who couldn’t appreciate the karmic justice of it. “So, Doc, when I said I wanted you to make things up to me, what did you think I meant?”

“You know what I thought.” Her words were like ice.

“Yeah, well, I’m interested in your *mind*. The information I need to get my life back is locked in that pretty head of yours and you need to tell me what you know. That’s the only way you can make things up to me.”

“I just told you that I have amnesia. But if what you’re saying is true, there has to be a record of what happened in your case somewhere. Maybe you should file a request under the Freedom of Information Act.”

“A FOIA request? That’s your brilliant solution? Sweetheart, I didn’t even get a lawyer, much less a trial. No, the only way to prove my innocence is to find my accuser and you know who that was.”

“I don’t know who gave evidence against you. I don’t remember.”

“Maybe you don’t want to remember,” he snapped.

She shrank away as if she thought he might strike her, or ravish her, or worse. Though it scalded his tongue to comfort her, he found himself saying, “Look, you don't have to be afraid that I'm going to…take advantage of you."

Her green eyes looked haunted and lost. "Maybe I'm afraid I *want* you to."

What kind of game was she playing with him now? It was like a matador snapping a red cape in front of a wounded bull. Heat seared through his body and tinted his vision with scarlet need. It'd been one thing to meet the alluring lioness in her mindscape, the one who tempted him with her blatant sensuality. But to see the confusion of the buttoned-up woman in front of him was an entirely new kind of torment. One that dizzied him.

"You're bleeding again," Layla said softly as Ray swayed on his feet.

He'd obviously used his powers too many times in the past few days. It was all catching up with him. There was never a time when he hadn't experienced pain and blood in the aftermath, but Layla was harder to control than anyone he'd encountered before. Keeping her here with him was taxing him beyond endurance.

"You should let me go, Ray," she said softly.

"I didn't just snatch you off the street for my own reasons, okay? You're being followed."

He could see that she didn't believe him. "Those men that you yanked me away from, they looked like federal agents. Which makes me think they aren't after me. They're after you."

Ray shook his head, hand coming to rest on the back of his neck. His control over her was fraying. "No, Doc. I'm telling you, they were watching *you*."

"Well, I'm not afraid of government officials."

"Goddammit, Layla! People with badges aren't always the good guys. Do you think that with skin like yours, with a last name like yours, that professional courtesy is going to save you if they've decided you're a threat to national security? Did the fact that I fought for my country matter a damn when I was being tortured?"

Suddenly, he was breathing faster. The world seemed to narrow into some dark tunnel, and if she gave any answer to his question, he didn't hear it.

Layla watched him collapse. He toppled like some felled animal at sacrifice. He fell hard, his head bouncing when it struck the floor, his mouth going lax. Instinctively, Layla rushed to his side, stooping to feel for a pulse. She found one, but he didn't respond when she said his name.

What was wrong with him? She remembered that he'd suffered a nosebleed the first time she saw him in her office. He was bleeding from the nose again now. Maybe he was suffering from high blood pressure or some far more serious ailment.

She should call an ambulance. No. He'd kidnapped her. She should call the police. But if she did, it was all going to come out. All of it. They'd find out that she'd been hiding her amnesia for two years, and no one would believe her when she told them about the mental powers that Rayhan Stavrakis had exerted over her. They'd think that she'd gone crazy.

Maybe she had.

This was her chance to escape, but she couldn't just leave him here bleeding on the floor. She pushed on his shoulder, trying to roll him over. He was brawny, heavy, hard to move. She managed to angle his mouth toward the ground so that he wouldn't choke on his own tongue but she didn't know what else to do. She had a doctorate in psychology; she wasn't a medical doctor.

But Nate Jaffe was.

Layla fumbled for her cell phone in her purse and dialed. After five rings it went to voice mail. Why wouldn't he pick up? Okay, he was obviously still smarting from their breakup. She'd just have to go get him. Nate's apartment wasn't far from here and her captor didn't look like he was going to regain consciousness anytime soon, so Layla bolted for the door. If there really were other men out there following her, then she'd just have to risk it.

Chapter 5

A barren woman with skin cracked and dry, still enchants men though none know why.

Though Seth was a desert god, he hated the Mojave. Not just because it was a New World desert, far and remote from his own Egyptian home. He also hated the Mojave because as a war god, he believed that a desert should *devour*. A desert should *destroy*.

A desert shouldn't give birth to a neon monstrosity like Las Vegas.

The city was like no proper desert metropolis of old. It had no citadel; it sent no chariots into the sands to conquer. It didn't join with the sand and sun and powerful ring of mountains. Instead the Vegas architecture was a blend of archaic myth with modern excess—an adult fantasy-scape at the very edge of reality, where magic blurred with the mundane. With its garish lights and glitter, the city beckoned visitors and residents to worship the myriad relics of man's gloried past. It became a fertile oasis for washed-up immortals. And why not? Where else but Vegas could deities walk comfortably amongst the mortals without fear of discovery? Here a primitive goddess of dancing could easily take on the guise of a showgirl. Where else but Vegas could a trickster god hide in plain sight, running a casino? Where else could a god of revelry gorge himself in an actual bacchanalia, but at Caesar's Palace?

This is what made Las Vegas the singular, perfect refuge for the old immortals.

Except for Seth. He'd never make his home here. He still had his pride. He had his powers too—some of them anyway—and there were still wars for him to feed upon. He still enjoyed the look in the eyes of men as he parched their tongues and stole the breath from them, leaving them to gasp, choking on their dry mortality.

Crouching by the road where it met the desert, the once mighty war god let sand slip through his hands. It felt like the hair of the woman who belonged to him. It felt like the silken sheets she used to lay upon in their cold, cold bed. He had only come here for Layla, and she had already betrayed him. Again.

Layla knocked on Nate Jaffe's door. He didn't answer. She rang the bell. She couldn't blame him for not wanting to talk to her right now, but this wasn't about her. "Nate!"

She rang the bell again and knocked at the same time. Then Layla remembered that he kept an extra key under the mat. She'd never used it when they were together, but while Rayhan Stavrakis lay bleeding, now wasn't the time to worry about emotional boundaries. What's more, the door wasn't even locked....

The apartment was dark and Layla felt foolish. Ridiculous. Maybe he wasn't home.

A sliver of light cut across the floor from under his bedroom door. "Nate, I'm really sorry about tonight, about storming into your apartment, about everything, but—"

Her words cut off as she swung open the bedroom door and saw the swaying shadow pass over her feet. A moment later, she realized that she was staring at a dead body.

This time Layla did call the police.

Now she sat in Nate Jaffe's kitchen wrapped in a blanket because she couldn't stop shivering. Yellow crime-scene tape cordoned off the bedroom but forensics were on-site. They'd offered to call a grief counselor, but Layla asked them to call Isabel instead. Her assistant was the closest thing that she had to an actual friend.

While she waited, the police officer sat beside her, a notebook in hand. "Dr. Bahset, can you tell us why you let yourself into the apartment tonight?"

"I already told you," Layla whispered.

"Ma'am, you said that a guy with mind control powers abducted you, then passed out, and you were coming to get him help. Is that really the story you're sticking with?"

"Dude, she's in shock," one of the younger officers said.

Fine. Let them think she was in shock. She probably

was. But that didn't mean Ray Stavrakis didn't need help. She'd already let one man die tonight. She wasn't going to sit idly by while another suffered. "You have to listen to me," Layla insisted. "Send paramedics to room 513 at the Golden Calf. You'll find an unconscious man, bleeding from the nose."

"We already sent an ambulance over there," the officer said, slapping his notebook shut in frustration. "There's nobody in that room and it's registered to an elderly gentleman."

Layla put her face in her hands. Maybe she'd imagined everything. Maybe she'd had a complete breakdown. That was the joke about mental health professionals, wasn't it? That they were the *real* crazies of society.

"Looks like suicide," someone said, coming out of Nate Jaffe's bedroom, and Layla swallowed the anguished sound in her throat. That he was dead was horrifying enough, but that he might have killed himself was unspeakably so.

She'd seen him hanging there in his closet at the end of a rope, his eyes bulging and his face discolored. She'd never be able to shake the image of his arms so limp at his sides, gently swaying with the rest of his body. If she could have burst into tears at the memory of it, she would have. Grief and guilt lashed violently against her insides, but no tears would come.

She hadn't loved Nate Jaffe, but he'd been good to her. He'd been gentle and patient. What's more, he'd been a good therapist. He counseled people who were unwell and made them whole again. And yet, no one had helped him. She certainly hadn't. She hadn't seen a single clue that he was capable of this. What kind of therapist did that make her? What kind of *person* did that make her?

"We just want to know what kind of frame of mind he was in," the police officer was saying. "Did you quarrel at dinner?"

Layla groaned, not even wanting to speak the words. "We ended our relationship."

And he'd seemed hurt, yes. But enough to take his own life?

Sitting in the passenger seat of Isabel's car, Layla watched the city skyline pass by in a neon blur. For two years now, she'd perfected the ruse that she was a competent psychologist. The cold truth was that she was a fraud. How could she help patients when she hadn't even been able to help the man who shared her bed? When she couldn't even help herself?

Fingering the sixpence coin at the end of its chain, Layla took a deep breath. "Isabel, I have something to tell you, and it's important. It's just really hard for me to say."

"*¿Por qué?* What could you say that would shock *me?*"

Oh, after tonight, Layla could imagine a thing or two that would surprise even Isabel. But the words of her confession stalled on her tongue. Isabel was the only friend she had and Layla was fairly certain they wouldn't be friends anymore once she told the truth. Nonetheless, the truth was what Isabel deserved. "Isabel, I don't have any memories of my life before I came to Las Vegas. I woke up in a car in the desert with this coin in my hand…"

Isabel gave it a glance, then her eyes went back to the road.

"I also had my wallet, a checkbook and a few boxes of my belongings. The diplomas and certificates I found told me that I was a psychologist, and as it turned out, I had enough money in the bank to open a practice, but I don't know who I am."

"You just don't know who you *were,*" Isabel said quietly, without any show of surprise. "There's a difference."

Layla felt herself blink. "You knew?"

"Do you think you could've pretended without me?" Isabel asked.

"But why? Why would you help me to pretend that everything was fine?"

"What harm were you doing to anyone?"

Layla squeezed her eyes shut. She felt certain that the life she'd led here in Vegas was a better one than she'd been living before, but now her past was coming back to haunt her. "The stranger who came to the office the other day. He's a man from my past. He's stalking me. He's left threatening messages in the office, and tonight he grabbed me off the street and…" Did she dare tell Isabel what she'd told the police about Ray's abilities to control her? They hadn't believed her and she couldn't bear to hear Isabel laugh at her. "The point is, I'm no good to my patients like this. I need to find them new therapists and make sure that they're cared for. Then I have to close down the practice."

Isabel looked dismayed.

Layla rushed to add, "I realize this puts you in a bad spot, but I'll have a generous severance package for you and a glowing recommendation." After all, Layla had money—lots of it—and she'd make sure that Isabel wasn't out of a job for long.

"But you love what you do, no? It's your calling. You were becoming your own woman."

Becoming was a strange word. One that felt as wet and salty and unfinished as the tears Layla couldn't cry. Maybe Isabel was right, but she couldn't go on like this.

"You were like a butterfly just coming out of her cocoon," Isabel continued. "You were just starting to find yourself…."

Maybe so, but Rayhan Stavrakis had found her first. Now everything had changed. "Isabel, I just need a few days to get everything in order. I'm going to attend Dr. Jaffe's funeral. Then I think I'll need to check myself into a facility for evaluation, and maybe I can get my memories back."

"Lo siento," Isabel said softly. "I'm sorry. If that's what you need to do, I'll help you, but be sure you *want* to remember…"

That night, Layla was afraid to sleep. Afraid that she'd dream of the way she'd found Nate's body hanging in his closet. Even more afraid that Ray would enter her mind, and that this time, he'd leave more than her headboard in shreds.

Chapter 6

It screams with no voice, and when it ends we rejoice.

Pain. Ray was holed up in his motel-room-by-the-hour with a bottle of bourbon, a handful of aspirin and a crushing headache. He'd managed to slip out of the hotel room before the cops showed up, but he wouldn't have been surprised if they broke down his door any minute now. Ray swallowed the pills down with a big swig of liquor in the vain hope that it would at least take some of the edge off the agony.

"Thanks for following Layla to the Luxor," Ray said to Missy. "Now get the hell out of here."

"It's Layla now, is it?" The teenaged hooker whistled. "Do you really think you should be taking the booze and the pills together? Maybe you should stop using your powers so much. It's like, you know, maybe you're burning your brain out."

Maybe. Or maybe Layla was killing him. It wasn't just that her mind was different than anyone else's. It was that controlling her was a struggle every time... as if she had powers of her own. "I've got no choice," Ray decided. "She's the only one who can help me clear my name."

Missy shrugged. "Did you ever think about maybe just taking her to lunch and asking her some questions like a normal person would?" He shot Missy a look and it actually shut her up for at least one whole minute before she added, "You still need me to spy on her?"

It'd probably be smarter for him to get out of town, but now that Layla had called the police, time was running out. He'd try to get to her, at least one more time. "Yeah. Go to her office. Make an appointment or whatever. She counsels troubled youth, and you definitely fit the bill."

"You're a real ass, Ray," Missy said, but he knew she'd do what he asked.

The war god found the atmosphere of Layla's office to be utterly detestable. The sterility of the place was marred by burning candles and vibrant pots of flowers. As water bubbled over a faux rock garden, the war god tried not to scowl. Seth couldn't abide the shabby-looking young man with paint on his fingers sitting in the waiting room next to a girl who looked like a streetwalker. It didn't better his mood to see that Layla's choice in associates hadn't improved.

As the two teenagers flirted with one another in the waiting room, Seth furtively glanced down at the folders on the receptionist's desk, looking for names. *Carson Tremblay. Artemisia Sloan.* No one he should know or care about. Instead, he centered his attention on the receptionist, whose lush curves annoyed him. The sign on her desk said that her name was Isabel.

Her pupils widened as if she took pleasure in just the sight of him. "I was just gonna tell the kids over there," she said. "Dr. Bahset isn't seeing patients today. She's having a rough week."

"I'm afraid it's about to get rougher," the god said, flipping open his wallet. "I'm Seth Carey. I work for the U.S. government."

"¡Qué interesante!" Isabel smirked, standing up to get a look at his identification. "Scorpion Group? Like Navy SEALS?"

As she drew close, Seth was disturbed by the scent of her, so feminine and fertile. He was even more disturbed that he'd come here himself, in his mortal guise. Normally, he had minions to do these kinds of things, but this matter with Layla was very personal. "Scorpion Group is a defense contracting firm. We work in counterterrorism alongside the Department of Homeland Security."

Isabel looked less impressed than she ought to have been. When she brushed a lock of hair out of her eyes, a red bracelet fluttered down to her elbow like a butterfly in flight. He noticed that her blouse was patterned like snakeskin, and fell open to expose the tops of her breasts. He shouldn't have noticed either of these things, but there was something potent about her. Something powerful. Something not entirely… mortal.

He knew most of the old gods, but Isabel was a stranger to him. *Could it be?* Had Layla somehow acquired herself a divine companion? Shaking off his curiosity, he assured himself that it was of no consequence. Las Vegas was filled with cast-off deities of bygone eras; he ought not ascribe too much significance to Isabel, so he continued the ruse. “Dr. Bahset may be in danger, ma’am. That’s why I’m here. It’s important that I speak with her.”

“Maybe you can come back *mañana,*” Isabel said, leaning provocatively across the desk to reach her calendar, briefly exposing her belly. “Let me write your name on her schedule.”

Again, her sensuality shouldn’t have caught his attention. She had some powerful magic indeed if she could make anything stir inside him at all. This intrigued him because most of the old gods had lost all their powers altogether. Even the once great Osiris now lived amongst the mortals as a funeral director and Horus had become an ordinary airplane pilot. Unfortunately, Seth couldn’t even take pleasure in seeing his old rivals reduced to such circumstances; he feared becoming like them. It was bad enough that he’d been forgotten, but as long as wars were fought he still had power. There was just no one left to appreciate it anymore, no challenges for him, which was why he wanted his minion back....

Just then, Layla appeared in the doorway to her office, startling him from his thoughts. If Seth had a heart, surely it would have seized in his chest at the sight of her. Layla looked drawn and pale, completely unsteady. But she wasn’t reacting to him. She didn’t remember him. *Couldn’t* remember him. He’d seen to that. He’d buried her pleasures and joys, her ability to know herself and be known by others. And along with those lost pleasures, he’d locked away her memories, too. Even so, it still angered him that she didn't drop to her knees in supplication.

Layla's clothes angered him, too. The high-necked white blouse covered her well enough, but where was her modesty last night when she wore a red dress that exposed her arms and knees? When she actually kissed the cheek of that puny, pathetic, mortal man?

Disloyal whore.

"It's fine, Isabel," Layla said, motioning for the man to come into her office, where she'd been organizing her case files. She wanted to have everything in order when she broke the news to her patients that she couldn't treat them anymore. Most of them would take it well, but she'd worked hard to earn Carson Tremblay's trust. She knew the young artist was in the waiting room, and she needed a few more minutes before she could face him. She was sure that talking to Mr. Carey would be easier. He claimed to be affiliated with the government. Maybe he had something to do with the men she'd seen in the casino last night. She actually hoped so; maybe Mr. Carey could make some sense of it all.

However, just as Mr. Carey took a seat, too rude even to remove his shades, Layla was struck by something terribly familiar in the way he folded his hands. She'd seen those hands before, those bony knuckles and elegantly cruel fingers. Somehow she was certain that if she touched them, his palms would be dry.

She knew him.

He was another man risen from the ashes of her past, and his dark presence frightened her to her core. Her heart seemed to have gone dead and dull in her chest, but she wasn't ready to admit she didn't remember him. "It's good to see you again, Mr. Carey," she said with as much bravado as she could muster.

He took off his sunglasses and looked at her. He didn't gaze at her with the gentle respect Nate Jaffe had always shown her. He didn't even stare at her like Ray did—with primal rage and animal need. No, Seth Carey looked at her as if he had every right to let his eyes roam over her body. He took his time, his scrutiny harsh and judging, as if finding every line on her face and every unwanted spare inch of flesh on her hips. "How long has it been, Layla?"

So they were on a first-name basis, then. Layla's mind raced. They were colleagues, perhaps, but not friends. No. They *couldn't* have been friends because everything about him made her want to run. She remembered that he'd asked her a question. How long *had* it been since they'd last seen one another? "At least two years ago…"

He was silent, as if he expected her to simply wait patiently for him to speak. All the while, something inside her thrashed madly, like a wild animal in a trap.

"Layla, I thought you might like to know that Rayhan Stavrakis escaped prison. He's come for revenge. He's already attacked his jailers and—let's just say, they wish they were dead. Now he's likely after you. He may have killed Dr. Jaffe last night in an effort to get to you. I understand you had a relationship with the deceased…" The *deceased.* What a horrible word. Sadness over Nate Jaffe's death welled inside Layla again, the tears she couldn't cry all but drowning her on the inside. "You think Rayhan Stavrakis killed Nate Jaffe?"

That wasn't possible, because Ray had been with her last night. She should say that. She should tell him that. Somehow, she couldn't make her mouth form the words.

"Don't you remember the Stavrakis case?" he asked with a smile, teeth sharp and threatening.

Layla realized he was toying with her, as if he knew she couldn't remember. "Of course."

"Then you know he's a madman. There's no telling what he could do. We don't know who his coconspirators are, or what act of violence he's planning here in the homeland."

Something about the way he said the word *homeland* was antithetical to every ideal of the nation he was supposedly trying to protect. It set her teeth on edge and made it easier to lie. "I hope you catch him."

"We hope you'll use your intimate knowledge about him to *help* us catch him."

Intimate knowledge? What was he implying? There was no mistaking the note of contempt in his voice when he said it. Mr. Carey leaned forward so that his bald head gleamed ruddy in the light from the window. "Just because you parted with Scorpion Group on less than amicable terms, doesn't mean you're not a patriot anymore, does it? He's a monster, Layla. Do you really want more deaths on your conscience?"

Layla faltered, instinctively fingering the edge of the sixpence dangling from her neck. What exactly was Scorpion Group and just how many deaths *were* on her conscience? What if Mr. Carey was right? Layla had already experienced Ray's strange powers firsthand. He hadn't hurt her last night, but maybe that was only because he'd collapsed before he could. Ray was a huge, violent and troubled man; if everything he'd told her was true, he had every reason in the world to hate her.

"I want you to come to a safe house with me," Mr. Carey said, reaching for her hand. "Somewhere we can protect you." Layla had never believed that someone could make her flesh crawl until that moment, and she pulled away. Her every instinct screamed that she shouldn't trust him. Especially when he added, "You're not safe on your own."

She'd studied sociopaths long enough to know that he wanted her to be afraid. He wanted her to be terrified. It fed something in him. And it fed something in her too: a wild defiance. "I'm not afraid," she lied. She *was* afraid of Rayhan Stavrakis, but she was even more afraid of Seth Carey. "But thank you for the warning. I'll be extra careful."

"Layla, even with all the locks and bolts on your condo door, you're not safe."

It wasn't an offhanded comment. She understood the subtext perfectly. *I know where you live. I can get to you.* He reached for her hand again and this time, she was too frightened to pull away. "He's coming for you, Layla, and there's going to be a reckoning."

A reckoning. That's what the note had said, and looking now into the sand-swept eyes of the man sitting across her, she realized that *this* was her stalker. This terrifying man who carried not only a gun, but a badge. The blood drained away from her face as she desperately tried to steady herself. Layla had counseled abuse victims. She would have told them to get out of this situation without enflaming it. She just never thought she'd be in a position to have to take her own advice.

"I'm sure you're right," Layla said with as much calmness as she could. "Can you leave me your card and contact information so we can arrange something?"

He grinned, as if she'd amused him. He took a business card from his pocket and handed it to her. It was white ink on black with a scorpion design and she recognized it instantly. She'd had cards like this once, too. "I have a lunch appointment," Layla said, grabbing her purse and willing him not to see through her deception. "But I promise I'll call you right after and you can take me to the safe house."

"Layla—"

She didn't wait to hear whatever it was that he had to say. She wouldn't call him. Not after lunch. Not ever. And by the time he called her, she'd be long gone.

Layla murmured something to Isabel about pushing appointments back, but she didn't break stride. It wasn't until she was out of the building that someone caught up with her on the sidewalk. It was Carson Tremblay. "Wait! Dr. Bahset!"

Gratified to see that it wasn't Mr. Carey on her heels, she kept walking. "Carson, I'm sorry but I can't see you today."

The young man kept up with her, practically running at her side. "But I have a show. My artwork is going to be on display." He handed her a flyer advertising the exhibition, as if to prove it. "I'm worried about what I might do."

"You'll be fine," she said, with a wary glance over

her shoulder. "I'll—I'll call you. I'll talk you through it. But right now, I have to go." Layla folded the flyer and thrust it into her skirt pocket, picking up her pace. She hated the look on the young man's face as she left him standing there beside the glass windows of a bank, but it couldn't be helped. She had to leave. *Now.* It was a matter of survival.

The walk to the parking garage wasn't very far, but it seemed miles and miles too long when her cell phone started ringing. The display said SCORPION GROUP. She wondered if she should answer it. If she should stall for time. Maybe tell Mr. Carey to meet her somewhere in the opposite direction from where she was going. But to answer the phone was to risk he might hear the fear in her voice. Besides, she had to get rid of her phone. It had a GPS system that could be used to track her.

She didn't have time to wonder how she knew this. She just threw it into the nearest trash can and hurried toward her car. She'd parked on the lowest deck, in the basement, away from the crowds. It was quiet enough for her to hear someone murmur into a crackling radio. It was probably just parking garage security, she told herself, but some instinct made her look before she took another step. Crouching low on the stairs, she peered between the metal railings down into the garage and saw the blinking blue lights of the security camera. Beyond that, two men wearing dark suits and sunglasses watched her car.

They were the same men that had been following her the night Dr. Jaffe died.

She hadn't believed Rayhan Stavrakis when he told her that she was being followed, but now she did.

What's more, she knew that these were Mr. Carey's men. Men who worked for Scorpion Group. The knowledge made the small hairs on the nape of her neck stand on end.

She'd leave her car behind. The only thing that mattered was escaping. She had to get out of this parking garage, out of this city, maybe even out of this country. And she had to do it today. Right now. Rising, Layla slowly backed her way up the stairs. She dared not breathe when she heard a heavier footfall behind her. Just two floors to go and she'd be back at street level. Layla increased her pace, her hand skidding along the metal railing. The footsteps behind her picked up pace, too, and Layla's heel caught in the stairs, sending her to her knees. She yelped with pain as her hands hit the concrete, skin scraping as a pair of hands grasped her around the waist.

"I've got her!" the man shouted.

What happened next was nothing Layla could explain. With a violent economy of motion, she slammed her head back sharply into her attacker's face and heard his nose break with a sickening crunch. He let out a startled cry and held his nose as red blood spurted between his fingers. Then she shoved him back and delivered a roundhouse kick that sent him tumbling down the stairs.

Layla hovered there, momentarily stunned. How had she known how to do that? Did she know martial arts? There wasn't time to figure it out, because another of Seth Carey's men was right behind him. This one leaped over his partner to get at her.

Desperate to find something—anything—to defend herself, Layla saw a fire extinguisher inside a glass case. Without a conscious thought, she smashed both fists into the glass case and pulled it out. She swung the cannister at her pursuer, nailing him in the forehead and making him stumble.

"Crazy bitch!"

He was after her again, but not before Layla whispered, *"I'm too heavy to carry, too light to put down, a stain on your soul, a thorn in your crown."*

At hearing the riddle, he crumpled as if she'd hit him. He just lay there, moaning.

Why did she say that? And why did it give her such satisfaction to see him fall? The uncharacteristic savagery swept away her fear, and mixed with an unbidden desire to tear him from limb to limb. It was a primal instinct, something that wasn't like her at all—but then, how well did she really know herself? She heard more footsteps coming and turned, still desperate to get away.

Instead of climbing another flight of stairs, she burst out the door on the mezzanine level. The air exploded out of her lungs as she slammed the metal door open against the wall of the parking garage. She must look ridiculous, red-faced and panting, her hands bleeding from the cut glass. But that couldn't be helped now as she threaded her way between cars. She was disoriented. Lost in a maze of shadows and automobiles.

The sleeve of her blouse snagged on the door handle of a truck and tore, but she didn't let it stop her. The footsteps behind her were louder now, thundering. She could hear her pursuer panting, hear his unintelligible curse. She ducked behind a large SUV and tried to catch her breath. The industrial lights overhead illuminated a shadow on the far wall. She'd thought a man was chasing her, but the shadow of a horned shape emerged in darkness like an animal come to devour her.

She heard a low growl. She smelled the musk of it mingled with the other base and earthy scents here. She could even smell her own fear, as much a lure for a predator as the blood that dripped down her wrist. She spun, frantic to find an exit. That's when he caught her, wrenching a terrified scream from her throat that he silenced by pressing his mouth against hers.

She wasn't expecting it. Not the way he swallowed her scream, crushing the terror beneath the fervor of his lips. Not the masculine way he tasted. Not the heat of his breath on her face, churning from his nostrils as if he couldn't decide whether to kill her or kiss her or both. She clawed at him, her nails extending into the flesh of his forearms as if *she* were the predator, not he. She smelled his blood, heard his flesh tear, and still he kept kissing her. Her thoughts spun away and she tried to latch onto one solid thing to steady her, but the primal desire that flowed from his kiss crowded everything else out.

That kiss became the heated core of her, layers of civility melting away. He seemed to sense the exact moment when she surrendered to it, and deepened the kiss, his tongue capturing her own. She knew, even without opening her eyes, that it was Rayhan Stavrakis. And kissing him was a revelation. A thing of discovery. It was as if she'd never been kissed before, and maybe she hadn't been. Not like this. Not with the promise and pain that tugged between her body and his.

"I'm not going to hurt you," he said as she thrashed in his grip.

"Yes, you will," she choked out. "You killed Dr. Jaffe last night!"

"I didn't kill anyone last night, and you know it," he said, his outrage at the accusation too sincere to be feigned. "Who are you running from?"

"You!" she said, still clawing at him blindly, deluged with a flood of memories, flashes of her past that flowed over her. It was as if his kiss had opened the floodgates, and it would take all her strength to close them again.

"You're lying," he said shaking her. "Who are you running from?"

"Seth," she said with a sudden, heart-stopping clarity. "And if you knew better, you'd run from him, too."

Chapter 7

With fingers like bone and a kiss like ice, it grabs hold of strong men and turns them to mice.

Ray knew what people sounded like when they were overcome with terror and on the edge of breaking. He'd heard that same terror in his own voice when he was being tortured and in spite of everything she'd done to him, hearing Layla's terror made him feel protective. If this Seth guy was after her, if he was going to hurt her, Ray would put a bullet between his eyes. "Where is he?"

"He's not…he's not here. But he's coming for me and he's coming for you, too," Layla said, her nails still digging painfully into his arms.

"Stop it," he said, grabbing her by the wrists. She'd already raked him so badly he was bleeding. Or they both were. He'd worry about that later. "Let's get out of here."

"I'm not going anywhere with you." She closed her eyes against him, which made controlling her that much more difficult.

"You'd rather that I left you behind to face this Seth guy?"

He felt Layla flail and then she said, "No. I'll go with you."

"Dude," Missy said, leaning against the passenger door of the beat-up old junker he'd bought with stolen cash. "What happened to you? You're bleeding like crazy!"

Ray herded Layla forward. "Didn't I tell you to stay in the car, Missy?"

"You also told me to follow her," Missy said. "So I figured you'd want me to keep an eye on things. There are cops, or rent-a-cops, or some kind of enforcement crawling all over the parking garage across the street!"

"You sent a young girl to spy on me?" Layla asked, trying to wrench out of his grip.

"Look," Ray told her, catching Layla's green eyes and grabbing hold of her mind. "I don't need to touch you to make you do what I want to, Doc. Now get in the car." But as he flung the passenger door open with every intention of shoving her inside, he couldn't even stop Layla from clawing at him again. "Easy there, Kitty Kat. Haven't you already left me with enough scars?"

It seemed to shame Layla, and all the fight went out of her. "But you're not listening to me. If Seth sees you with me, he'll kill you… Besides, the authorities are looking for you."

"Really? This is my shocked face," Ray said, deadpan, pushing her legs into the passenger seat.

That's when she started in on the kid. "Are you really that kind of girl? You're going to let him kidnap me?"

To Ray's surprise, Missy burst into tears. "He's just a freak. He won't hurt you. He just needs to ask you some questions."

"Leave her alone, Layla," Ray snapped. "She's trying to help me get a little justice, a concept you're not all that familiar with."

But he didn't want Missy any more involved in this than she already was. He took a wad of cash from his pocket and threw it to her. "You did good, Jailbait. I've got it from here."

Missy caught the money in one hand, but her attention was on Layla. "Don't be scared. He won't hurt you. Will you, Ray?"

Ray sighed. Nobody ever used to think that he was the type to hurt people. Sure, he carried a gun, but he was an interpreter. People looked to him for help. Now even Missy seemed to think he was a brute. He slammed the door, trapping Layla inside the car, and was about to launch into a tirade in answer to Missy's question when he saw her smeared makeup and tearstained face. Layla's questions seem to have really upset her and it wasn't a simple case of teenaged moodiness. "Hey, Missy, are you okay?"

"I'm not the kind of girl that she thinks I am. I'm not a bad person."

Damn it. He didn't have time for drama. "I know

that. Listen, you've really helped me out. You're a good kid. Thanks for everything."

"Sure," she said, sniffling and pulling up one of her exposed bra straps.

He didn't like leaving her upset like this, but it was for her sake as much as his that he didn't want her involved. "Be good," he said, then got in the car.

"You're just going to leave your girlfriend behind?" Layla asked as Ray turned the ignition.

"She's not my girlfriend," Ray growled, pulling out of the parking spot. "She's a hooker."

Sarcasm curled over Layla's lips as she said one single, condemning word. "Nice."

He felt himself flush. "I'm not a client, but it's nice to know you're jealous."

Layla shot him a look—one that was decidedly not calm, cool, or collected. He was starting to see sides of her he didn't know existed, and he was kind of looking forward to a snippy denial, some witty banter. But she didn't say anything. She was too scared. He could see it in the tightness around her eyes.

"So who is Seth?" Ray asked while he drove, though he suspected that he knew. Odds were good that the guy she was running from was the same guy who had buried her memories in sand. "Why has he got you so spooked?"

"He's very dangerous," Layla said, her voice hollow. "He's jealous, and petty, and cruel. I think I must have been married to him."

That wasn't the answer Ray was expecting. He almost choked on it. He'd suspected that whoever ruined her memory had been someone more like him—someone else she'd interrogated and turned into a monster. The possibility of an abusive ex-husband hadn't crossed his mind and the shock of it forced him to say, "*Married?* You *think* you were married to him?"

"I don't know," she murmured. "I don't know why I said that. I don't know anything. I just know that he'll kill you if he finds you with me. Or worse."

"Is that supposed to scare me off? Lady, I did four tours of duty and escaped two years of torture. I've had people trying to kill me or worse for my entire adult life."

"Fine," she said. "Then just drive. Please, just get me as far away from here as you can."

Seth thought that if war gods could have vices, pride would have been his. He'd been so sure that Layla's memories were safely buried that he hadn't expected her to run. The betraying little slut *should* have been begging for his help. Instead, she'd disappeared.

He stormed back into Layla's office, ready to interrogate her assistant within an inch of her life. "When is Dr. Bahset's next appointment?"

Isabel rose up tall from behind her desk, imperious, as if she had a right to meet his eyes as an equal and only now, face-to-face, did he appreciate her truly Amazonian stature. "Why don't you leave her alone?"

Seth felt the corner of his lip furl at her impudence but remembered that he was here in mortal guise. "We're just trying to protect her, ma'am."

"No, I know who you are..." Isabel said. "*¡Bastardo!*"

Now this was interesting. At Seth's sudden focus of concentration, the candles in the room flickered out, leaving only the harsher overhead office light to illuminate her face, and yet, she was beyond beautiful. He'd suspected she was an immortal. Now he was sure of it. "*Do* you know who I am?"

"I've sensed you for a while now," Isabel said, pointing at the flower vase on the low table. "But I only suspected. Now I see that my lilies have died. Mortal things wilt in your presence, so I'm sure."

Her acknowledgment of his nature gave him pleasure. It made his eyelids lower, in the manner of a lazy crocodile. Seth was the dread god of Egyptians, a civilization older than most on earth. Everything in creation should fear him and venerate him, so when Isabel did neither, he warned, "I think that if you really knew who I was, you'd flinch away from me."

"I said *mortal* things wilt in your presence." Isabel smiled coyly. "But I'm not a mortal thing." As she said this, the bracelet on her wrist became a swarm of red butterflies. The candles flickered with new flame and the lilies came to life again.

It was a pretty but petty display. He could kill all her butterflies and flowers with a glance, but he was too busy contemplating the meaning of this. She wanted to show him that she still had powers. Perhaps not many—perhaps only decorative in nature—but she did have them. To the unspoken question in his eyes, she replied, "I'm *Xochiquetzal*."

This was entirely unexpected. Seth knew her only by name. In fact, the young goddess was born of a civilization much newer than his own, but he still felt an instant kinship with her. She didn't have his age, or Layla's wisdom, but she had a vitality that was infectious even to a deity of his stature. And now he wanted to know more. "An Aztec goddess, yet you speak Spanish?"

"And you speak English. What of it?" she asked. "We all adapt. Besides, my real name is a mouthful for *foreigners*. So you may call me Isabel."

He didn't smile, even though she'd so cleverly alluded to his identity—Seth the destroyer, the other, the *foreigner*. She was too brash to reveal herself to him like this, too sure of her frivolous charms. He shouldn't encourage her. "I'll call you what you are. A harlot. A goddess of prostitutes… No wonder you were drawn to Layla."

His sharp rebuke didn't even give her pause. "Yes, I'm a patroness of all those girls who work on the street. But not only them and that's not why I was drawn to Layla."

"She's *my* minion," Seth said harshly. "You can't have her. Content yourself with birds and butterflies."

"Why should you care who Layla belongs to now? You cast her away. Two years now, she's been foundering in this desert by herself, struggling to embrace her own sexuality. *That's* why I was drawn to her."

"And now you want to make her into a painted trollop like you?"

Isabel tilted her head. "Again, why you should care? There are other creatures in the world to add to your stable."

Yes, there were others. War forged some men into monsters—literally—and Seth was eager to add them to his menagerie and exploit their supernatural abilities. But Layla wasn't war-forged. She was war-*born*. More importantly… "She's mine!"

"I pity the wretches that belong to you," Isabel said.

"You took a strong, womanly creature and you buried all her emotions and covered her in a shroud of forgetfulness. Now you won't even leave her in peace. She doesn't even know who she is. She doesn't know *what* she is."

"And she never will," Seth snapped. "I'm taking her away from you and the mortal men she debases herself with. It's for their benefit as well as hers. She could ask the wrong question and drive yet another man to take his life."

Isabel's eyes went soft, and he felt himself momentarily pulled into them. They were like chocolate and cinnamon, vibrant and rich. Too earthy and fertile for his tastes, so why didn't he look away? "You're not worried about saving lives," Isabel said quietly.

He didn't have to explain himself. Certainly not to a washed-up Mexican goddess. Yet, he found himself asking, "Aren't I, though? A new minotaur has been unleashed. With his mental powers, he's already destroyed several mortals, and in his desire to take revenge, he may kill a few more."

"A *minotaur,*" she repeated slowly. "There hasn't been one of those in a very long time."

"He'll come for Layla and when he does, I'll capture him and bind him to me."

"So you intend to use Layla as bait?"

Seth didn't deny it. "If you dare to interfere..." He didn't have to voice the threat. All the old immortals abided by rules of divine etiquette that circumscribed their behavior. Layla had been his minion long before *Xochiquetzal* was born. Layla *belonged* to him, and no other god could take her away unless he released her. Which he had not, and would not.

Seth brushed past Isabel and reached for the door when vibrant green vines suddenly wound about his wrist, buds blossoming into giant orange flowers. She was actually trying to keep him here! She *dared?* He turned on her in a rage, and blustered, "Trifle with me and I'll bury this whole city in sand."

"I just want you to answer one question," Isabel said. "What did Layla do to deserve such punishment?"

"She defied me," he said, the memory of it still a burning hole of anger in his heart. "All for the sake of a mortal man."

"Why didn't you smite her where she stood?"

Seth withered the vines on his arm and threw them to the ground, a heap of dried husk. "Because she's all but immortal. Besides, death doesn't frighten her. There's only one thing that would kill her, and it's the one thing she wanted most."

Isabel understood immediately. "The one thing you can't give her."

She reached out for his cheek. His skin wicked away the moisture on her fingertips and Seth considered biting her with his savage teeth. It made him angry to be comforted by her. To be pitied by her. "Unhand me, you filthy whore."

She smiled sadly and withdrew her touch. "As you wish, Scorpion King."

Nothing was as Seth wished it. Nothing had been as he wished it to be for a very long time.

But when he captured Layla and the minotaur, that would all change.

Chapter 8

What's worthless when stolen, priceless when shared, a token of love when two souls are bared?

Sitting in a car next to a possible terrorist, Layla couldn't forget the way she'd felt the moment he kissed her. The scent of him had been like straw and sweat. Then there was the disturbing imagery. In the dream-like shadowy haze, Ray's nose had been a flat broad expanse, almost as wet and black as his eyes. His skin was almost like hide, soft to the touch, but somehow sleeker than skin. She'd felt the powerful muscles that bulged beneath, the cords of his neck tightening with unspeakable power. It had made her feel like he could tear her to pieces with his bare hands, but it also made her feel as if he was the one man who could protect her from anything.

She'd gone with him, fear and all, because some part

of her wondered—in the arms of a beast like Ray—would she ever have to fear anyone else? "You're not going to hurt me," she said, as if realizing it for the first time.

"I told you that I wouldn't. We'll be at my motel in a minute, we'll have a nice leisurely chat, and then you won't ever have to see me again."

"No," Layla said instantly. "We can't stay here in Vegas. We have to just get on the highway and keep driving."

He glanced at her for a moment, then shook his head. "This car wouldn't make it an hour into the desert. I'd have to buy a new car and there's not a dealership in the world—not even one in Vegas—that's going to sell us anything looking like we do."

That was when Layla first noticed the blood. Her cut hands had bled freely and stained her blouse. The scratches on Ray's forearms were starting to scab over, but he too was smeared and filthy. They'd have to clean up before they went anywhere.

Given the pinched expression on Layla's face, Ray was pretty sure that she hadn't ever been to a place that rented rooms by the hour. "What's the matter, Princess Jasmine?" he taunted, shutting the motel room door and locking it behind them. "A little too low-rent for you? The good news is that nobody saw us come in together, and even if they did, nobody thinks you're on the run. They'd just think you're here with me for a quick roll in the hay." He'd only meant it as a joke—to lighten the mood—but she turned her head as if he'd slapped her. "Hey, I was just teasing. I told you before that I wouldn't use my powers to take advantage of you."

She didn't even smile. "Then why did you kiss me in the parking garage?"

Okay, so she had him there. "I kissed you to shut you up and keep you from screaming," he said, though he was pretty sure that was a complete lie. He'd kissed her because her face had haunted his dreams for years. And because he could. What's more, she'd liked it, so he wasn't about to apologize.

He watched her cross the room and pick up the receiver of the phone. He was on her heels and caught her by the hand. "Who the hell are you calling?"

Her green eyes blinked. Once. Twice. "I was just checking to see if there was a dial tone. If Seth followed us—if he's planning to storm this place with his thugs—one of the first things he'll do is cut the phone lines."

"You're not going to try to call the police?"

"The police can't protect me," Layla said, breaking free of him. "Not from Seth and obviously not from you, either. After all, you were able to get past security and into my apartment without unbolting the locks, weren't you?"

"I was never in your apartment," Ray explained, sitting on the edge of the bed. "I was in your mind. In your dreams."

"No, you *were* in my bedroom," Layla insisted. "My headboard was slashed open!"

"That was all you, sweetheart," Ray said, a hint of smugness at the corners of his mouth as he lifted his gouged arms. "You like to scratch in moments of passion."

Passion. Even the word sounded foreign to Layla's ears. Like something forbidden and wonderful. Like something she'd once wanted very much but could never have.

She glanced down at his bed, which looked like it'd been shredded by some wild animal. The sheets were torn rags. "I guess you're going to tell me that I did this too, then?"

"No," Ray confessed, with another rueful twist to his lips. "But it *was* your fault. When I went into your dream— You do remember your dream, don't you?"

"Just in bits and pieces." Embarrassed at the memory of their near intimacy, she looked down at herself and sighed. "I'm going to need a change of clothes."

"What you need to do is sit down and answer some questions for me."

"I will. I promise. I'll tell you anything I can remember. But not here. Get me a change of clothes and then we can go. There's a dealership in the valley. We can trade in your car for something that'll make the trip to California. Or New York. Yes. The East Coast. The farther we can get from here the better."

"Who says I'm letting you go anywhere?" Ray asked. "Besides, we can't trade in the car tonight. By the time I get you a change of clothing, the dealerships will be closed."

"I have a lot of money," she said, hugging herself. "We could bribe someone."

"I thought you were a smart lady. If you interrupt some used car salesman at dinner by waving around a ton of cash on the way out of town, he's going to remember your face. And mine. The best thing to do is hunker down here until morning."

Until morning. Surely he didn't expect her to stay here with him until morning. On the other hand, maybe it was the smart thing to do. She needed time to calm down and think things through.

"But what if he finds us?" Layla asked. "What if Seth somehow finds us here?"

Ray pulled his gun out of the waistband of his jeans and held it up. "Then I'll kill him."

Layla put both hands over her mouth. Two things had shocked her. The first was that this time, she was able to identify his gun on sight. It was a Makarov semiautomatic pistol. The second thing that shocked her was the calm way in which he promised to kill someone. Ray was a soldier. Maybe killing came easy to him. Yet, the idea that he might kill for *her,* to protect *her,* was more comforting than she wanted to admit.

She'd stay here with him, then. Just until morning.

He seemed to realize without her having to say so that they'd come to some kind of truce and he took off his bloody shirt, dropping it in a disorderly heap on the floor. Then she watched him plod over to the sink and turn on the faucet. She drew closer, marveling at what she'd done to him. He looked as if he'd been clawed by a wild animal. Both exhilarated and sickened by the deep gouges she'd scratched into his arm, she drew closer. "Here, let me help you," she said, reaching for the soap.

He tried to shrug her off, but then their hands twined in the warm, sudsy water. He stilled, then looked away as she cleaned his wounds. His silence only emphasized the sound of their breathing. His deep and sonorous, hers quick and airy. She'd only intended to help slough the blood off his arms and fetch him a towel, but her efficient lathering slowed until his hands joined with hers. Then they were washing together.

Before this place and time, she hadn't known if he was a guilty man. For that matter, neither did she know if she were an innocent woman. In this moment, something changed between them.

Their shoulders touched, but it was more than that. She was leaning against his bare chest as if she'd been running lost through a wilderness and finally come to rest against the base of a mighty tree. She'd been so frightened, for so long, and against all reason, she felt safe with him. In the warm flowing water, his big thumbs caressed her palms, stroking her with a gentleness that belied the animal savagery she'd seen before. It was as if the sins of their past were washing away down the drain with the blood and dirt.

When he tangled her tawny fingers with his darker ones and held them…she let him. She'd never had anyone hold her hands like that. Like the lines of her palms could tell the story of her soul. And she wanted to linger here, with the scent of soap in her nostrils, poised in that perfect moment where she felt like the darkest parts of her were finally starting to come clean. But Ray was still bleeding, and she couldn't bear that he was in any more pain. "I need to find something to bandage your arms…."

"It's nothing." He shrugged as if he'd suffered so much that he'd grown detached from his flesh.

"Maybe there are some Band-Aids or something in here," she said.

He reached for a towel. "I said it was nothing. You don't need to play nursemaid."

It might be nothing to him, but she wanted to bandage him. Heal him somehow. Prove to him that she'd changed. "Please just let me do something for you."

He worked his jaw, as if the decision didn't come easy. "There's a first-aid kit in my pack."

She fetched it, trying not to think too hard about the other things she found inside—like duct tape and bourbon. When she returned, he extended his arms to her but it was several moments more before the tension left his shoulders and he fully surrendered, which made it easier to rub salve into the lacerations and bandage him. He watched her as she worked, lowering his head so that their foreheads almost touched, and something tightened in her throat. "I'm sorry I did this to you, Ray. You grabbed me. You frightened me."

He still couldn't look at her. "I know."

"I just wanted to get free...."

"I understand."

She supposed he, of all people, would. She taped the bandages in place around each wrist and stepped back to admire her handiwork. That's when he reached for her again. "Now let me take a look at the cuts on your hands. It looked like the glass sliced you pretty deep."

She let him take her hands again, searching for wounds she knew he wouldn't find. He turned her palms over, first this way, then that, fingertips probing. When a puzzled look crossed his face, she said, "I heal quickly."

He stared in disbelief. "You broke open that fire extinguisher case with your bare hands and now there's not a mark on you."

"My flesh mends like magic. I don't know how."

He arched a curious brow, his voice low and even. "A girl like you, with all those diplomas, doesn't even have a theory?"

"Can *you* explain everything that *you* can do?"

He shook his head, slowly. "No. I guess I can't. That doesn't keep me from trying to come up with explanations. How long have you had this ability?"

"Since as far back as I can remember. Which, admittedly, isn't that long."

"No? You seemed like you remembered something before." Before she could deny it, he took her chin between his thumb and forefinger and made her look at him. "You remembered something when I kissed you. Maybe if I do it again, you'll give me something more useful than the name of your psycho ex-husband."

She *had* remembered things when he kissed her, but now, more than anything, she was remembering that kiss. One of her hands still rested in his big calloused palm, and she felt herself lean in to him. It startled her to realize how hungry she was to be kissed again. Maybe it startled him too because his damp fingers went to the sides of her neck, thumbs on her cheeks, like he wasn't quite sure what to do with her.

But Layla knew. She didn't want to think, or plan, or fear. She just wanted this.

"You shouldn't look at me like that," he rasped. "Do you know how many times I fantasized about wrapping my hands around your neck, just like this, and choking the life out of you?"

She wanted to tell him that she wasn't that person he remembered anymore. She wasn't the kind of person who would hurt anyone, but how could she even say such a thing when both of his arms bore the bandaged evidence to the contrary? "I'm sorry I made you hate me, Ray. I don't remember it, but I'm sorry that I pushed you to fantasize about strangling me."

His gaze settled on her with unmistakable sensual

weight. "That's not the only thing I fantasized about doing to you."

"Show me," she whispered. She wanted to understand. She wanted to *feel.* Every time he touched her, something inside of her started blooming to life. She wanted to know what the blossom would look like. Every petal and grain of pollen.

Ray looked as if something were twisting inside him. "I can't."

"Why not?" she asked softly. "Do you want to hurt me? Is that what you want?"

His eyes closed, as if it shamed him to say, "No."

"Then what do you want?" It was only a question, but it made something inside him snap. It was almost an audible thing—as if she could hear the crack of his self-control when he jerked her against him, drawing her lips against his. It wasn't wild and savage as it had been in the parking garage. This kiss wasn't meant to silence a scream, or to capture the cornered creature she'd been. This time, his lips claimed her, explored her, encouraging her to do the same.

When she did, she heard his breath grow ragged. His big hands drifted down her throat to the collar of her blouse, clumsy fingers fumbling with the tie. She reached up to help him, trembling as they worked at the buttons together. She shivered when the silk slid from her shoulders and fell to the floor, baring her to the air. He didn't rush to undo her bra, but let his mouth drift down her neck to nuzzle the hollow of her collarbone.

It didn't seem possible that skin could be so soft. *This was madness,* Ray thought. He shouldn't be doing this, shouldn't be touching her, shouldn't be kissing her. But he didn't want to think about anything but her skin, lest it return him to sanity. Ever since he'd changed in that dungeon, he'd lived a thing apart from society, an outsider even to himself. Touching her pulled him back into his body. His physical desire for her grounded him. He wanted to have her, take her, taste her and lose himself inside her if she'd let him.

He tried to be gentle, tried not to maul her, but pent-up need made him brutish. He grabbed her, molding her body against his, smothering her tiny, womanly cries. He wanted to gently slide her skirt down, but instead he yanked it up over her hips then thrust his fingers into her panties. She was so wet that it made him groan, and as soon as he touched her there, she made a needy sound that he was sure would be his undoing.

Dim light filtered through the high bathroom window, chasing away the shadows between them. The scent of salve and soap now mixed with a more earthy musk of desire. Layla shuddered as he touched the forbidden place at her core, not knowing if she should push his hand away or not. The intimidating bulge of his erection pressed against her belly, bringing with it an unfamiliar sensation, both sickly and sweet. Was this *arousal?* How could it hover so close to the edge of pleasure and pain? She needed something. She needed, wanted, ached. Those were words she never used, words that hadn't applied to her before now. But in his arms, wearing little more than her bra and panties, the steadiness of his hands on her waist emboldened her. She felt the brazen urge to stroke him. She wanted to grab for his zipper. She'd done it before, but now her fingers faltered.

He encouraged her with his eyes, and whispered, "My scars aren't contagious, you know."

She glanced up from beneath her lashes. "It's not that I don't want to, it's that I *can't.*" Something was stopping her. She couldn't lift her own hand to do it. She didn't know if it was fear or shame or something else. All she knew was that whatever force it was that had made her sleep through the past two years of her life still had her in its thrall. Maybe she was still dreaming. Maybe Ray could wake her. "You need to *make* me do it, Ray. Make me touch you."

He looked at her as if she'd suggested he strangle her. "No way."

"You've already used your powers to make me do things I *didn't* want to do," she argued. "Why can't you use them to make me do things I *want* to do?"

"Layla." He said her name like a warning. Like she was putting him to some kind of test. "This is different."

She was so afraid it was all going to slip away. If she didn't seize this one moment of pure heat and passion, she might never have another one. "Help me, Ray. Please *make* me touch you."

She couldn't have asked him again if he'd refused. She was too vulnerable. But he didn't refuse. He lifted his dark eyes to hers and she felt the penetration as keenly as if he'd grasped her with both hands. Her world slid off its axis, but this time she opened her mind to him and fell into his control as if gravity had drawn her there. She was floating, disoriented, not in possession of herself. He had her now....

"Touch me," Ray said. A hoarse, terse command.

She'd never be able to describe the way it felt that first time—to feel his sexual mastery over her as she unzipped him. She was free of all fear she might do anything wrong. She'd felt the bulging rigid line beneath his clothes, but it was different to touch his bare erection, and she was startled by its size. Her fingertips didn't come close to meeting her thumb as they wrapped around his girth. He was hot and hard, pulsing in her palm as her hand moved.

It would never have occurred to her that a man would want such a firm grip, such a rough jerking motion, but that's how he must have wanted it as she worked her closed fist over his shaft. And it thrilled her. She had no control over the way she touched him, no control over her own hands, and yet, she felt completely free. The absurdity of it made her sputter with laughter and unexpected joy.

"Is that okay?" he asked, startled by her response. It was so much more than okay. It was the most erotic thing Layla had ever known, and she thought her knees might buckle from the sheer pleasure of it.

"Layla." He said her name again, a harsh whisper, but she'd never heard her own name sound so beautiful before. She could see in his eyes that he wanted her, desired her. She hadn't realized how powerful it would make her feel. It made no sense that she was so completely under his control, and yet, felt like...like some kind of object of worship. She hadn't known that a man could make her feel like something he *must* have. Like something he might die without.

While she stroked him, his fingers searched for the center of her, swirling beneath her underwear in a way that made her squirm. It was all too much. "I need..."

"To come?" he asked, fingers still dancing over her most sensitive spot.

"Yes. No. I don't know," Layla said raggedly. "I don't even know what it would feel like."

"You've never had an orgasm?" he asked, as if he'd misunderstood.

It wasn't that men hadn't tried. It wasn't even that she hadn't tried to do it herself. It's just that she *couldn't*. How could she explain that to him? His gaze intensified and something started building inside her. She realized that he was doing it. He was trying to make her come with his mind. In the past, she'd shut down, shut off. But Ray didn't let her. "You're going to come for *me* though, aren't you?"

This couldn't be happening, but it was. The heat of it boiled up inside her. It wasn't something she could do for herself, but it was a gift he was giving her. He forced her to feel the pleasure, to open herself up to it, and she gasped. Just then, sexual intensity blossomed, bursting open in vivid color. She never closed her eyes, not even when her head lolled back from the orgasmic pleasure. It was so powerful as it rolled over her, that she lost all threads of self-restraint. A startled cry escaped her lips, then deepened into a moan as her body tensed and released in waves.

Her knees buckled beneath her, her entire body shaking with the intensity of it.

She slumped against him. "You okay?" he asked.

"I don't know," she said, and honestly she didn't. She was like some teenager experiencing everything for the first time.

The water was still running in the sink. Their bodies were still tightly pressed together, and Ray braced himself to steady her. Her hair had all come down around her face, framing it in disheveled wisps, and

Ray realized that he'd *made* her come. He'd made her do it. The exhilaration of controlling her like this, the thrill of having this kind of power swirled together with his arousal in a way that made him fear he was going to take it too far. That he could do this to her, that he could do *anything* to her, was almost as exciting as knowing that she wanted him to.

Staring into her eyes like this, he could force her thighs open without having to touch her and he wanted her so much that he didn't trust himself. If this was going to happen, it had to be the old-fashioned way. He took her by the shoulders and turned her around so that he couldn't look into her eyes, then placed her hands flat on the countertop. The break in mental connection was abrupt and painful, something that he eased by rubbing his erection between her thighs, and against her pantied ass. She arched back for him in clear invitation. She even rubbed against him, like an affectionate cat.

She was ready for him and he didn't have to make her do this. She wanted him. With that heady thought, he pulled her cotton underwear to the side, brushing the shadowy curve of her belly with both hands. She smelled so good, and when the dark curls between her legs came into view, he felt drunk with need. Intoxicated. He pressed between her thighs, slicking himself in her wetness before attempting to push inside.

And that's when she went cold.

Chapter 9

I watch you, I mock you
And you just stare.
Break me into pieces—
Now many of us are there.

Layla wished she hadn't looked at herself in the mirror. She didn't even recognize the woman she saw there bent forward over the sink, arching her back like some animal in heat. Her pupils were so dilated that her eyes were nearly black. Her hair was tousled and her body was shaking with the aftermath of orgasm. She was wild and hungry, like a stranger who'd waited in the desert a thousand years for someone to happen by and solve her riddle. But who was that in the reflection? Certainly no one she'd ever seen before. "I look…"

"Sexy," Ray said, his body still positioned to mount her.

"I look like a slut," Layla said, shame choking her like a mouthful of sand.

Ray paused, his hand still warm on the small of her back. "No—"

"Yes I do," she snapped, straightening up and hugging herself, her bare arms no substitute for the protection of clothing. A maelstrom of self-loathing swirled in her mind. *Slut. Whore. Tramp.* "I look like a half-naked prostitute and I'm behaving like one, too, so it's really no wonder that you'd treat me this way."

Ray blanched. He started to say something, but Layla didn't hear it. She pushed past him into the bedroom looking for something, anything to wear. He followed, lumbering after her as if he couldn't quite get the blood back into his brain. When he finally spoke, he said, "Layla, what the hell is going on?"

She shrugged, sitting on the edge of the motel bed, pulling the quilt around her body. The memories were coming back now. All the men she'd questioned. All the things she'd done. "I remembered something." That shook him out of his sluggishness. He was at her side in two steps, crouching in front of her.

"I remembered *you,*" she said, biting her lower lip. "I remember questioning you, day after day. I remember all the confessions you signed saying that you'd worked for the enemy."

His expression darkened, both hands rubbing the stubble of his face. "They were lies, Layla. I'd have signed anything to get out of that hole."

"So I *was* an interrogator just like you said. I asked you questions. I tried to earn your trust. I tried to get close to you and find your vulnerabilities. You wanted to know my real name and I almost told you. I knew you were developing feelings for me…" She watched him swallow, his pride too strong to allow him to admit it. "And I *used* that."

"Why?" he asked, his expression pained. "Why did you do that?"

Layla lifted her chin. "To help the U.S. government break you before another soldier or civilian died."

Ray slammed his hand against the bedside table. "I was innocent, damn you!"

Her accusation obviously infuriated him, instantly and powerfully. He looked like he could tear the whole room apart, like he could kill her, but when he reached for her, he just took her face in his hands. "Layla, you need to listen to me. I didn't do anything but risk my life for my country. Someone told you otherwise, and I need to know *who*. What was the evidence against me?"

"I don't know," Layla said. "I don't remember."

Fury burned higher and hotter in his eyes. "I need you to remember. I'll *make* you remember."

In her half-naked humiliation, she felt angry and defiant. "Oh? How are you going to manage that?"

"I have an idea or two," he said with a dark laugh. "Every time I get your pulse racing, you seem to remember something else. The first time I touched you, you whispered my name. I kissed you, and you remembered your ex. I bent you over a sink, and now you remember questioning me. What happens if I throw you down on this bed and give you what you really need?"

"Don't," she said, putting her hand on his chest.

He grabbed it and twisted it just to the edge of pain. "You know I can do it. In fact, you *want* me to do it. All that crap you said in there about how you looked like a slut, that's just an excuse. You're just scared, and maybe you should be, because let me tell you something, I've done worse things to unlock people's memories than get them off."

The coarseness of his language seemed to physically scrape her skin. All the bravado went out of her, and she was left only with her vulnerability. "You don't understand," she whispered. "I'm not like this. I'm not this person who...who...has sex in a stranger's motel room."

"We're not strangers," Ray said. "And it's pretty clear to me you don't know who the hell you really are. You think you're some demure little rabbit, but do you want to know what I saw inside your mind?"

Layla inhaled sharply. "What?"

"I saw a lioness."

"A lioness?" It sounded wrong in every way. She wasn't anything like a lioness. Layla was wary and restrained, not wild and free. She was a creature of order and logic, not instinct. It's true that when she'd defended herself in the stairwell she'd felt like a fierce predator, but she hadn't known that part of herself. She also didn't know the part of herself that wanted this man. She was a stranger to the part of herself that quivered and ached for him.

"Then make me remember, if you think you can," she said. "Do it."

He pressed her down onto the mattress with a kiss that left her breathless. Her bra and panties, and the skirt bunched at her waist offered little barrier between his body and her own. Even so, she let him remove her clothes, and then his own. She squeezed her eyes shut, but her thighs parted for him anyway, and her back arched as he positioned himself. She wanted to say that it was all his doing, that he was controlling her, but it had gone well beyond that now. She wanted to give in to this before grief and fear and wisdom and sadness chased it all away.

She was mesmerized by the scars on his body and by her own need to touch him, soothe him, as if her fingers could erase the burn marks and the slashes of pale flesh across his muscular back. His erection pressed between her legs and it suddenly seemed impossible that he would fit inside her. Ray was a big man in every sense of the word, and she gasped as he tried to slide forward into her. The pressure built and it wasn't altogether pleasurable. Resting his weight on his elbows, he readjusted, probing her wetness. He was stretching her and she squeezed her eyes shut against the discomfort.

"Am I hurting you?" he whispered.

"No," she lied. But then, biting her lip, she whispered, "A little, but don't stop."

Layla wouldn't have wanted him to stop even if she were in agony. She wanted to give him her body, as if it could heal what had been done to him. As if it could somehow make up for what had been done to *her*. Ray slowly sank down until he was within her.

Then he groaned. She loved the sounds he made, the way he looked at her in amazement. He was the burning center of her now and she struggled to adjust to his thickness. She didn't have her memories, but she knew that she'd never been stretched so far. Her insides throbbed as if her heart had somehow fallen between her legs. If he'd started thrusting, if he'd moved at all, she would've screamed. But he didn't move. He stilled, gritting his teeth as if he were the one in pain, and maybe he was.

His shoulders shook from the effort and that's when she realized he was waiting for some signal from her. She gave it to him by lifting her hips. Another groan, and he was withdrawing, leaving a stinging emptiness behind that she found more unbearable than anything. "No, please," she whimpered, rocking up against him. "More."

"Careful what you wish for," he said through gritted teeth, but he wasn't too much of a gentleman to accommodate her. He hoisted one of her knees over his hip, then started the slow and steady pistoning motion. She reeled as if he'd breached some barrier, and she supposed he had, because sex had never felt like this before. Heat spread through her belly and the tension in her thighs eased. This wasn't the kind of sensation that a woman like her should've wanted. But she did want it, and it changed her.

He was so big that he left no room inside her for doubts or self-consciousness, no room for second thoughts or self-control. There was only room inside her for this.

He rocked her, heedless of the rickety headboard that banged against the wall with each thrust. It was so good now, so thrilling, that her skin tingled. Before he'd seemed like too much, but now she wasn't sure she could get enough as her body coiled and coiled with so much pleasure she thought it might kill her.

"Come," he whispered, nudging some fleshy spot near her womb that made her cry out. She wrapped her legs tighter around his waist, desperate for it.

Sweat-damp dark hair fell over his face as their eyes locked and he took control of her mind so gently it was like a kiss upon her forehead. He pushed her over that edge, right into orgasm.

She bucked beneath him as he took possession of her muscles, and made them all release at once into a climax that left her raw and screaming. If it'd only been the one time, perhaps she'd have been able to retain some semblance of decorum. But he did it to her again, and again, until her cries sounded like sobs and she lost all sense of time and place. Her nails raked his back. Her teeth sank into his shoulder as if she really were the lioness he saw inside her.

When he finally found his own release, he gave a shuddering moan, flooding her. She felt the warmth of him settle, like rain on a fertile plain. She gasped again as if something quickened inside her, her newfound discovery of pleasure like the gasp of a newborn infant.

Then they collapsed together, in a tangle of panting, sweaty flesh.

"I'm sorry," Layla said, twining her fingers in the hair on his chest, marveling at its texture. "For scratching…"

"Don't apologize," Ray said, still breathing hard. "There's a lot of stuff you should be sorry about, but not this. Maybe I need to get you declawed but—" Then he saw her expression and went serious. "To see a woman like you do that was damned sexy."

"Seth didn't like it." Layla hadn't meant to say it, and she bit her lip once the words were out. She knew that the mere mention of another lover could send a man into a rage, and Ray seemed like a man with more anger than he knew what to do with.

She expected him to lash out, but he just rolled over onto his side so that he could look at her. He brushed the hair out of her eyes. "You're already remembering more."

Layla nodded. "Not the specifics, but impressions. Nothing useful to you."

"Okay." His frustration was plain. "So tell me what else you remember about your asshole ex-husband, then."

"He used to call me names." *Whore, slut, tramp.* She could hear them still. Given that she was in bed with a man she barely knew, it was hard not to think those words about herself now and let them stain her cheeks with shame.

Ray's expression soured. "I'll never get why women marry guys like that in the first place."

"I loved him." It clearly wasn't the answer Ray had been expecting. Certainly it wasn't the answer Layla had been expecting either. She'd thought herself incapable of any emotion as strong as love. Now a sharp pain stabbed her chest at the realization that she'd felt love before. That maybe she could feel it again and that it might hurt her just as badly. "He broke my heart."

"What'd he do? Cheat on you?"

Layla let out a little laugh. As if being betrayed in such a banal way could have possibly caused this much damage. She didn't know how Seth had broken her heart; she only knew that he'd shattered it like glass on a cement floor. Now with so many jagged edges, she was afraid she'd slice open anyone who tried to pick up the pieces. Maybe that's what had happened to Nate Jaffe, and why she couldn't cry over his death. Maybe that's what would happen to Ray if he came to care for her.

"He didn't want me," Layla said.

"Bullshit." He looked completely bewildered, as if he couldn't comprehend that any man might not want her. His fingers closed protectively around her arm and her body felt as marked by his lovemaking as his was marked by torture. Maybe it was this moment that she started to fall in love with him.

"There were things I wanted that Seth couldn't give me," Layla tried to explain.

"Like an orgasm?" Ray asked, and she wasn't sure if he was joking.

"I don't know. I only know that everything I did, I did to please him. He owns Scorpion Group and he has multibillion-dollar contracts with the government. If I wanted to be a part of his life, I had to be a part of that. So I learned how to use every weapon I could get my hands on. I learned to move in his world. I helped catch bad guys. I helped ensure the war effort went well. Seth liked that. He appreciated my competence, but the more I made myself into what he said I wanted, the more bored he seemed to be. Like the thrill of the chase was gone, and then he only seemed to want me if someone else did. But if someone did want me… he'd become so jealous. *Murderously* jealous, Ray."

"I told you before, I'm not scared of him. But let me ask you something. Did you go with other guys just to piss him off? To get his attention?"

"I don't know."

"Is that why you're in bed with me now?"

She all but hissed with indignation, but didn't he

have every right to question her motives? Ray had no reason to trust her, and even less reason to trust whatever it was between them. "I wanted you, and you have no idea how foreign a thing that is to me. To want something and take it for myself, without his permission..."

Ray's eyebrow arched at the way she phrased that. "He sounds like the kind of abusive asshole who would have eventually killed you."

"He can do worse than that, Ray," she said. "He *did* do worse than that. When I was with Seth, I thought I knew who I was. I told myself that I was doing good things to help the war effort and make the world a better place, but obviously I was wrong."

He glanced away. It was still there in the room between them. They'd each seen the monster in one another. "Layla, I used to imagine what it would be like if you believed me. If you believed in my innocence. I used to imagine that you'd *beg* for my forgiveness."

"When you imagined it, did you forgive me?" she wondered. The answer seemed terribly important.

"Yeah." The one single word sounded like it had been torn from his throat. "But not before I had you naked and on your knees."

"Having sex with me was what you needed to forgive me?" she asked.

Ray looked queasy. "Layla, don't even say that. Can you stop being a shrink for just a minute and stop analyzing?"

Layla braved his anger anyway. "You started it. Besides, I just want to know why you fantasized about me naked."

He winced. "Because I just wanted to have power

over you for a change. Because it felt good to think about sex. Because it was a distraction from prison. Because if I was thinking about pleasure, then I wasn't thinking about pain. It helped me forget the fear. It made me feel just a little bit free."

"Then I'm glad you did," Layla said, pressing a kiss to his palm.

"Are you?" Ray asked. She could see that he was wondering if it had been part of her game. Maybe he was wondering if what they'd just done together was still some new kind of manipulation. If she was just trying to earn his trust, so that she could send him back to a dark dungeon. He squeezed his eyes shut a few times, as if he were literally in pain, and then she saw that he was.

"Ray?"

He shook his head and pinched the bridge of his nose. "It's nothing."

"It's not nothing. You're bleeding."

A few droplets of blood had leaked from his ear onto the pillow and his jaw clenched. "When I use my power to control people, it always hurts after. More so with you."

She felt guilty for encouraging him to use his powers during sex. Her heart hammered in her chest at the thought that something that had felt so right between them could have hurt him. "Can I get something for you?"

"I just need to rest a little," Ray whispered. "Just stay with me."

The war god struggled to keep his expression appropriately somber as the police allowed him into the parking garage to look over the crime scene. Layla was gone. Vanished. Her car abandoned. That should've been enough to fix Seth's mouth into a scowl, but the dangling body of one of his men was a sight that unexpectedly delighted him. The limp body hung loosely from the stairway railing; the police thought it was a clear case of suicide, but Seth knew better. This was Layla's handiwork, and he wanted to pause and admire her skill.

Seth had always believed that blood was the best irrigation for the soil, but there was something to be said for the clean and sterile kill of a sphinx, too. Every man had secret sins and a guilty heart. Some men had shame too great to live with, and that made them vulnerable to a riddler like Layla. Obviously, the men who worked for Seth—men who agreed to kill for profit—were easy prey.

Even if Seth could feel pity for a mortal, he wouldn't have felt it for this man. It was difficult for him to even *pretend* to be grief-stricken.

Isabel had no such difficulties. She was already sniffling into a tissue. He didn't have to guess how the strumpet had managed to charm her way past the police tape. There wasn't a mortal man alive who could walk by her without a second look, and a police detective was already at her elbow, comforting her. "You shouldn't have to see this, Miss Flores. Why don't you let me take you back inside and we can go over your statement again about the last time you saw Dr. Bahset."

"¡Qué horror!" Isabel cried, eyeing the dead man and shaking her head.

The worst part was that Seth sensed that the Aztec's

emotions were genuine. How could the goddess possibly be upset about the death of one of Seth's men? Had she known his hapless employee? Worse, had she *touched* him? Had they been lovers? The possibility was surprisingly unsettling. It was a good thing the man was dead, because Seth may well have killed him just for the brief flicker of...what was it? *Jealousy?*

No. Isabel was a filthy whore. Why should he want what so many other men had obviously already enjoyed? Worse, she was a goddess. No minion that he could control and keep under his thumb. If she displeased him, he couldn't simply punish her. Isabel would be his equal. Well, not *exactly* his equal. He was older than her, and stronger by far. The fact remained that she wouldn't submit to his commands and Layla's rebellion was already more trouble than Seth wanted to contend with.

"It isn't suicide," Seth told the police. "Rayhan Stavrakis did this. He's an escaped enemy combatant and he has a score to settle with Dr. Bahset and now he's kidnapped her."

"But first he took the time to hang this guy?" the detective asked. "Kind of a lot of trouble to go to when a bullet would work just as easily."

Seth hated to be questioned by petty mortals. "It's his modus operandi."

"So you think Stavrakis hanged her boyfriend, too? What was his name? Dr. Jaffe?"

Seth winced at the word *boyfriend.* It was such a juvenile word, and it implied intimacies that Layla shouldn't have engaged in with anyone, much less the pathetic psychiatrist. Then again, Layla was proving to be as unpredictable and elusive as the minotaur. Oh, how Seth looked forward to capturing them both.

"I think you'd be smart to put all your resources into finding him. He has information vital to our national security so we need him alive."

In truth, the minotaur had never given up useful information in the dungeon. He may have even been innocent of the crimes he was accused of. Not that it had mattered at all to Seth. The important thing about Rayhan Stavrakis was that he'd been a perfect specimen. It hadn't been difficult to turn him into just the kind of pet Seth had always wanted for his very own. Seth doubted the Las Vegas police force would be able to catch him, but a manhunt would increase the pressure.

Back out on the street, Isabel was waiting for him. "Is Layla in danger from the minotaur?"

It irritated Seth that he wanted to reassure her. "No mortal man can hurt Layla."

"Rayhan isn't *just* a mortal man, he's also a monster. What if he really *has* taken her? What are you going to do about it?"

"I'm going to find them both and add them to my collection of creatures. I'll use them to make war, to grow more powerful, to put the world back the way it was supposed to be. Maybe you should help me. Perhaps if men understood the power of the old gods again, you'd have a worshipper or two."

"Do you really think I don't have worshippers?" Isabel asked, her pretty eyes hot with offense.

"Besides slobbering fools who want to take you to bed?" He glanced angrily at a man on the street who ogled her.

"Sex can be worship," Isabel countered, fearless of his wrath. "Lovemaking is. When a man worships a woman's body, he's worshipping me, too."

Ah, he could see it now. Whereas he fed off war and mayhem, she fed off sex, and with all the rutting in this sinful city, he could see why she'd make it her new home.

"I think," Isabel said, her eyes half-lidded and voice sultry, "that *you* would even worship me a little bit, if I came to your bed."

It wasn't possible that he should want her. She was the embodiment of everything he despised in a woman. Where he was the sterile sand, she was lush and fertile. Where he inspired hatred, she inspired lust. Maybe even love. He controlled storms and crocodiles and venomous scorpions that burrowed under sand and rock, whereas she commanded flowers and hummingbirds and butterflies that fluttered delicately through the air. Yet, the thought of conquering her stirred something in his blood that he hadn't felt for centuries. "If you came to my bed, perhaps you'd do the worshipping, *Xochiquetzal*."

She smiled at the use of her true name. "It's a pity you'll never find out."

"I could have you if I wanted you," Seth assured her.

"No," she replied. "No man puts his hands on me unless he's earned the right."

Earned the right? He didn't need her permission to enjoy whatever pleasures her body offered. He could *take* them. "I'm more powerful than you," Seth warned. "I can bend you to my will."

She should've stepped back from the thunder in

his eyes, but instead, Isabel whispered, "Are you sure about that?"

In an effort to soothe his ego and satisfy his pride, Seth had come to Vegas to fetch his wayward minion. Now Layla had made a fool of him again, and the young Aztec goddess had been on hand to witness it. It had emboldened her to taunt him like this, and it made him furious. She was too young a goddess to truly understand the world, but he would teach her. She'd either submit to him now or he'd take her right here on the street like the whore that she was. He'd tear the clothes from her body with the scouring winds of a sandstorm. He'd scorch her lips with his desert heat and make her wilt in supplication!

With a sharp breath, he summoned his powers and the sky began to cloud over. An unseasonal gust of wind rattled windows of the nearby building. It also pressed Isabel against the wall while fat droplets of rain spattered at her feet. At the sudden storm, the city's residents and tourists fled indoors, but Seth wasn't thinking about any of them. At the moment, his attention was wholly and solely on Isabel. Her skirt fluttered around her hands as she fought to stay covered and Seth gloried in the way rain drove like needles into her. "Don't test me—"

He got no further than that before her hair blossomed into a wreath of orchids and Isabel laughed. "Rain makes the earth fertile. I'm not afraid of your storms."

Her laughter was too much to endure. He considered calling an army of scorpions from the desert to carry her somewhere he could have her at his mercy, but she was exhausting his reserves, and he didn't want the mortals to see this display. It was foolish to spend so much power over this little spat. And what's more, she seemed to be enjoying it. "It's been a long time since you've had a worthy rival, Seth, hasn't it been?"

"Nonsense," he told her, letting the storm clouds drift away. "The mayhem and bloodshed of this world still sustains war gods like me. I have plenty of competition. There are the Greeks, like Ares and Athena. I vie with Ogun in Africa..." He trailed off because it seemed as if he'd named them as equals, and they weren't.

"Those aren't your true rivals," Isabel said. "All of you want the same thing. War, battle, violence. You're all jackals of the same pack fighting over the bones. I'm something completely different."

Yes, she was different. In all the most interesting ways. He'd always thrived in his epic battles with Osiris and Horus. He missed those days, and longed to taste them again. Was it possible to recapture with her?

"I propose a wager," she said. "Layla has vanished and we both want to find her. If I find her first, I want you to release her as your minion and give her to me."

Seth snorted. "Layla is a betraying bitch. She'll be no more obedient to you than she was to me."

"I don't want her obedience," Isabel said, slicking the raindrops from her skin.

"Then why do you want her?"

"Do you really care?" Isabel asked. "Or are you just afraid to lose?"

She pricked at his pride. "What do I get if I win?"

"Me." Isabel leaned forward to press a very provocative kiss on his mouth.

He let it happen. It was a way of sealing their bargain, but it was more than that too, and soon he'd make her regret having trifled with him.

Chapter 10

I get inside your house at night
I lurk beneath your bed
Close your eyes: you still see me
Light a torch: I'm dead.

A few hours later, in the darkness, there was a soreness between Layla's legs—a physical reminder of what she'd done with Ray. She clamped her thighs together as if to savor it before she went back to feeling nothing at all. With Ray, she'd experienced all the things people always talked about, but she hadn't understood. How was she supposed to go back to the numbness of life before?

A vague sense of regret formed at the realization that she'd just had unprotected sex. Nate Jaffe had always been diligent about using protection and Layla had made it a practice to be responsible. So why had all reason fled the moment Ray touched her?

Ray slept soundly, his face half on her pillow, his big frame taking up the bulk of the bed. She couldn't sleep, but didn't want to wake him either, so she found the remote control, flipped on the television, and pressed the mute button. She should've known better. Photos of Nate Jaffe flashed on the screen, stabbing her in the heart. Then her own image flickered across the screen. Underneath her photo, red letters spelled out the word KIDNAPPED.

Seeing Ray's picture on the news was even harder to take. The red letters under his photo said AMERICAN TERRORIST. Layla turned up the sound just loud enough to hear the newsmen compare him to John Walker Lindh and proclaim that Ray was armed and dangerous.

That wasn't a lie. Ray had made love to her, yes. He'd shown her a side to him that was gentle and vulnerable. She'd also seen the other side of him, too. She'd seen the coldness in his eyes when he'd shown her his gun, and though he protested his innocence, Layla wasn't sure she believed him. She might not remember everything about herself, but she remembered enough to know that she wasn't a malicious person. She wouldn't have interrogated someone she thought was wrongfully accused.

Ray had to have done *something* to make the government arrest him. Breaking out of prison to terrorize people didn't sound like the actions of an innocent man. People didn't just get thrown into places like Gitmo by mistake, did they? So what was she doing here, in his bed? Layla took a deep breath, wondering what version of the Stockholm syndrome had led her to not only go willingly with her captor, but to sleep with him, too. Logic and reason were coming back to her, and she was horrified.

She'd walked out on her patients today. Walked out on Isabel. And now what? Was she literally sleeping with the enemy? She couldn't go back to her office or her old life until she remembered exactly who Seth was and why she was so afraid of him. She couldn't stay with Ray either. Some sense, deep and foreboding, told her that if she stayed with Ray, he'd end up dangling from a rope or strangled. That's what happened to people who got close to her….

Where could she go?

Her fingers itched for the sixpence that she'd kept since the day she woke up with it in her hand. It comforted her. Steadied her. Helped her to think. Helped her feel safe. Safe… The memory teased itself out of her mind slowly. She'd left herself a clue, as if the information were too secret to write down, as if she knew she were losing her memory. Six pence. She'd always thought it was just a coin, but it was more than that. It was an address!

6 Pence Road.

A safe house in the mountains that she'd set up for herself long ago.

Layla carefully slipped out from under Ray's arm and crept across the floor, gathering her clothes and dressing silently. Her skirt was salvageable, but her bloody blouse was beyond saving so she pulled one of Ray's black T-shirts over her head. It looked sloppy on her, and smelled like him. It was also too big. She was swimming in it, but nothing could be done about that. The keys were in the pocket of Ray's jeans. She pulled them out very carefully, so as not to wake him, then slipped out the door.

Ray had actually slept without nightmares for a change. He couldn't remember the last time that had happened. No dreams of finding his brother's dead body. No dreams of dungeons or village massacres. Just pure, blessed sleep. He would've liked to turn over and catch a few more winks, but he knew Layla would be anxious to be up and out of here before daybreak. He reached for her, liking the way her scent was on the pillow, but not liking it so much when his outstretched hand found an empty bed beside him.

"Layla?" He sat up, trying to shake his sex-sated stupor. It was a small hotel room; she couldn't have gone far. He glanced at the bathroom, half expecting to see her fixing her hair in front of the mirror, but it was empty. He launched himself out of bed. "Layla!" Her name echoed off the walls as he pulled on his jeans. Stumbling toward the door, he threw it open and blinked into dawn's light. His car was gone. His keys were gone, too. *"Motherf—"*

His own curse was cut off by the pain in his arm as he repeatedly bashed it against the motel door in fury. She'd played him. *Again.* Last night had been about luring him into a false sense of security so that she could get away without telling him what he needed to know. Where the hell would she go now? She wouldn't go to the police—he knew that much, but it was of small comfort. Knowing her, she'd probably decided to chance a trek out of town in that rust bucket, which meant she could be stalled somewhere in the middle of the desert without water, terrified and alone.

Why should he care? She'd taken off again. And this time was almost worse than the first time, when she'd left him behind to rot in Syria. At least then he only had an illusion that there was something between them. He hadn't slept with her.

But with his powers, she couldn't *really* run from him, could she?

Layla's cabin was in the mountains, at the edge of the desert. It was a well-hidden and well-chosen safe house. The car she'd stolen from Ray shuddered to a stop then stalled out completely in that driveway. *Great.* There was no sign of anyone else living here, and the place looked near-abandoned. She found the key under the gutter spout, where she expected it, but worried that there would be an alarm inside. There wasn't one. There wasn't electricity either but there was a generator, a well for water, and a wood-burning stove in the kitchen. Everything she'd need to live off the grid for a while.

Off the grid? Who said things like that?

It was one of the many unfamiliar thoughts that had been rushing through her mind. The first thing she did was find a flashlight, and that led her to some lanterns. The second thing she did was check the bedroom, where she found a few changes of clothing. Casual clothing. Mostly jeans and cotton tops. These outfits didn't look like anything she would wear, but they would have to do.

She got the generator working and once the power was on and the water was pumping, she decided to take a shower. It was with a bittersweet feeling that she washed Ray's scent off of her. Once she was clean, she changed into her new clothes, surprised that they were a little big.

Had she lost weight? It seemed as if she hadn't really been very hungry for the past two years of her life, but now she was ravenous. It must have taken her a half hour to figure out how to get the woodstove burning and put on a kettle of hot water. There wasn't any tea in the pantry. Just coffee, soup, and a lot of beans. She hoped it would be enough to still her growling stomach. She'd heard that a watched pot never boils, so she went back into the bedroom and rummaged around, curious and awed by each new discovery.

In the large walk-in closet, she found an enormous safe. It was big enough to lock a man inside of it. She didn't remember the combination, but her fingers did, and a moment later, she was staring at the unnerving contents. A metal briefcase full of cash lay open before her, but her eyes were immediately drawn to the weapons and ammunition. She found not one, not two, but *three* different guns. Steeling her courage, she picked one up and realized that she knew how to clean it, how to load it, how to turn off the safety. She knew how to shoot it, too.

Under some clips of ammunition, she found a few cell phones. All prepaid. All she had to do was charge them up and activate them with one of the many credit cards she found in a manila envelope that also contained several passports. Layla opened one of the passports and it had her picture, but a different name. *Berenice Neferet.* It didn't sound familiar. Layla opened another passport, and then another, all with her photo.

Isadora Asar. Alexandra Khaldun. Nila Odji.

The names were alarming enough, but it was the dates that disturbed her. One passport had expired fifteen years before. Layla could have been no more than a teenager in that photo, and yet, she looked exactly as she did now. Who the hell was she? *What* was she?

Layla pulled out a sealed envelope. She hadn't liked what she found in that safe, and she was sure she wasn't going to like what she found in this envelope. Breaking the seal, she pulled out a series of photos. Pictures of strangled men, bodies dangling from the end of ropes, corpses with bags over their faces. Suffocations. Asphyxia. People who had somehow stopped breathing… maybe because of her.

Nate Jaffe had died this way too, but she was sure she hadn't killed him. When it came to the men in the pictures, she wasn't so sure. All she'd done to that Scorpion Group flunky in the stairwell was whisper a riddle to him, and he'd crumpled on the ground as if he'd been struck by lightning. What had she said? *I'm too heavy to carry, too light to put down, a stain on your soul, a thorn in your crown.* The answer to that was guilt. *Guilt*. And there was certainly enough of that to go around.

Layla went into the kitchen to make herself a cup of coffee and think. What if Ray's car wouldn't start again when she tried it? Layla took a sip of the coffee, letting her mind work over the problem, and was rewarded with a rich roasted flavor rolling over her tongue. Wow. A flavor at once deep, dark and buoyant. How had she never noticed how good coffee was before?

It wasn't just the coffee either. It's like the whole world was coming alive for her all at once—all the horrible things and the beautiful things all mixed together. Ray was like that for her. Someone whose nature seemed so awful and wonderful that she hadn't known how to be with him for even one more moment. Now, she couldn't stop thinking about him and wondering if she'd made a mistake.

Ever since Seth had walked into her office, she'd been running scared, reacting and letting emotions crowd out her more reasoned, deliberate nature. For the first time in more than twenty-four hours, Layla started to analyze her situation like the therapist she was. And the first thing she had to do was make a very important call.

Holding one of the prepaid cell phones she'd found in the safe, she unfolded the mangled flyer she'd tucked into her pocket the day before. It was the one advertising Carson Tremblay's art show, and it had a phone number. A few moments later, she had him on the phone.

"Holy crap, Dr. Bahset! Are you okay? You're all over the news."

"I'm fine, but I want you to know that I'm so sorry for walking away from you yesterday—"

"They're saying you were kidnapped!"

"I wasn't," Layla said. "I'm having personal problems right now and I can't treat you anymore. I need you to get a pen and paper and write down the name that I'm going to give you of another psychologist—"

"I don't want another therapist."

"Trust me, I wish this wasn't happening. I know how hard it was for you to trust me, and I don't want to do anything to betray that, but I have to make sure that you're cared for if something happens to me."

"What's going to happen to you?" Carson asked. "Where are you? Do you want me to call the police?"

"No," she said. "I don't want you to get involved. I don't want to put you in any danger. This phone call isn't about me. It's about you. Are you experiencing any anxiety?"

"Yeah, I guess. But just the normal kind," he said.

"If you start to feel an attack coming on when you look at the artwork, do you think you can practice the techniques we talked about?"

There was a pause on the other end of the line. "Dr. Bahset, my dad is a reporter. Maybe he can help you."

It broke her heart to know that she'd put him in a position to worry about her. "You can help me by getting well, Carson. Before I called, what were you focusing on?"

He cleared his throat, as if he were embarrassed. She could almost see him shuffling his feet and digging one hand down into his pocket with a shy shrug. "I was thinking about the girl I met in your office."

Layla was confused. "Isabel?"

"No. Artemisia. Missy. Isn't she a patient of yours?"

Layla bit her lower lip. She didn't have a patient by that name, but she remembered the young prostitute that Ray had hired to follow her. Wasn't her name Missy?

"Anyway," Carson continued, "Missy and I talked for a while in your waiting room and I showed her some of my stuff. She said that nothing beautiful is unblemished and that maybe I've gotta learn to see the flaws in the art, too."

"What do you think?"

"I think that sounds kinda like what my dad does. Always uncovering the ugly secrets of everything. I'd rather focus on the good, ya know?" There was some static on the line and then Carson said, "My show is starting soon, so I gotta go, but you should really call the police and tell them you're okay."

Chapter 11

Without me, you have everything.
I dwell inside your deepest core.
Without me, you are nothing.
Wanting only makes me more.

"I thought you didn't need me anymore," Missy said, posing in the doorway of Ray's motel room like some twisted version of Lolita. He motioned her inside and that's when he noticed the bruises on her face. Someone had busted her lip open and bruised her jaw. Someone had roughed her up.

"What the hell happened to you?" Ray demanded to know.

She shrugged. "My pimp. He's not happy about my extracurricular activities. He only let me come here because I told him you were a big spender."

Ray rolled his shoulders, ready for a fight. "Is he outside?"

"What are you going to do if he is?"

"I'm going to beat him to death."

Ray was as serious as a heart attack and it must have showed because Missy paled. "I don't want you to kill anybody, Ray."

Missy was one of the few people left in the world who didn't think of Ray as a monster. Her good opinion actually meant something to him, so he decided to let it go. For now anyway. "I need to find Layla."

"Again?" Missy eyed the rumpled bed with a knowing glance.

Ray didn't want to look at the bed. Some part of him couldn't believe that last night was real. He couldn't quite wrap his mind around the fact that he'd been inside Layla in every way, but he couldn't stop remembering it either. It made him feel angry and betrayed. He'd been a sucker to think that anything that happened there actually meant something. "I'm going to try to get into her head, and I need you to make sure that I find my way back."

"Got it," Missy said, swaggering over to the mini fridge for a cold soda. "I'll wake you up in one hour, like before. You got something I can read while I wait?" She caught his sidelong glance. "What? You think I don't know how to read?"

"I didn't say that."

"You didn't have to. You think I'm just some stupid bimbo because I turn tricks."

Ray ran a hand through his hair. "I think you've made some bad choices with your life, that's all. What would your family think about how you make money?"

"I don't have family," Missy said, flipping the tab on her soda so viciously that it foamed over the lip. "And you don't know *shit*. My life isn't your business so maybe you should shut up about it before I walk out and leave you stuck in your shrink's head."

She was right. He needed to focus on getting his own life back, and right now that meant hunting down the woman he'd gone to bed with the night before. Ray lay back on the bed, focusing his concentration on his memory of betraying green eyes.

Ray wasn't surprised that Layla's mindscape was still sand as far as the horizon, but now there were some signs of life, too. Greenery dotted the landscape. Spiked aloe plants had clawed their way toward the sunshine and as Ray trudged through the dunes, he saw prickly brush and flowering cacti ringed by thorns. Layla was like that, he thought. Lush and vibrant beauty that would cut you if you dared to get too close.

Her inner pyramid was fully exposed now, and it wasn't the only thing. Broken chariots lay strewn about, the wind having swept some of the sand away to reveal them. He found arrows, too, and broken spears. Not just ancient weapons, but modern ones, too. A hollowed-out tank lay upside down like a rotting carcass in the sun.

He didn't see the lioness, but knew she was lurking. The entrance of the pyramid beckoned like the maw of a wounded animal gasping its last breath. Ray stormed into the pyramid and raced up its twisting passages. There was an antechamber. His nostrils flared as the monster rose within him. He felt his bulk expand and bulge, his skin turn to hide. His skull reshaped itself, the horns pushing through his scalp. He was an animal now, vicious and more dangerous than before, and the fortress that held Layla's memories no longer looked so impregnable.

With a furious snort, he charged forward, ramming into the weak spot. It was a clash of stone and horn and hoof. The pain of it, a hammer to the brain. Still, he charged again. Gravel and stone fell into his eyes, and by the time he shook it out, the lioness had appeared in the dark passageway, illuminated by the light from a brazier that flashed with sudden fire. The lioness's fur was as tawny and golden as Layla's skin, and her eyes just as green.

"Let me inside," Ray said.

"I told you that I can't," the lioness said. "I told you the way..."

Ray remembered what she'd said. *Make me want something. Make my pulse quicken with excitement. Make me sigh with longing. Make my body weak with pleasure. Make me, make me, make me...* Well, he'd done all that, and Layla had walked out on him anyway. Now he'd do things his way. He'd *make* Layla remember just as he'd made her cry out underneath him.

"There's a gentler way in," the lioness warned, a line of fur rigid upon her back.

"I'm done being gentle with you, Layla. I'm going to unlock your memories even if it kills me. Or you." When he rose to charge again, the lioness leaped upon his back. Her powerful legs straddled him as her teeth found the bulging flesh of his back. They went down together, sending a wild spray of sand into the air with their bulk. She tore at his flesh. He bucked, trampling her beneath him. There was a wild raking of claw and horn. She was trying to get her strong jaws around his throat, trying to suffocate him like the huntress that she was.

It'd been a long time since Ray had felt like her prey and his outrage rose like hot red lava in his veins. If he couldn't break into her memories, he'd use his powers to drag her into his.

Layla gasped as some nightmare enveloped her. She couldn't breathe. She couldn't see. It was as if Ray had her by the throat and was forcing her to look into the stench-filled blackness that had a weight of its own. She wasn't a lioness now. She wasn't even sure she was herself.

That's when she knew. She was inside Ray, inside *his* memories, inside his prison cell. Layla reached her hands to the sides, trying to feel for an exit and felt metal walls instead. It was just a box and there was no light. Only pain and shivering and sweat. Someone was screaming. She heard the beating, the sickening sound of breaking flesh and bone.

Ray was here, too. She heard him panting. A slat in the cell opened, and something was pushed through it. Something soft and pulpy spattered to the floor. "Your dinner," someone said. "Have some meat."

Layla *felt* Ray's hunger—the starvation that was hollowing out his stomach and driving him mad. He scrambled for the meat blindly, grasping it with filthy fingers and tearing into it with his teeth. Then she heard him gag, and spit, as he said, "It's raw…"

"It's the only thing you're getting until you confess," was the unseen guard's reply.

She heard Ray take another bite, choking it down. She smelled the blood of it in her nostrils. Then Ray gagged. "What is it? Dead rat?"

"It's your nephew," the guard said. "We cut off his little arm to feed to you and if you don't tell us what we want to know, we're going to cut out his heart and make you eat it, too."

At hearing that, the sound Ray made wasn't human.

He dropped the flesh in his hands and cried out, a shattering sound that shook the walls.

"Food fit for a monster," his guard said, only his eyes showing through the slat. "Why shouldn't your family have to pay for what you've done?"

"I've done nothing!" Ray shouted, his grimy hands pounding on the walls.

Then it all came up. He regurgitated the bites of flesh he'd eaten and sprayed the floor with bile. It didn't matter if the guard had been lying or telling the truth. It only mattered that Ray's mind couldn't sort out the fact from the fantasy. The sour scent of vomit was everywhere, and that's when it happened.

That's when Ray first became the minotaur. He couldn't reach through the bars, but he seized hold of the guard's mind with the force of his anger alone.

"I'll kill you!" Ray shouted.

Layla saw the fear in the guard's eyes. The guard scrambled for his keys, unable to fight Ray. Unable to stop himself from opening the door, and when he did, Ray beat him bloody. Layla didn't stay to see if Ray had killed the man. She felt the roiling of her own stomach that she'd been any part of this, and she ran.

Ray's memories were a labyrinth. They twisted and doubled back upon one another. There were a thousand other versions of Ray here, in a thousand more memories. She saw him being beaten. She saw him sitting in an orange jumpsuit in a metal room under bright lights, and she was there, too. She had a folder in her hands, and glasses perched on the end of her nose, and she was saying, "Just give me something, Ray. A name, an address, something that will help me make a deal for you. You know that you're special to me. Help me save you."

"Ray?" she whispered, feeling the taurine shadow of his inner minotaur fall across her. But her voice was drowned out by another sound. Someone else's call was echoing through the cavernous insides of Ray's mind.

"Wake up, Ray." It was a girl's voice, frantic, terrified. "Wake up, Ray. Wake up!"

Ray opened his eyes to see Missy fighting off some pasty-faced white guy with a knife who slapped her across the face and sent her sprawling to the floor. Ray pulled the gun out from beneath his pillow as he tried to shake off the dizziness and disorientation. He didn't pull the trigger.

He didn't have to. His attacker hadn't expected to be looking down the barrel of a Makarov semiautomatic. The pale and lanky intruder put his hands up in surprise. "Easy, dawg. I was just checking to see how strung out you were. I don't need my slut getting herself in trouble with no junkie."

Great. So the guy was Missy's pimp. He was here to rob Ray or kill him or both of them. "Drop the knife, Vanilla Ice."

The pimp took a few steps backward, but didn't drop the knife. Ray didn't want to have to fire his gun.

Didn't want to make any sounds that would draw attention, didn't want to deal with a dead body, but he could almost see the calculation in the pimp's eyes as Missy sobbed on the floor.

Okay, then. Ray was up out of the bed in one swift motion, knocking the knife out of the pimp's hand and slamming him against the wall. He delivered a brutal punch to the guy's kidney, then another to the other side. Missy's pimp howled in pain, but Ray didn't stop punching. His fist hammered into the guy's face. He was *tasting* the pungent fuel of rage. It felt good to actually hit something with his bare hands.

"Stop it!" Missy yelled as her pimp curled into a fetal position, moaning and groaning. Ray kept hitting him until a solid blow to the face made the guy's eyes roll up in his head. He was out cold. Even so, Ray pulled back for another punch. "Ray!" Missy was screaming, clutching him, crying, hanging from his arm with all her weight. "Stop it, or you'll kill him."

"Why should you care?" Ray asked. "He's a sick fuck who gets off on exploiting little girls. Look what he did to your face. The guy is scum. He's not even human."

"You're wrong," Missy said, her lower lip trembling. "He's a person, okay? You're not his judge, jury and executioner."

Ray's nostrils flared once more, but he dropped his arm. Missy had just saved his life. The last thing Ray wanted to do was kill this bastard in front of her and traumatize her. Ray stood up, retrieved the knife and the gun, and shoved them into his duffel bag where he found a roll of duct tape. He tossed it to Missy. "Tape him to the chair. I'm going to clean up, then we're out of here."

* * *

Ray's hands were shaking and it wasn't just because he'd nearly beat a man to death. He could taste the blood in the back of his throat from his mental war with Layla. Luckily, the adrenaline seemed to be keeping him conscious. The pain was bad. Worse, the bathroom walls suddenly seemed too close. Crowded. It hadn't seemed so small when he was with Layla, but now the idea of showering was more than he could handle. Stepping into that shower would be like climbing back into a prison cell. Goddamn, this anxiety was getting worse every day.

He wiped himself down with soap and a washcloth, rinsing his hair in the sink. He was toweling himself off when Missy finished duct-taping her pimp to the chair. "We can't just leave him here, Ray. He needs a doctor."

What that asshole needed was another beating, but Ray held his tongue.

"I can just call an ambulance," she said, flipping her pink cell phone open to show Ray. "They wouldn't even trace it back to you."

"Hello Kitty?" Ray asked as he glanced at the cartoon-character-themed phone. "Seriously?"

The hard-edged teenager blushed. "Maybe I could get someone else to call an ambulance. There's this boy I met at Dr. Bahset's office. Cool name. Carson something. He's an artist and he said if I ever needed anything, he'd be happy to help."

Young love. Just what Ray needed. "Missy, it's better that we just get out of here first. We'll take a bus to my friend Jack's house in Virginia. We'll be safe there until I figure out how to find Layla again."

"Dude, you've got a *friend?*" Missy asked sarcastically. "Get outta town!"

The pimp made a horrible gurgling noise, obviously in pain.

"Come on, Missy. Let's go."

They were halfway out the door when the phone on the motel end table rang. Might be the cops. Might be motel management. The one person he didn't expect it to be was Layla Bahset.

Chapter 12

No puzzle stands before me. No riddle bars my way. When questions cloud the meaning, I chase the doubt away.

Layla held her breath, cradling the phone on her shoulder, waiting for Ray to answer.

"Nice disappearing act you did this morning," he finally said, his words guarded.

Layla exhaled then took a deep, steadying breath. "Ray, I want you to come find me."

"You can be sure that I will, sweetheart. I can find you anywhere. I just proved that to you by dragging you into my memories, didn't I?"

"You don't understand," she said. "I'm going to tell you *where* you can find me. There's a manhunt on for you. For both of us. You have to get out of Vegas, but until you do, I have somewhere you can stay and be safe. With me."

He laughed and it was a bitter laugh. "So what's the catch? What's the game this time?"

"There isn't one," Layla said. "I saw a lot of things in your memories, Ray, but the one thing I didn't see was treason. I want to help you clear your name if I can."

She let the silence settle, not wanting to push, but finally asked, "Ray?"

"I'm thinking."

It wasn't the most hopeful sign. "I know. You're thinking about last night and wondering what it all meant, thinking—"

"I'm thinking about how I'm going to get to you, since my face is all over the news and you stole my car."

"She could be luring you into a trap, you know," Missy said, unwrapping an ice pop she got from the bus stop vending machine.

Maybe the kid was right. It wouldn't be the first time that Layla had tried to trick him, but Ray had to take the chance; it might be the only one he got. "Listen, I emptied your pimp's pockets. Take the cash and keep yourself out of trouble until you get to Virginia."

"If you give me your money then you're helping to transport an underage hooker across state lines," she said, slowly sucking on her frozen treat in a provocative way that made him worry about her future. "It's a violation of the Mann Act, you know."

"There's something freakish about you, Missy."

"Right back atcha, *Rage-a-tron*." She snatched the

money from his hand. "Anyway, it was nice knowing you."

So she was still pissed. "Don't be like that, Missy."

She turned to face him. "You never asked me if I wanted to leave Vegas, Ray. You never asked me if I *wanted* a new life."

His skull-crushing headache seemed to get worse, so he popped a few more aspirin in the hopes that it would stave off the pain. "Look, Missy, I'm not abandoning you. Jack's going to take care of you, and not in a sexual way. He's a good friend, and he owes me."

"Yeah, well, you beat the crap out of my pimp, so I don't have much choice now."

"You've always got a choice," Ray said. "Just try it out, okay? See what it feels like to follow the rules and do stuff you can be proud of."

She snorted at his hypocrisy and he supposed he couldn't blame her. He wasn't exactly the poster child for following the rules. But he *would* be. When he got his life back, he'd never skirt that line again. Everything he ever did would be one hundred percent legit.

"So, Ray, if it all turns out to be a bust, how will I get in touch with you?"

He'd planned to get a new cell phone at the convenience store—one of those disposable, prepaid ones. But by the time he'd have a number to give her, they'd already be out of touch. "Tell ya what, Jailbait. Gimme your phone. I'll carry it with me, and if you need me, you call it."

She gasped. "Not my Hello Kitty!"

"When I find Layla and this is all over, I'll buy you a new one."

"Careful what you promise. I want a touch screen one that costs a bajillion dollars."

If Ray managed to get himself out of this mess, he'd be happy to buy Missy one of those phones. Hell, he'd buy some for his nephews, too. "You know how to follow the bus schedule and get to Virginia, right?"

Missy didn't answer him, distracted by the moth that landed on her outstretched hand. "Hey, cool…"

"It's a bug, Missy. I need you to pay attention to what I'm telling you here."

"It's not a bug," was her indignant reply as the thing spread its colorful orange wings like it was preening. "It's an American Painted Lady. See the white spot in the forewing subapical field? That's how you can tell it apart from a regular Painted Lady."

Ray stared at her. "What are you, an entomologist now?"

"Artemisia's a plant that attracts butterflies," Missy explained. "That's where I got my name."

"So?"

"So, before my mom became a raging drunk, she used to read me all these butterfly books at night. But you go on thinking I'm just some dumb hooker."

"I'm sorry."

"Forget it," Missy said as the butterfly fluttered away.

"No, really. Missy, I'm sorry." He was. What she'd been through, what she'd done to make a living, wasn't the sum total of who she was. Prostitution didn't define her. No more than what Ray had been through in the past two years defined him. Right now people saw her as a hooker and they saw him as a fugitive. It was time for both of them to do better. He kissed the top of Missy's head as people started getting on the bus. "Take care of yourself, Jailbait."

He'd come for answers—not for Layla—but the moment she opened the cabin door, he was once again rendered a stammering fool. On the drive up into the mountains in his newly stolen vehicle, Ray had promised he'd steel himself against her and harden his heart. But now that he saw her again in the flesh, he was stricken.

Layla was wearing a thin cotton shirt that clung to her curves and a denim skirt that left her legs bare. She stood in the doorway, her hair loose around her shoulders, and she didn't even have shoes on. Her perfection had crumbled and the woman beneath the facade was even sexier. He'd thought—maybe hoped—that one night would've been enough to break his fascination with her. Especially after she ran off and left him behind. Again.

Yet, he still wanted her. In fact, he wanted her so much his mouth went dry. Nothing should matter to him as much as clearing his name, but desire for Layla somehow moved up the hierarchy of his basic needs. He was like a man dying of thirst, and for him, she was an oasis.

She noticed him staring, and self-consciously tucked an errant strand of hair behind her ear. "Are you going to come in?"

"That depends," Ray said. "Are you going to run away from me again?"

"No." Her voice strained with emotion and she reached for him. "Ray…"

He squeezed his eyes shut, because he couldn't bear

for her to see how much he liked hearing her say his name. He'd pulled her into his dungeon memories because he wanted to force her to remember, but now he wished he hadn't. She'd seen his powerlessness. She'd seen him as he never wanted anyone to see him. It'd been more intimate than anything else they'd done together.

"I'm so sorry," she whispered, taking his hands and drawing him into the cabin. "I'm sorry for what I saw inside your memories, and I'm sorry I ran from you. When I turned on the news, they were calling you a kidnapper, and a murderer, and a terrorist. I just got scared."

He forced himself to shrug. "Even after what we did last night, you didn't trust me?"

"I didn't trust myself. I don't even know who I am. I can't trust my memory. I can't even believe in my own sense of right or wrong. I used to think that I didn't remember my life but at least I had values that were important to me. Now I find out that I've been involved with things I can't accept. So I didn't know what to believe."

"And now?" Ray asked, closing the door behind him and locking it.

She put her hand on his shoulder, her lips brushing his neck. "The only thing I trust is this."

It was like that for him, too. Maybe it was because he'd been deprived of the most basic human contact for so long. Imprisoned, the only time anyone else's skin ever touched his was when it came in the form of a closed fist. Touching Layla was more than sex; it helped him remember his basic humanity.

The scent of her hair was in his nostrils and he had

to back away to get himself under control. She'd been his interrogator, his tormenter, and now she was his lover. None of it made any sense. "Are you still afraid of me?" he asked quietly, his voice a whisper by her ear. "Of my powers."

"Yes," Layla replied softly. "But I'm afraid of everything. I'm afraid of Seth. I'm afraid of my past. And I'm afraid of you, because when I'm with you, I feel things. I want things. I remember things, and I don't know if it's going to be my destruction or my salvation."

It was a perfect echo of his own emotions. She'd already helped steal two years of his life from him and now he was wanted for kidnapping her. She could be the ruin of him. Yet, he hungered for the soothing balm of her caress as if she could save him from the raging monster inside. His hands went to her hair, threading through the dark strands as he kissed her. They stumbled back together and he pressed her against the door. They were aligned now, chest to chest, thigh to thigh, his hardness pressing against her belly. He thought she might stop him, but her fingers unfastened his buckle as if she were more eager for this than he was. He wasn't controlling her now. She was doing this on her own, and it made something squeeze in his chest. "Layla, I don't want you to do this because you feel guilty."

She answered him by slipping out of her panties and letting them fall to her ankles.

That was the end of his self-control. He plucked her up so that she had no choice but to wrap her arms around his shoulders. She felt featherlight in his arms, but he worried that the weight of his desire might crush them both. He wanted to be inside her. Needed to be. He pressed her against the wall and anchored her pelvis with his, feeling the beckoning heat between her thighs. He used one hand to unfasten his pants and pull himself out. She was still a very tight fit, but gravity helped draw her down onto him this time. She whimpered and he felt her insides spasm around him.

He didn't want to hurt her. He didn't ever want to hurt her, so he tried to go slow, but her mouth found his ear. "Don't stop," she whispered, wrapping her bare legs around his waist.

"I didn't kidnap you," Ray said, not sure what he was saying, only that he needed to say it.

"I know," she whispered.

The pace of her breathing and the way she clenched around him threatened to make him unravel, but there were still things he had to say. "I'm not a traitor."

"Ray, I believe you," she whispered. "I believe in you."

It made all the difference. She knew what he could do. What he could make her do. Yet, she was giving herself to him completely. He braced himself, ignoring the jingling of his belt buckle around his legs, and banged her back against the wood-paneled wall.

Layla felt as if she might never touch the ground again; they hadn't even bothered to undress. She hadn't taken the time to think or consider or analyze it. It just happened. It wasn't perverse or demeaning; her body simply recognized the demands of his and wanted to meet them. Now he was inside her so deeply that it edged upon discomfort before easing into bliss.

If either of them had protection with them, maybe

she'd have asked him to use it, but what happened with Ray crossed boundaries of skin and bone. A latex barrier would have seemed like an abomination. As before, Ray filled her, leaving no room for doubts.

"You're so sexy," Ray murmured.

What's more, she *felt* sexy. Every time her back hit the wall, she marveled at the way lust tightened in her belly, how her nipples hardened, how her skin burned. She thrilled at each discovery. She delighted in the way that her body wasn't just a prison. It wasn't just a container to keep her from escaping. It was an instrument of pleasure. It was made of give and take. Hands that stroked the flexing muscles of his broad back as he moved. Thighs that strained around his waist, urging his release and her own. Wet folds that made him groan. She was doing this and it belonged to her. The sweat, the sighs, the shivers and chills.

All hers.

"I'm close," Ray said by her ear, as he moved inside her.

She wanted to beg him to look into her eyes and send her into soaring orgasm, but she wouldn't ever ask him to use his powers again. "Don't wait for me," she said. "You know I can't."

She thought he'd accept that answer, but Ray somehow found it within himself to stop. Shuffling through the tangle of his pants, he carried her to the bed where they collapsed on the mattress together, never separating. He positioned himself over her so that every time he stroked into her, his thumb brushed against her in the most sharply pleasurable way. "Oh, God." She moaned frantically, rotating her hips, not sure if she were trying to escape him or get closer. "What are you doing?"

"Turning you on," he said, slow strokes sending a screaming need up and down her body. "Stop fighting it."

She wasn't fighting it! She wanted it, ached for it, but some part of her wouldn't let it happen. A stuttering breath forced its way up from inside her as her climax danced tauntingly close but just out of reach. The rush of arousal was in her ears like the roar of a waterfall, but she couldn't get over the edge. "Please," she whimpered.

"Layla, this time you have to do it. It's not real unless you let go completely."

Her nails dug into the mattress, fists closing on the quilt beneath her as he stroked slow and steady inside. Her thighs were locked around his waist, but she could feel them quiver. The shadow of his broad shoulders moved over her, again and again as he thrust into her, and animal sounds came from her throat.

She thought she heard him say, "You're going to come, Layla. You are."

"No, I can't," she wailed. She felt defenseless, left wide open and raw. The closer she got to the edge, the more exposed she felt. "Just stop."

"You're safe with me," Ray said. "Whatever you show me."

"No, no, I can't!" she cried.

Then she did. The orgasm wrestled its way up until she broke the surface with it, gasping for air like a drowning woman. The sensation churned her insides with exquisite pleasure until she was pulled fully into the undertow. This orgasm was hers, and she claimed it, as if she had every right to it. *Every right.* Her screams harmonized with his sharp cry as he shuddered into a climax of his own, emptying himself inside her.

She didn't remember exactly what happened next. She only remembered the after-spasms that rocked her as Ray enveloped her in his arms.

Chapter 13

My touch starves the guilty
My army feeds the poor
The preachers use me weekly
But the sinners need me more.

Salvation or damnation. Looking at Layla, he still couldn't say which she was. He only knew that she'd wrecked him. Utterly wrecked him. He'd been desperate for her, but she'd been more desperate for him. He'd never felt needed in bed before. Wanted, yes. Lusted after, sure. But needed? No.

She'd let herself be safe in his arms, and now he felt a very real responsibility to never, ever let her down. Watching her as she slept, he thought he'd kill anyone who ever tried to hurt her.

When her eyelashes finally fluttered open, she said,

"You don't have to keep watch. I'm not going to run away."

He felt himself flush. "Maybe I just like looking at you."

She lowered her lashes. "I'm not a statue."

"No," he said. "You're a puzzle. This whole thing is a puzzle. A little new for me."

"You've never slept with a woman before me?"

"Sure, I have," he said, and he wasn't lying. Serving four tours of duty made it difficult to maintain relationships, but there'd always been willing women that he cared about. Maybe even thought that he loved. It just hadn't been like this.

"For some reason, I thought you were a Muslim," Layla murmured.

"I am… I was. I dunno," he fumbled to explain, caught off guard. "My family practiced progressive Islam. My mother only wore a *hijab* to the mosque. My father and I were less devout. He liked to say that he's more Greek than Syrian."

Thinking about his family made him wonder how they'd reacted to his disappearance. It may have been his mother's instinct to wear down her knees in prayer, but he was equally sure that his father would have seen Ray's disappearance as one more reason not to believe in God. And Ray wasn't sure he could blame him.

"Mostly, I grew up just like everybody else," Ray said.

"Ah. All very Americanized."

Was that judgment he heard in her voice? He'd spent two years being told how un-American he was. He didn't feel like debating whether or not he was a bad

Muslim. "Yeah. Well, I drink but I don't get drunk. I don't eat bacon if that's what you're wondering."

He knew that wasn't what she was wondering. Strict Muslims weren't supposed to have sex outside of marriage. Then again neither were Christians or Jews but nobody seemed to bat an eyelash when they lived their lives according to their own rules. His family had always fasted during Ramadan and venerated all the prophets including Mohammed, Moses and Jesus. But Ray had also been raised to believe in the autonomy of the individual in interpreting the *Qur'an.* Ray had never seen anything wrong with enjoying a woman's company in bed or out of it.

Layla shifted so that her head was on his shoulder. He liked the way her hair fanned out on his arm. It was dark and shiny as ebony. She pressed her lips to an old, faded military tattoo on his arm. A bald eagle. "Your family must have been proud of you when you joined the army."

"They were actually pretty pissed," Ray confessed, and not just about the tattoo, which his mother denounced as a defacement of his body. They were also angry that he enlisted. He was supposed to be an engineer like his father, or a lawyer like his brother. He was supposed to go to college and get the fancy education his parents had saved up for all their lives. Instead, the day after his eighteenth birthday—ten days after his brother blew his brains out—the Twin Towers in New York City came tumbling down. The whole world seemed to be falling apart, and enlisting seemed like the only way to fix it. He didn't know how to explain all that to Layla, so he said, "The military needed translators and I spoke Arabic. It made sense at the time.

Each tour of duty, I spent about eighteen months fighting in the Sandbox, then a year stateside training other soldiers."

Her fingers idly traced his arm. "With skills like yours, you could've made a lot more money as a civilian contractor…"

"Probably, but I'm not a damned mercenary." He hadn't meant it as a rebuke but the wounded look in her eye told him that she'd taken it personally. He just kept talking, hoping to push past it. "In any case, eventually the army bonuses were lucrative enough that I could help my parents out. They've had a tough time raising my nephews. Kids are expensive."

"I wouldn't know," she murmured, and disentangled herself from his arms. He was already blowing it, and he wished he knew what he'd said wrong, but before he could ask, she said, "There's something I need to show you. I don't know if it will give you the answers you're looking for, but maybe you can make more sense of it than I can."

He sat up and his gaze was still lazy and lustful as he watched her smooth her denim skirt back over her hips. It gratified him to see that she stood on shaky legs. She padded over to the closet and showed him the safe, opening it to reveal a stash that would be the envy of any government operative. Money. Guns. Official documents under different aliases. His eyes widened and he pulled his pants back on, coming to her side in three strides.

"What do you think it means?" Layla asked.

"I dunno," he said, flipping through her passports. "You don't recognize any of this stuff?"

"I was hoping you might."

Ray explained, “I helped gather intel but I don’t know shit about serious spook stuff.” That’s when he noticed she was holding a folder. Clutching it, really. “You gonna show me what’s in that?”

She drew her lips together and shook her head, but didn’t stop him when he pulled the folder from her fingers. Ray wasn’t sure what he was expecting to see inside, but the photos of the dead men shook him. Strangled men, hanged men, asphyxiated men. “What the hell is this?”

“I don’t know,” she breathed. “Suicides. I think some of them are men who killed themselves at black ops sites. I think I questioned them.”

Ray slammed the folder shut, trying to block out the way the word *suicide* still echoed in his ears. It was an ugly word. One that sent his mother into shrieking hysterics. One that left him with a hollowness inside that wouldn’t ever go away. Sweat broke out across his brow and the air seemed stifled. How hadn’t he noticed how small this room was before?

It didn’t seem possible that it could fit the two of them and the bed, too. “I need some air.”

She followed him out onto the deck in the back, and he had a hard time looking at her. He kept his gaze steady over the desert below. “I’m sorry. I have trouble with—”

“Enclosed spaces,” she finished for him.

Ray marveled at the grandness of the view, the golden arc of beauty as the sun set over the mountains. They really were alone out here. There wasn’t another cabin for miles. “I guess I’m claustrophobic.”

“It’s post-traumatic stress disorder,” Layla said. “I

know what you've been through, Ray. I saw it in your mind."

"Is there a cure?"

She hesitated. "Sometimes. Therapy sometimes helps. After what you've been through, I think you're going to need a lot of it. When all this is over, you're going to need to trust somebody."

"Right now, I only trust this," Ray said, pulling her into his lap, and she smiled at the way he echoed her earlier words. They sat together watching butterflies dancing amongst the desert flowers, when her stomach growled.

"Are you hungry?" Ray asked.

She nodded and looked a little bit astonished. "I actually think I am. I want to shower, and get dressed, and eat something...delicious."

"I didn't see anything but beans and soup in your pantry," Ray said. "But I'll give it a shot if you want to go ahead and get cleaned up while I cook."

"You want to cook? For me?"

"Don't expect five-star service, but I can heat up some soup." He took another deep breath of the great outdoors. It steadied him. "Just go and shower and it'll give me a few minutes to get myself together."

In the shower, Layla *remembered.* She remembered all of it.

Like a crumbling antechamber of an ancient pyramid, something inside her gave way and the buried treasure came spilling forth in all its beauty and horror. One minute the warm water of the shower was running down her back. The next moment, Layla was the cracked earth of the desert, soaking up the rain. She was made of sand and stone. Her veins were the burrows of scarab beetles and the blood that flowed inside her was that which had been spilled in the war above, the red syrup of mortal life that soaked into the ground. Her heartbeat had been the thunder of chariots, the march of men, with spears and swords. Her only tears, the milk of the cactus and her only companions had been the swift-striking vipers that slithered over her skin.

Seth had changed all that. She remembered that now. He was no stalker ex-husband, no shadowy government contractor, no mortal man at all. He was the Scorpion King, god of Egypt, ruler of the desert, and her creator. With his hands running red with the blood of his vanquished foe, Seth had pushed them into the sand and molded her to life. Layla's first breath had been the arid one he'd breathed into her. Layla had lived thousands of lives in thousands of years, and never aged. She was *war-born,* created to serve a war god.

There was nothing that could have prepared her for this truth. No notes that she could have left herself that would have ever convinced her that she wasn't human. As the memories continued to flow over her, Layla pressed herself against the shower wall and slid to the floor. She crouched there, in the steamy shower. A wretched noise heaved itself out of her, something keening and filled with loss.

"Layla?" She heard Ray's voice from the other room. She didn't answer. She just went to her knees, unsteady and sick, wondering—if she were really made of sand—why the water didn't just wash her down the drain. Seth had fashioned her into something lasting, something to serve him through the ages, that's why.

And she'd been a fool to ever think there was a way to escape him.

The door in the bathroom creaked open and Ray hesitated. "Layla, are you okay?"

She made another sound, like a wounded animal in pain.

"Shit," Ray said, crossing the threshold. "Are you hurt? What's happening to you?"

"I'm remembering," Layla choked out. The shampoo had long since washed from her hair, but something still stung her eyes. Another sound came out of her. It was a sob.

Ray's voice softened. "Layla, come on out of there. Let me help you."

"You can't help me," Layla said, near-hysterical laughter bubbling up in her throat. "You said you saw inside me. You said you saw a lioness. That's not what I am. I'm not a woman and I'm not a lioness. I'm both. I'm an abomination. I'm a *sphinx*." It was a relief to hear the truth spoken aloud after all this time. Her secret name. Her secret self.

"You're not making any sense," Ray told her, pulling open the shower door. She saw that his hands were shaking. The confines of the bathroom were like kryptonite for him and he must have felt as if the walls were already closing in. Somehow, in spite of this, he made himself crouch down and reach for her. "Come on out of the shower. Let me help you."

Layla pulled away, feeling the sting of the needles as the water beat down on her back. "I told you, you can't help me. I'm not even a mortal woman, don't you understand? Please just go, Ray. Get away from me before you end up dead. Like Nate Jaffe or the men in those pictures."

Ray shifted on his heels, jaw clenched, eyes narrowed. "I'm not leaving you like this."

But he'd have to. Layla would just stay here in this shower until the end of time. She might just live that long. She'd go on and on, long after Ray and his soulful eyes had turned to dust, and the only one who would know her was the loathsome god of the desert.

Seth. Her mate. Her maker. Her *master*.

"I'm not coming out," Layla whispered.

Ray muttered a dark curse, unintelligible. "Then I'm coming in."

It was a hollow threat. There was no way he'd be able to make himself climb into the shower with her. She could see the way his body tightened in rebellion, the way his knuckles went white on the shower door. "Just go away, Ray, before you have another panic attack. Go away before Seth finds you and kills you. Or before I do."

Ray snorted. "You're not going to kill me."

Then, with a slow heave, he pushed himself into the shower with her, his body low to the ground as he squeezed inside. She knew what it cost him. She heard the pace of his breathing double. She felt how cold his skin was as he brushed past her. She felt the erratic beat of his heart as he enfolded her against his chest and smothered his anxiety under the steam and water. Water ran over both of them now, soaking his clothes. His shirt sucked tightly against the muscles of his chest and his jeans went to soggy dark indigo. He smoothed her hair back, holding her face away from the spray.

He'd done this for her sake—*for her*—and now his

voice was a shaky whisper. "Whatever it is, Layla, you can tell me...."

"No, I can't," she said, burrowing her face against him. The burning in her eyes was nearly unbearable now. That's when she realized that the water on her face wasn't just from the shower. All those pent-up tears breached the barrier, spilling from her lashes and scalding her cheeks. She was crying. Sobbing, really, and couldn't stop.

"It's gonna be all right," Ray said bracing against the shower wall with his boots so that his wet, denim-clad knees made a cradle for her.

It wasn't going to be all right. She was the twisted minion of an evil god. What comfort could a mortal man like Ray really offer her? And yet his arms were the only safe place that she'd ever known. "Oh, Ray... you have no idea who I am or what I've done..."

"I know what you've done. I was there, remember?"

"I'm nothing, nothing but what he made me!"

"Don't say that," Ray murmured against her lips. "Don't ever say that again. It's not true."

It was true, Layla thought. Until Seth had breathed life into her, she'd been nothing but sand. Is it any wonder that without Seth she'd felt nothing but fear? Yet, as Ray rocked her, it was more than fear that surged through her. Steam had clouded the air around them, shutting out the rest of the world, and as he mopped water off her face, she tilted her head and kissed him. She kissed him because words failed her. She kissed him because he was good, and loyal, and loving, and brave. She kissed him because it might be the last time she could.

She'd never thought that Ray was hers to keep, but

she hadn't realized before now that she wasn't even her own to give. As they kissed, the warm water pooled between them where her breasts pressed against his chest. It seemed to ease him a little bit, but as she ran her hands down his arms, she realized that his fists were balled. It was taking all the strength he had to sit here in this glass box.

"Layla," he finally said, "are you gonna let me get you out of here? I'm kinda buggin' out."

She nodded, her whole body limp. He got to his feet, then hoisted her into his arms. His boots squeaked on the tile as he stepped out of the shower, and she was afraid he'd slip, but Ray managed to stay on his feet even when every force in the world conspired to knock him down.

He found a towel and dried her off, from head to foot, and she let him. It felt somehow wrong to have someone take care of her like this, but she didn't have the strength to protest. If it made her selfish and childish and needy…well, those were small crimes next to the others.

Then he carried her to the bed. Only when he'd wrapped her up in blankets and made sure she was safe and warm, did he strip out of his wet clothes and find something dry to wear. If he'd crawled into bed beside her naked, she would've run. The intimacy of what they'd shared before was now too raw for her, and he seemed to know it. Instead, he pulled the chair close enough to the bed that he could touch her. "Layla, you need to tell me what you remembered."

"I'm a sphinx," she said again.

Ray was part Greek. The history wasn't lost on him. "Like the one in Oedipus? The one who wouldn't let any traveler pass into Thebes without solving her riddle?"

"That was a different sphinx, but yes. We aren't just mythical creatures or monuments of stone. We're real."

He ran a hand through his wet hair. "Look, it's not that I don't know that a lot of unexplained shit goes down in this world. I can do things that shouldn't be possible, but I stopped believing in God a long time ago—"

"Gods," Layla corrected. "There are lots of them."

Ray's jaw tightened. "You know, if I was going to believe, I was taught the *Shahada* which says, 'There is no God but Allah and Muhammad is His prophet.'"

"Some say the more rightful interpretation is, 'There is no God worthy of worship above Allah, and Muhammad is His prophet.' For the Christians and Jews it's, 'Thou shalt have no other gods before me.' It doesn't say that there aren't any other gods. It doesn't say what happened to the old ones when people stopped believing in them. I can tell you. They're here, living amongst the mortals. And Seth is one of those gods. A terrible one."

"What about you?" Ray asked.

"I'm not a goddess, but I'm not mortal either."

"That's why you heal." It was the one solid fact that he'd seen for his own eyes, and he seemed to cling to it. "Do you have other powers?"

"Yes," she said, though she couldn't force herself to speak them over the lump in her throat. What she could do to men—what she *had* done to men—was difficult to admit. "I'm a riddler."

He looked puzzled. "Can you show me?"

"It's not a parlor trick. With my questions, I can

force people to answer me. I can put them into a trance. I can hurt them, or cause them to hurt themselves…"

He nodded slowly, no doubt remembering all the times she'd used her powers against him before he was tortured. What he finally said was, "So you get into people's heads. You're like me."

"No. Seth fashioned me from the sand and breathed me to life. But you were born of flesh and blood. You're human. You're mortal. You're war-*forged*. But I'm war-*born* and I belong to the desert. I belong to Seth."

"The *hell* you do."

She recognized possessiveness when she saw it, and it was there, but more besides. Anger, confusion, and maybe even deeper feelings than that. She didn't dare probe them, didn't dare ask. "Ray, don't you want to know if I remember anything about you?"

He should've latched onto that. He should've been more concerned with his own welfare than hers. But she couldn't seem to dissuade him from the direction of his thoughts. "Don't change the subject. You don't belong to Seth. He scares the shit out of you—"

"Of course he does. In his prime, he was the fiercest god of the world. He wrought such bloodshed and chaos that no nation wanted to own him. Even the Egyptians called him a foreigner, and when they depicted him in the hieroglyphics of their tombs, his face was a creature none recognized. He's not as powerful as he used to be, but there's still plenty of war in the modern world and bloodshed for him to feed on. Men may not mean to worship him, but they do. With their bullets and their bombs. They call for him."

Ray pulled himself to the edge of the chair, so that he was nearly standing. "You're serious…"

"Dead serious. Seth's been an advisor to kings. He's been a battlefield general. He's been the wicked voice that whispers into the ears of men who crash planes into buildings. In every age, he becomes whatever he must to stay close to the forces of war, so right now, he's a government contractor." Layla laughed bitterly. "He was so sure that I wouldn't remember him that he actually gave me his card. It's on the dresser."

Ray stood, walked to the dresser and snapped up the card. "Scorpion Group. What is it?"

"It's a group of mercenaries that the government uses to do the things they don't want to do themselves. A way of avoiding accountability. Trust me, Scorpion Group isn't the only government contractor out there willing to interrogate and torture prisoners—it's just the only one run by a god with powerful minions. I was one of them. I questioned prisoners. I got them to trust me. I built a rapport with them, and I used all my training and all my powers to do it. I asked them questions, and I posed riddles to them, until they choked on their own guilt. Literally choked on it. Until you."

Ray stared. "What was so different about me?"

"You never reacted to my questions like a guilty man would…."

"Because I wasn't guilty," Ray snapped.

"I was sure you had a secret and that I just wasn't asking the right questions," Layla said softly, and when she saw him wince, she hurried to add, "I know you're innocent now."

Ray clasped his hands together, staring down at them. "Do you?"

He seemed to go somewhere, his mind lost in the past. She hated to be the bearer of bad news, but he deserved to know the truth. "I can't prove your innocence, Ray. I never even knew who it was that accused you. Seth didn't want me to know because he didn't care."

Ray's eyes narrowed to dangerous slits. "But Seth knows, doesn't he? If he's a god, as you say, then he must know everything about why I was arrested."

"He's not omniscient. If he was, don't you think he'd have found us by now? If he knows why you were arrested, it's only because someone in the government gave him a file."

"A file?" Ray asked, eyes bulging. "You're saying that the Egyptian god of war and chaos keeps notes on paper?"

"Or on papyrus, or on a stone tablet, or written in blood," Layla said, thinking back over all her years. "Besides, the military can be surprisingly low-tech. There's usually a paper copy of everything. Contractors keep notes. I did."

"Where are your reports, then? Do you have them?"

"I'm sure they're stored away in some box at Scorpion Group. But what I do remember is that you weren't just accused of working with the enemy in Afghanistan. You supposedly set up an ambush that went wrong. When it did, you allegedly massacred a village full of civilian witnesses to shut them up."

He staggered back. The chair must have bumped the back of his legs and made him unsteady, because he collapsed down into it so heavily that all the air hissed out of the cushion. His face twisted in anguish. "That's not what happened…"

"Why don't you tell me what really happened?"

He looked away and she realized that not *all* the

boundaries between them had been breached. She watched his head stoop and his shoulders sag as some burden pressed down on him. He ran a hand through his hair, staring at the floor before he said, “I can’t talk about that.”

After everything she’d just told him about who and what she was, it seemed impossible that he could hold anything back. “You can’t or you won’t?”

“Either. Both. I dunno,” Ray said, then went silent.

Chapter 14

If you have one, you want to share it. But if you share it, you don't have one.

"Ray, you helped me unlock my secrets," Layla said. "Let me help you with yours."

Her voice held the promise of healing, but what happened in Afghanistan wasn't Ray's secret to tell. What's more, he wasn't sure if she was using her powers as a sphinx on him or not. Certainly, her questions were tying him in knots. She'd given him a lot to think about and an entirely new way to look at the world. It was a lot to process.

"Ray," she pressed. "What happened in Afghanistan?"

"I said I'm not going to talk about it."

"Have you ever told anyone about it before?"

Yeah. Once. They'd kept him awake for more hours

than he could count, and he'd started hallucinating. He'd started to hope that he'd pass out when they zapped a current through him, because then he'd get some sleep. But the pain hadn't been bearable, and in his desperation to say something that would make the torment stop, he'd confessed everything that'd happened in Afghanistan. He'd given up Jack to stop the pain and his only consolation was that his captors only laughed; they hadn't believed him or maybe they hadn't cared.

"Ray?"

"I'm not your prisoner anymore, Layla. I don't have to answer your questions."

At that, her face fell, and she reached out to him. "If you don't want to talk about it, you don't have to. I just want you to know that when you're ready, I'll be here to listen."

He wanted to tell her, but there was a code soldiers lived by. To have each other's backs. To stand up for your brothers-in-arms when no one else would. Ray, more than anyone, lived by that. How was he going to explain it to her? As it turned out, he was spared the effort. It took Ray a moment to remember that he had Missy's phone and to realize that it was ringing.

"I've gotta take this," Ray said, flipping the phone open.

It wasn't Missy; it was Jack and he got right to the point. "We've got a problem, brother. The gal you sent to me for safekeeping just got herself arrested. I got in the truck and met up with her at a bus station. I was holding her bags when they nabbed her. She managed to give me this number to reach you."

Ray felt the veins at his temples throb and if he

hadn't needed the phone to actually speak, he'd have hurled it across the room. "Arrested? What the hell did she do? Turn tricks on the bus?"

"Naw, it wasn't local police or anything like that."

"Then who took her? FBI? Homeland Security?"

"That's just the thing," Jack said. "They had that look, but they didn't identify themselves, and they didn't show badges."

Scorpion Group. Given what Layla had just told him, there wasn't a doubt in Ray's mind. "Do you know where they took her?"

"No, but she's just a kid. Whatever she knows, she's going to spill. So, look, you know I got some money. I can get you out of the country and I think you better start fixin' to leave."

No, Ray thought. This was his country. He'd fought for it. He'd bled for it. Why should he have to leave? Ray closed his eyes.

"You can't prove your innocence from behind bars, brother," Jack said. "Pride's a bitch, Ray. Let's meet somewhere and come up with a plan. Just tell me where you are."

Ray didn't want to give an address over the phone. Whoever figured out that Missy had a connection to him had either been watching him or tapping the phone. "I'll be in touch." He hung up without another word.

Ray's frustration was a palpable presence in the room as he paced back and forth at the foot of her bed. The real world—not as Layla had seen it before, but as it really was—was crashing in on them both. This place had been their refuge. In this cabin, she'd found herself again, and just a little bit of happiness with Ray, but Seth always said that nothing good was meant to last. "What are you going to do, Ray?"

"I don't know!" With one broad arm, he swept everything off her dresser. A hand mirror shattered, a lamp crashed and sparked out, and a decorative wooden box hit the wall and exploded into splinters.

Layla didn't care about the mirror or the lamp or the decorative box. The only broken thing she cared about right now was Ray. He needed her to talk him through this. "We'll think it through, step by step."

His chest rose and fell, fists clenched at his sides as she slowly got through to him. "I need to find out where they took Missy."

"Okay. How can you do that?"

"I remember Missy's eyes. If I had a picture of her, or something to focus on, I could get into her mind. I could go into her dreams."

"Like you found me," Layla said, not liking the idea at all. It felt, somehow, too intimate a thing for him to do with anyone else. Besides, it was dangerous. Every time he used his powers, it damaged him a little more. "And once you find her, what will you do?"

"Something crazy, probably."

She needed to get through to him. "Ray, does it even make any sense that anyone would have taken her? What does she really know about you?"

"She knows about *you,*" he said, still seething with anger. "She knows that you called me to meet you. Given when I dropped her off at the bus stop, someone could use that information to track me here."

"If that's true, then the most important thing for us to do is leave immediately and not worry about the girl. Missy's young. The authorities will probably just let her go."

"What if it's not the authorities that took her? What if it's Seth? Would he kill her?"

Layla could read his unspoken thoughts. Missy wasn't brown, or Muslim, or any of the things that Ray believed to be at the root of how easily he'd been disappeared. But Missy was a prostitute. She was someone without a family to fight for her. Someone who lived at the edge of the law. Someone that society saw as *disposable.*

Luckily, Layla knew that Seth didn't enjoy killing people half as much as he loved forcing people to kill each other. He wasn't a god of murder; he was a god of war. "He won't kill her unless she gives him a reason to. He wouldn't have taken her unless she was useful to him, unless he thought she knew something that would help them track us down."

"Or he took her to flush me out, to lure me into a trap..."

"I don't think so," Layla said quietly, preparing to lay out her arguments rationally, even though she knew they'd offend him. "The authorities think you're a terrorist. A killer. Given Missy's age, they probably even think you're a pedophile. They aren't likely to think that you're sentimental enough to come rescue her."

"What about Seth?"

Layla bit her lower lip. "He thinks you're a raging monster bent on revenge. If he'd dangle anyone in front of you as bait, it'd be me."

He glanced at her in surprise, those dark eyes peering up from the shadows of his face, the unspoken question on his parted lips. She could see him trying to form the question in a way that wouldn't open up old wounds. "In Syria, when you were interrogating me, when you told me that you had feelings for me… that was his idea?"

"Partly." Seth had encouraged her to toy with Ray's emotions. He'd told her to pretend to care about Ray, but somewhere along the way she didn't have to pretend anymore and when Seth found out, he'd punished her. Layla didn't want to blame anyone else for the things she'd done, so she said, "He saw everything on camera and when you escaped, he knew you'd hunt me down…"

"That's why he was having you watched?"

"You mean, besides his desire to terrorize me? Yes."

Ray squinted. Layla knew all of this was a lot for a mortal to understand—even a special one like Ray. "I don't get it."

"He wants to capture you, Ray, and not just because you escaped. It's not just a matter of government contracts or professional pride. He knows about your powers. He wants to make you use your powers to do his bidding, just as he made me use mine."

"And you were supposed to lure me in."

She hadn't betrayed him. Not this time. So she didn't flinch. "He just didn't think I'd run away with you."

Ray almost smiled at that. She saw the corners of his lips quirk up as if he was going to make a flirtatious remark, but his mind was on the hapless young prostitute who had helped him and was now paying the price. "If Seth captured Missy, where would he keep her? Does Scorpion Group have a headquarters, or are we talking about Mount Olympus or some fairy-tale palace in the sky?"

"Scorpion Group headquarters is in Dubai, but there's an office in Arlington and another in Washington. If Scorpion Group is responsible for nabbing Missy, they might hold her there."

"What's the security like?" he asked her.

Layla arched a brow. "Why? You're not seriously thinking of breaking her out, are you?"

"You got a better idea?"

"Yes," Layla said, biting her lower lip. "Let me do it."

"I'm not letting you do this," Ray said, watching with scarcely contained amazement as the woman who claimed to be a sphinx dressed herself and gathered her things with military precision.

Layla tucked a small pistol into her boot and another at the small of her back. "I told you. I have security passes. They're expired but they might still get me into the building. People might remember me there and let me inside."

She'd handled her weapons like a pro, and he'd be lying if he said that her sudden proficiency with firearms wasn't a turn-on, but the change in her was enough to give him whiplash. "It's too dangerous."

"For me?" She glanced up at him. "Ray, it doesn't matter if I walk into a hail of bullets. You saw how my skin heals. I'm a sphinx. Nothing can kill me. Well, *almost* nothing anyway."

"I'm not talking about bullets, Layla. I'm talking about Seth. If everything you've remembered is true, you were right to run from him. He broke your mind and left what remained of your identity swirling down a shower drain while you sobbed. You've said that he could do worse things to you than kill you, but suddenly, you want to just turn around and risk falling back into his hands?"

Slinging a backpack over one shoulder Layla said, "He's after you, too, but you're the one who is determined to break into Scorpion Group buildings."

"That's because I have to find Missy. She shouldn't be involved in any of this. The kid *wouldn't* be involved in any of this if it weren't for me. She trusted me and I put her in harm's way. But you don't have to put yourself at risk for Missy. She doesn't mean anything to you."

"Yes, she does. She means something to me, because she means something to you."

He didn't know what to say to that. It humbled him a little bit.

"We need to get going, Ray," Layla said. "We'll be spotted if we go anywhere near an airport so we're going to have to drive, and it'll take more than thirty-eight hours to get to D.C. even if we trade off driving in shifts."

It wasn't until they'd reached the border of Utah and Colorado that Ray finally turned to her and asked, "What did you mean when you said *almost* nothing could kill you?"

She'd been hoping he'd glossed over that slip of the tongue. "What do you think I meant?"

"Don't answer a question with a question, Layla. Can something kill you or not?"

It was a complicated question. "Not now. Not the way I am. I'm immortal unless I pass my life force on to someone else."

"Pass your life force onto somebody else?" Ray eyed her suspiciously, his hands tightening on the wheel. "Like who?"

"Like a child," she said, staring out the passenger side window at the passing road signs. She'd always wanted a child—a family—even if it meant that she wouldn't live forever, but Seth was the god of the sterile desert, the veritable patron of infertility. He couldn't give her a child and her desire to be a mother was blasphemy against her creator. "If I give birth, I pass on the breath that Seth gave to me, and become a normal human woman who ages and dies." When Ray was silent, she asked, "You don't believe any of this, do you? You don't believe what I just told you and you don't even believe I'm a sphinx."

"It's not that I don't believe you." Ray rubbed the stubble on his unshaven chin. "Okay, I don't know what the hell to believe, Layla. But what you're saying makes as much sense as anything else I've been through in the past few years. It's just the whole idea that you think of yourself as not human. That Seth created you..."

"He created you, too."

He looked at her and the expression on his face wasn't pretty. "What do you mean?"

"Seth fashioned me from sand, from nothing. But just as surely as he made me a sphinx, he used the horrors of that dungeon to turn you into a minotaur."

It seemed as if Ray had only heard one word, and now he repeated it, his lips moving slowly. *"Minotaur."* He probably knew about the monster of Crete, the one that the ancient king locked in a labyrinth. The one that hunted down and devoured youths until Theseus slew him. Even schoolchildren knew that story, and the way

Ray's eyes blazed, she could see that he didn't like the comparison.

"The minotaur in the Greek myths wasn't the first minotaur and won't be the last," Layla explained. "It wasn't just happenstance that you became this way, Ray. Seth made you into what you are."

"There were hundreds of prisoners in that Syrian jail," Ray protested. "You're saying that someone is turning them all into minotaurs?"

"Just you," Layla whispered. "You had the right ancestry. The right circumstances…"

"What circumstances?" His fingers flexed around the steering wheel in annoyance. "The minotaur was a flesh-eating monster locked in a labyrinth under some Greek palace. So what? It's got nothing to do with me."

"It has everything to do with you. The minotaur you've read about was a bastard child and so are you."

Ray glared at her. "My mother—"

"Not literally, Ray. *Figuratively* a bastard. Because of your skin, your upbringing, your religion, the languages you speak. Your countrymen couldn't decide if you belonged to them or to the enemy they're fighting. You're the unwanted offspring of mixed heritage and they locked you up. They didn't have the courage to torture you themselves, so they brought in Scorpion Group to do it for them. That's when Seth saw an opportunity to twist you into a creature that could serve him."

"And you knew this?" Ray asked.

Layla shook her head quickly, violently. "No. I'd never willingly help Seth create another monster and I'd never help him use someone else the way he's used me. When I found out what he was doing to you, I demanded your release."

Layla trailed off, not wanting to tell him how Seth had laughed at her demand. She'd refused to interrogate Ray anymore and promised to defy Seth until he was forced to return her to the desert sand from whence she'd come. So he'd done just that. He'd taken her memories from her and buried every desire she'd ever had.

It almost comforted Seth that so many of the old gods were without power and influence in the world, because if they knew just how many ways his minion had betrayed him, their mocking laughter would go on for eternity. Layla had been *here.* He could smell her deceit in every crevice of this cabin. How many years had it taken his clever little sphinx to find a remote spot like this one and squirrel away supplies? To set up a safe house like this one meant that she must have been planning to run away from him even before her heart softened toward Rayhan Stavrakis. It meant she'd been planning her escape even before he decided to destroy her memory. It was a shame he only had the power to bury memories, not read them, or he might have predicted this.

Seth found a Hello Kitty phone tossed haphazardly on the bed, no doubt hastily ditched so that the authorities couldn't track them. The bed looked rumpled and slept-in, which made Seth scowl. It wasn't like Layla to leave her bedsheets askew. Had she shared this bed with the minotaur? No, surely not. He put the horrifying thought out of his mind at once, then stooped down to survey the wreckage.

Glass shards and wood splinters littered the floor, and a broken lamp lay sprawled like a corpse. It looked like there'd been some kind of violence here, perhaps a fight. Now *that* was an idea more to his liking. It would be inconvenient if his all-but-immortal sphinx managed to kill his very mortal minotaur, but it was hard for him not to delight in imagining what would have been a powerful clash between the two.

The war god heard a sound at the door, and he thrilled at the notion he might have captured his quarry after all. Perhaps she'd not abandoned the cabin, merely gone for supplies or returned from burying the minotaur's body. Oh, it would be so sweet to capture Layla and not just because of the way he'd enjoy crushing her beneath his thumb. It also meant that he'd win the wager with *Xochiquetzal.* With the promise of victory humming through his veins, Seth stalked silently toward the entryway, positioning himself so that he could take his prey by surprise.

The door opened and just as he reached to grab her, he saw a flash of the woman's hair. It was a wild tangle of brown curls, not Layla's jet-black mane.

"You!" Seth growled, grabbing her by the wrist.

"You!" Isabel said at the same moment, whirling to face him.

They stared at each other for a moment, then he let go of her as if he'd caught a serpent by the tail. He was stunned to find her so close on his trail. He'd used all his government connections to get here ahead of the authorities. "How did you find this cabin?"

"You have your minions, *Papi,*" she said with an enigmatic smile. "And I have mine."

Seth glanced out the picture window where several

butterflies danced on the wind, but he had difficulty believing that the winged creatures were as effective as global positioning satellites. "Layla's not here."

"Qué lástima," Isabel said with a heartfelt sigh, then walked to the sliding glass door. "You can see the whole of the Mojave from here. It looks so barren…."

"You'd be surprised at how much life you can find in a desert."

"Tell me about the desert you ruled, Seth. Were you very powerful?"

"I'm still powerful," he said through gritted teeth.

"But lonely," Isabel replied.

It was true that the modern world was a lonely place for war gods. The violence remained but the glory was gone. It was chaos that thrilled Seth, so he also despaired of the modern mortal obsession with laws. Men even tried to fashion rules for war; it was exhausting to subvert those rules and unbearable that he should have to. To whom could he turn for solace? Could Isabel understand?

"And you? What did the Queen of Whores rule?"

"A verdant jungle teeming with beauty," she said, turning back toward him so that he could see her eyes light up to remember. "There were tribal festivals in my honor, where the silversmiths would come to ply their trade. The weavers and the sculptors would come, too. All the people who created things loved me. But especially the prostitutes who danced with flowers in their hair…"

"I heard they'd sacrifice a girl and flay her skin off her body in tribute to you," Seth said, for he knew more about her than he'd admitted. "That sounds like something I would have enjoyed. Did you?"

"No." Isabel scowled. "The mortals seem to always get it wrong and lead the religion astray."

He enjoyed having wiped the smile off her face. In fact, he enjoyed the sparring altogether too much. "Those days are gone now, Isabel, but if you must live amongst the mortals why take such a menial job?"

"Helping people is never menial," Isabel said. "I'm studying to become a sex therapist. Working for Layla was good clinical training."

"A *sex therapist,*" he said, a bitter taste in his mouth. If she must feed off sex, why not become a celebrity starlet? Why not own a pornographic media empire? "How can you disgrace yourself? Aren't you better than this?"

"Better than what?" Isabel said with a teasing grin, leaning back against the window so that the light radiated around her curvaceous form. "Better than you? I think I am. I think I'll find Layla before you do, and then we'll see who is a disgrace."

Chapter 15

I fly in the air
And rarely touch the earth
Men die for me
Protecting home and hearth

In all the years Ray had been fighting under its flag, he'd never seen much of the nation of his birth. Now, driving cross-country with Layla, he was mesmerized by its beauty. The reds and browns of the desert and mountains faded into the plains states and their amber waves of grain. By the time they got to Topeka, Kansas, there was nobody on the road and he'd never seen so many stars in the sky.

"It's sooo good," Layla said, with a sensual moan. She literally writhed in the passenger seat, her well-manicured fingers flexing around her soda bottle with pleasure.

She'd been doing that with every bite of the cookie Ray had picked up for her in a convenience store and her enthusiasm was starting to turn him on. He glanced over in time to see her licking chocolate from her fingers in a way that made him twitch. She aroused him so easily, under any circumstance, without even trying. Maybe especially when she wasn't trying.

For as long as he'd known her, she'd been a serious woman, but now she started laughing. It reminded him of how she'd sputtered with joy in the bathroom of that crappy little motel when she'd first touched him. The pleasure of the memory—of being touched in a way that didn't bring pain—set him off balance. "What's so funny?"

"It's just that I can't believe I've gone two years without eating anything sweeter than a bran muffin!" Her laughter cut off suddenly, and she stammered, "Oh—oh, Ray. I'm sorry. Next to what you've been through…"

"Don't do that," he said. It's true that he'd spent two years eating any slop they shoved through the slats of his prison cell, but she'd been in a kind of prison, too. He was glad she was finally free of it. "Don't walk on eggshells like you pity me, Layla, or like you think I'm going to explode at any moment."

"Okay," she said, offering him a bite of the dessert as a peace offering. "Do you want some?"

"No, thanks. I'm not big on sweets unless it's my mother's baklava. The way she brushes the phyllo dough with butter and spices the nuts… My whole family goes crazy for it."

Layla stared at him. "What's it like to have a family?" It was an odd question, and his expression must have said so, because she explained, "When I didn't have my memories, I always hoped that there was a family out there somewhere looking for me. Now I know that I don't have parents. I don't have siblings or children. Just Seth."

"What's it like having family?" Ray repeated, struggling for an answer. "It's like asking someone what it's like to have an arm or a leg. You can explain what it's like to lose it, but you take it for granted when you have one."

"They must be so worried about you."

Ray was pretty sure that his family couldn't be more worried about him than he was about *them*. It had to have been terrible for them when he just disappeared. How much worse it must be now with his picture all over the news, every other commentator calling him a terrorist. "It kills me to think of what my nephews must be thinking about me right now."

Layla offered him a sip of her soda and this time he took it. "Ray, I'm sure their parents tell them that you're a good man."

"They don't have parents," Ray explained, the familiar ache in his chest. "Their mother died in childbirth."

"She was your sister?"

"My sister-in-law. When Ayisha died, my brother just— He'd never been the most stable guy, okay? He went off his meds and he got it into his head that the boys would be better off without him. So he checked out."

"He abandoned them?"

Ray worked his jaw. "He killed himself, Layla."

They drove in silence for a little while, and he

thought maybe she'd let that be the end of it, but instead, she said, "Was he in therapy?"

"You really think that would have made a damned bit of difference? Some people just can't hack it."

"You sound angry at your brother."

"I guess I am. I guess I think he was a fucking coward to leave two little kids behind like that…not to mention what it did to my parents. My mother thinks that his soul is burning for eternity. The day of my brother's funeral, my father said he didn't believe in God anymore. He said he'd never step foot in another mosque again and he never has."

"What about what your brother's suicide did to you?"

Ray shifted in his seat. "Stop being a shrink."

"I'm not asking as your therapist. I'm asking because I care about you. I want to know."

"You want to know what his suicide did to me? It kept me from bashing my skull open against the metal walls of that dungeon. There were days when killing myself seemed like the only way I was ever going to get out of that coffin, but I just kept thinking about my brother and how two little boys were going to spend their lives wondering why they weren't good enough for him to stick around."

"Is that what you think? That you weren't good enough to keep him here in this life?"

Ray would have glared at her, but he was too afraid to take his eyes off the road and too afraid she'd see the truth of it in his features. He'd spent his whole life trying to prove he was good enough. A good enough brother and son to keep his family together. A good enough friend that Jack shouldn't have lost his shit in

Afghanistan. A good enough soldier that his country should have loved him, too.

"Maybe you should call your family," Layla suggested. "I have a few phones that'd be hard to trace...."

"Save 'em. We might need them."

"What about a pay phone?" Layla asked. "There's one right there."

Leave it to Kansas to still be using old-fashioned phone booths in this age of Hello Kitty devices. Ray could call home. Just one call. It might be the last chance he'd ever have to hear their voices. He could just let them know that what they were hearing on the news wasn't true. Maybe he could even ask them to look for Missy in case he didn't find her at the Scorpion Group offices.

As the silver glint of the phone booth beckoned him to the side of the road, Ray jerked the truck to the shoulder, put it in Park and slammed the door when he got out. If he took the time to think better of this, he might change his mind.

He was in the phone booth within three long strides and had yanked the door closed behind him before he even knew what he was doing.

He should have known better.

As soon as he heard the metal close upon its latch, the air went out of his lungs. It was one of those old-fashioned booths with a phone book on a long chain, but for Ray, he was in the dark, alone and suffocating on the stench of his own sweat and urine. When he'd forced himself to climb into the shower with Layla, he'd been concentrating on helping *her*. Now Ray couldn't think. Couldn't breathe. He just started punching in a blind fury. He heaved with his shoulder, like some kind of creature bursting out of a shell. Something shattered beneath his fist. Something else screeched and warped, cutting him with its jagged edge. In blind terror he found a fist full of wires and pulled. More glass shattered and the whole frame of the booth creaked in collapse. The next thing he knew, he was scrambling his way out of the wreckage, safety glass crunching beneath his feet as blood dripped down both arms.

"Ray!" Layla put both hands over her face. "Are you okay?"

He was anything *but* okay. He was shaking all over, covered in sweat, yet cold as ice. His attacks were getting worse and worse. What if he couldn't stop it? What if next time, he was so blinded with panic he hurt somebody—somebody who didn't deserve to be hurt? Dazed, Ray stumbled to the truck, and Layla was at his elbow steadying him as he gasped for air.

"Layla, you gotta tell me something…"

"Count your breaths," Layla said calmly, her cool hand on his cheek.

One. Two. Three... Fuck if it didn't actually help. Or maybe it was her.

"You gotta tell me, Layla—" he broke off trying to catch his breath.

"I'll tell you anything you want to know, but not until you calm down."

She was steady—steely even—as she got him back into the truck somehow.

"Tell me about minotaurs," he said, still panting. "What happens? Do we go psycho?"

"Minotaurs have violent rages," she said without looking at him. Something in the ruined phone booth had cut through his T-shirt and tore his shoulder open.

Kneeling beside him in the front seat, using only the overhead car light to see, Layla inspected the wound. "Hold still, Ray."

"We have violent rages and what?" he asked. "Kill people?"

"Sometimes," she admitted, probing the wound. "Mostly, minotaurs don't live as long as the one Theseus killed. Using their powers, they burn out quickly and die. That's why Seth is so impatient to have you in his clutches. He wants to control you before you're worthless to him."

Great. The expression on Ray's face must have told her that he'd heard all he needed to know, and that he didn't want to discuss it further because when she leaned back to look at him, all she said was, "Your cut isn't too deep. You may not need stitches."

"There's no time for stitches."

"At least let me bandage it."

"I just need to drive," Ray snapped, but he was in no condition to take the wheel. His vision was swimming and his hands were shaky. It'd be just his luck to be picked up by the cops for weaving on the road. "We need to get to Missy."

"I'll get us there," Layla promised. "You just have to trust me."

And in spite of all reason, he did.

Scorpion Group's office was tucked back on D Street, just past L'Enfant Plaza, and the wedge-shaped gray and glass building was exactly as Layla had described it to him. Now, in the truck beside him, Layla was staring at the building with an expression of unease, her shoulders tense.

"So this is where you used to work?" Ray asked. "Will they recognize you?"

"I worked all over the world," Layla said, her voice a monotone. "Mostly at the compound in Arlington, but I spent some time here."

Seth may have wiped her memories to punish her, but Ray wondered if it had been a blessing in disguise. She'd run away from this life to make a new one in Las Vegas. She hadn't wanted to face these memories and maybe she wouldn't have ever had to if Ray hadn't tracked her down. "Layla, you don't have to do this. You don't have to relive your past…."

"I do have to, Ray. Seth took my memories, but now I think I want them back. All of them. Good and bad…"

Ray respected her determination, but was rethinking the wisdom of having her with him. "I still think it's too dangerous."

"You're the only one in danger here," Layla said, tying her hair back. "Every guard in that building could shoot me full of holes and I'd heal, but if you go in there, guns blazing—"

"Well, I wasn't planning on blasting my way in. I was going to use my powers. I just need you to tell me about the security in this building. I need to know how many minds I need to control at once. I've never had to do it to more than one person at a time."

"Don't be stupid, Ray," she said. "Every time you use your powers, it hurts you. I can do this."

"How? If Seth is looking for you, don't you think everyone on his payroll knows your face?"

"I'm going to riddle them," she said.

"You mean like that guy in the Vegas stairwell? The

one you left a gibbering idiot after you hit him with the fire extinguisher?"

Layla winced. "He was trying to hurt me. I acted on instinct. I posed too powerful a riddle."

"Is that what happened to Dr. Jaffe too?" He tried to ask it gently, but maybe there was no way of asking it that wouldn't hurt her.

"I didn't kill Nate Jaffe," she said firmly, getting out of the truck. "Seth did that because he's a jealous maniac. He wanted to spook me and to make me feel guilty, but I'm not groping around in the dark anymore. I know how to ask questions more like..."

"More like what you did to Missy when you made her cry," Ray finished for her. "More like what you did to me in Syria."

She nodded without meeting his eye. He saw her swallow, her fingers folding in her lap. "You have your monstrous powers, Ray, and I have mine."

When he thought she was a mortal woman, he'd been haunted by her. Obsessed with her. Now that he knew she too was afflicted with strange abilities, it only deepened the connection. He'd thought they were so different. His hot temper clashed with her cool reason. His brawn versus her brains. But the monster in her was someone else's creation, and he understood her struggle on the deepest level. She didn't want to riddle anyone, but she was going to do it for his sake. For him.

"Well, if we're gonna do this thing, then we're gonna do it together," Ray said.

At the front desk, Layla flashed her outdated badge for the security cameras, not for the guards. One of them seemed to recognize her and started to pick up his radio, but Layla wasn't about to let that happen. *"A maze without walls, turns or hidden doors. No map can chart it, no ship can sail it and only reflection can banish it."*

Confusion. That would keep their minds working for a while. The guard with the radio sat back down in his chair as if lost in concentration. The other guard blinked, his eyelids drooping.

With that, she and Ray walked right into the building. She didn't like Ray seeing her use her sphinx powers, but there was something exhilarating about what they were doing together as a team, and a look passed between them that made her melt. She'd never felt as if she had a partner in anything before. Now Ray knew her secrets, and he was still at her side.

Layla navigated the hallways quickly, threading her way to the storage room. If Seth was holding Missy prisoner in this building, he'd be keeping her there. When they reached the clerk on duty, the woman's eyes lit up with recognition. "Dr. Bahset?"

Now it was Ray's turn. He took one look at the woman, latched onto her mind, and said, "Push in the pass code."

"Just do what he says," Layla told her, but the woman's hand was already lifting and punching numbers of its own volition.

"Who are you?" the clerk asked Ray. "How are you doing this?"

"You don't know who I am," Ray replied, staring into her eyes. "You didn't see us come in and you don't remember punching in any access codes."

Layla winced. It was one thing for Ray to force

people to his will—quite another to see him toy with their memories. Seth had done it to her and she wasn't sure she could bear to see it happen to anyone else. The blood would follow, she knew. From his nose or his eyes or his ears. Minotaurs were short-lived creatures and she didn't want him to spend any more of his life than he needed to, so she didn't even ask him if he could undo the damage.

Meanwhile, Ray shoved the industrial door open. "Missy!"

But there wasn't anyone inside. Instead, the room was filled floor-to-ceiling with boxes. As the disappointment passed over his face, he asked, "Is there anywhere else they'd be keeping her?"

Layla shook her head.

"What about in Arlington? You said there was another facility there. A compound?"

"It's more private than this office, Ray, but it's also more secure." If Seth really had kidnapped the girl, she could be halfway around the world on a private jet to Dubai, but Layla didn't want to get Ray more worked up than he already was.

"What the hell is all of this?" Ray asked, pointing to the boxes.

"Notes from contractors in the field," Layla said.

"You think there's anything here about Missy? Maybe about my case?"

"Maybe," she said. "But we don't have time to look. We have maybe five or ten minutes."

"Let's make the most of them," Ray said, yanking down the nearest box and riffling through it.

Layla wanted to tell him not to bother. It was the needle in the proverbial haystack. On the other hand, she remembered one salient fact about her master. Seth's guise as an officious government contractor alone proved that he believed in security through obscurity. "If there's something here about your case, Seth would've mixed it in with something mundane, something that he thinks is clever."

"Like a yellow box?" Ray asked, yanking a banana-colored container from the shelf. "For Ray of Sunshine, since I'm such a sunny kind of guy?"

"Something like that," she answered, meandering down the rows looking for boxes with place names. She found one from Crete—home of the more famous minotaur. Another one from Spain, which was famous for its bullfighting. They dumped records all over the floor, and the more files Layla opened the more horrified she was. Ray wasn't the only man that Scorpion Group employees had tortured. He wasn't even Seth's only pet project.

It was Layla who found the file first. Plain manila with a black sail upon it. Just like the one that the hero Theseus mistakenly flew after having slain the Minotaur of Crete. "I think I found something," she whispered, flipping it open and gasping at the contents. "Ray, we have to get out of here now."

"What the hell is in that file?" Ray asked, trying to snatch it from her, but Layla was already at the door. She started at a full run and he chased her as she retraced their steps and exited the building before Seth's security team roused themselves from their puzzled stupor.

"Do you need to unriddle them, or whatever?" he

asked, glancing at the men who still sat behind the marble security desk, still as stone.

"They'll come out of it on their own," she said. "Now hurry!"

"What's in the file?" Ray asked, running by her side. "Is there anything about Missy?"

"No, nothing," she said, her boots pounding on the pavement as she raced to the truck.

Ray wasn't sure how many more dead ends he could come up against and retain any semblance of sanity. "Then why the hell are we running?"

"Because there's a note inside," she said. "In Seth's handwriting. It says 'Keep looking, Rayhan.' He knew you'd come for it."

They flung open the vehicle doors and leaped inside. As Ray peeled out of the parking spot and sped away, Layla kept her eyes on the rear window, as if convinced the dark god of Egypt was going to come lashing his chariot out into traffic. Instead, they both saw blue lights of security cars racing toward the Scorpion Group offices.

"So it was a trap," Ray said, grinding his teeth. Between the security footage and eyewitness accounts of their break-in, they'd gambled and lost. There was already a manhunt in progress for him—and now the authorities would have an even better idea where to look. In fact, he half expected to see a helicopter hovering overhead.

"No," Layla said, her knuckles white as she gripped the folder in her hands. "If it was a trap, we'd both have been caught. He's toying with you. He doesn't want to capture you in an office building in the middle of the city where people might hear you scream. He's egging you on, trying to lure you somewhere else."

"Like where?"

"Like the compound in Arlington," Layla snapped. "It's a little out of the way. He has medical facilities and panic rooms and all sorts of places he could torture you some more and no one would hear you scream. It's a good place to hold prisoners."

"Prisoners like Missy," Ray said. "Maybe we should have gone there first."

Layla twisted toward him in the passenger seat. "You're not going to break into Scorpion Group's compound in Arlington."

"What the hell other choice do I have?"

"Ray, I don't think Seth has Missy. Look at this note. He didn't think you'd come after the girl. He thought you'd come after a *file*. He thinks the most important thing to you is finding out who the informant was who turned you in."

"It is," Ray said, emotions roiling. Well, it *was* anyway. Ever since he'd found Layla again, his priorities had shifted.

"Ray, you can't fight a *god*. Neither of us can." Even over the roar of passing traffic, he heard the quaver in her voice. She was scared.

When he'd been down in that hole, Ray had forgotten other people. They'd kept him in darkness so long he wasn't sure he could even remember his own mother's face. He'd started to think only of himself, only of his survival, and only of his pain. They'd turned him into this, and he'd let them. These rages were making him more of a minotaur every day, but he wasn't a monster. Not completely. Not yet. Making love to Layla had reminded him of that.

He was still man enough to realize he wasn't the only one who had been hurt in all this. He'd involved Jack and Missy in his escape, and now they were both in danger. He'd be damned if Layla would suffer anymore than she already had. She'd remembered painful truths. She kept telling him that she didn't want to remember, and now he knew why. For his sake, she'd let him dredge up all the awful things that sent her down to the shower floor, broken and sobbing. And today she'd walked right into the belly of the beast—risking being captured by Seth.

He couldn't blame her for wanting it all to end here and now.

"You don't need to be involved in this anymore, Layla, but I've got to clear my name."

"No, you don't," Layla whispered. "You *want* to clear your name, but you don't *need* to. You can live a good life without a name. You could run. You could just leave the country."

The truth was, with his powers, Ray probably *could* get on a plane and disappear. Besides, after all his country had put him through, why should he care what people thought about him here? But he *did* care. He wasn't sure how to explain that to someone like Layla, who had lived long enough to see thousands of nations rise and fall and probably felt allegiance to none of them. He loved this country, in spite of everything. "Layla, I can't leave everything behind."

"I'd go with you," she said. "If you wanted me to."

As traffic crawled, Ray risked glancing over at her. It was too much to hope for. She was this timeless, exotic creature. How could she really want to stay with him? "Layla, how can I leave my family behind?"

"I think your family would rather know that you were safe and alive. They'd go on without you."

They'd go on without you. That's how his brother had justified killing himself, and Ray couldn't believe Layla had echoed the same sentiment. "You don't have any family, Layla, so how would you know a damned thing about it?"

Her mouth snapped shut and he caught a glimpse of pain flash behind her eyes before she lowered them. He'd been an ass. He'd hurt her feelings and had no idea how to fix it. "Layla—"

"No, you're right," she said, her voice icy. "I don't have a family and I can't pretend to understand mortals. I think that's why I went into psychology. I *wanted* to understand. I never could fathom how men could whip themselves up into such a frenzy that they'd kill complete strangers on a battlefield. I never was able to wrap my mind around the horrors of war that Seth loved so much. I never could understand how soldiers would slaughter civilians. Maybe you can explain it to me."

He felt his heartbeat skip. Did she know what'd happened? What he'd done for Jack Bouchier? In answer to his unspoken question, Layla flipped open the folder to reveal pictures of the massacre in Afghanistan. "Seth's note isn't the only thing in this file."

Ray couldn't bear to look at those pictures and hated the chill in her voice. If what she'd seen in that file made her doubt his innocence again, he wasn't sure he could bear it. "I'm not responsible for killing those people, Layla."

"Then who is?"

That was a question she'd never asked him when she'd been his interrogator. She probably could've forced him to answer her now. She could've used her riddler's power. But she didn't. "War isn't pretty, Layla. Bad things happen."

Tears hovered at the corners of her eyes. "*Bad things happen?* Ray, that's what everyone at Scorpion Group said about your imprisonment and torture. The government said, 'We've gotta get the bad guys before they get us, and if that means that a few innocent people have to suffer, so be it.' Is that the way you think?"

It hit him like a punch to the gut. He didn't know if she'd used her powers on him or not. He only knew that the breath went out of him. His chest seized with squeezing pain and it was as if the truck became a kaleidoscope of twisted metal and prison bars. He went hot, then cold, then hot again as he fought for control. What the hell was wrong with him?

"Ray?" she asked as the wheels slipped and the truck began to sway out of control.

Shit. It was happening again. Just like in the phone booth, but worse. He had to get out of the truck. He had to get some air. Frantically, he pressed the button to lower the window, hitting every one of them but the right one.

"Ray, you have to calm down."

That made it even worse. "Don't tell me to calm down!"

He managed to screech the vehicle to a halt on the shoulder of the road while angry commuters leaned on their horns. It didn't matter that he'd pulled over at the top of an overpass. It didn't matter that traffic was whizzing by dangerously close to his door. He had to get out. He had to get out or he was going to die right here. He shoved open the door and flung himself out.

"Ray!" Layla called after him.

It wasn't until he was standing by the side of the road, gulping deep breaths of air, that he even realized she'd followed him. "Count—"

"I don't want to count my fucking breaths!"

"Ray, you can't let yourself lose control. You need help. You need treatment."

"What do you suggest? A little couple's therapy for fugitives?"

"You need treatment for your anxiety. Maybe medication."

"I'll get right on that," he said, hands on his knees as he bent over, the pavement swimming before his eyes.

"I'm sorry," she said. "I shouldn't have pressed you."

He hated how she was always so willing to believe that everything was her fault. She'd only asked the same questions anyone would have asked him. She deserved an honest answer. Unfortunately, it was the one thing he couldn't find the courage to give her. He managed to stand up, buffeted by the force of air that passing cars sent his way. Layla's dark hair was whipping her face and his. "You have to get back in the truck, Ray. I'll drive and we'll keep all the windows open."

"No," Ray said, taking her cheeks in his hands, kissing her as if it would somehow substitute for all the things he wanted to say to her, but would never find the words to express. "You've done all you can for me. You need to take the truck and get out of here."

Her eyes flew wide. "A minute ago I told you I'd go anywhere with you and now you expect me to just leave you standing at the side of the road? And go where? Do what?"

Once, he'd felt entitled to hunt her down and drag her into this mess. Now all he wanted was for her to be free of it. He didn't want her to see him degenerate into some brutal, unthinking, rage-filled killing machine. He didn't want her to watch him bust into people's minds and slowly lose his own. Ray took her by the shoulders. "Listen, Layla, when I found you, you were desperate to get away from Seth, and if it weren't for me, you'd have escaped him. You need to go. Run. *You* leave the country."

He felt her tremble, then visibly calm herself, a fierce determination in her eyes. "I'm not leaving you here."

He traced her chin with his thumb, then gently pressed the keys into her hand. "You're going to have to leave me here because I can't get back in that truck. I just can't do it. It's too confined. What's more, I need you to get it off the side of the road before we attract any more attention."

He started to turn, but she grabbed his elbow. "We could meet somewhere. I'll get rid of the truck and we can find each other—"

"After all this is over, I promise I'll find you, Layla. But not until it's over."

She looked stricken. Abandoned. Ray knew that she'd loved Seth and he'd cast her away. Now she looked as if Ray were hurting her even worse. "Why are you doing this, Ray? Why won't you let me stay with you?"

Wasn't it plain as day? Did he have to spell it out for her? "Because I love you, Layla. And because you're the only one who *knows* I'm innocent. The truth of who I am needs to be safe with you."

With that, Ray started walking the shoulder of the road. Layla followed him a few steps, but then paused, as he knew she would. The truck was causing traffic to slow. It was the kind of disorder that someone like Layla couldn't abide. She called after him. "Ray!"

He dared not look back, but picked up his pace.

"Ray!" she shouted again, but her voice was warped by the wind and the passing cars.

Chapter 16

It's pleasure mixed with pain. On your heart it makes its claim.

Layla didn't know whether it stunned her more that Ray had said that he loved her, or that he'd left her standing there on the side of the road. Layla ditched Ray's truck, then set out on foot to find him, not realizing until she'd hit the National Mall that she had no idea where she was going. Now she meandered there, trying to make sense of it all.

Loved. Layla was loved. In all the thousands of years since Seth had shaped her from the sand, no one had ever loved her before and now the whole living world looked different to her. The flowers were in love with the sun, lifting their faces to gaze up in adoration. The passing traffic in the streets had a pulse of its own, like blood moving through the veins of a heated lover. The marble buildings were like the carved headboard of some giant bridal bed, with the silken sheets of grass folding out beneath it. Layla walked through it all in a daze.

Ray *loved* her. Rayhan Stavrakis—a man she'd interrogated, humiliated and manipulated—had not only forgiven her, but *loved* her. Yet, he'd also left her.

And he'd left her before she had a chance to tell him that she loved him right back. She shouldn't stay here now. Seth had destroyed her memories once before and if he caught her this time, he'd destroy her memories of Ray. What if she had to live the rest of her life never knowing that someone had loved her? That thought alone was more than Layla could bear standing up.

Luckily a park bench was nearby, and she collapsed onto it, staring at the children playing next to the reflecting pool. It was hard to believe that such a beautiful day could exist while her insides were in such turmoil. How could the sun be shining when Ray was out there somewhere, in danger?

Ray would go to the Scorpion Group compound in Arlington. He'd go there to look for Missy and he'd go there to find evidence of his innocence. Maybe he'd even go there to confront Seth for transforming him into a minotaur. And then he'd die, or worse. There had to be some way to stop him. Layla put her face in her hands, trying to focus. Trying to think calmly and rationally.

"It can't be as bad as that, *chica,*" someone said.

Layla looked up, squinting into the bright sunlight. Surely she was hallucinating. "Isabel?" Layla's eyes widened, staring at Isabel—seeing Isabel not as a mortal would, but through the eyes of a sphinx. She'd always sensed Isabel's feminine power, but how had she ever thought that Isabel was a simple administrative assistant? How had she never noticed the golden skin and supernatural aura? How blind she'd been!

"Wh-what are you?" Layla stammered.

"I'm your friend, *mija,* but I'm more than that, too."

Isabel was a goddess. It was all Layla could do to still the tremor that ran through her. Should she kneel in reverence? She didn't know how to behave in the presence of a deity who didn't own her.

"Relax," Isabel told her, and sat down on the bench.

"But how?" Layla was so startled, she blurted out, "It must have been so hard for you to pretend that you're an ordinary woman."

"Bite your tongue, riddler," Isabel said. "I never pretended to be *ordinary!*"

"You knew I was a sphinx? The whole time, you knew?"

"I knew you were a sphinx, but I didn't know who you belonged to until Seth walked in the door looking for the minotaur. He was hoping to catch you both together."

Somehow, against all odds, Isabel had found her first. "How did you find me?"

"I let my butterflies help me," Isabel said with a quirky little smile as if she had secrets. "Seth won't be happy about it."

Layla blanched. "I don't want to be his. I don't even want to be what Seth made me."

"Lucky for you that I won a wager," Isabel said.

Layla listened with scarcely contained shock as Isabel explained. When Isabel was finished, Layla asked, "So then…I belong to *you* now?"

"No, *mija*. I didn't make the wager so that I could have a sphinx of my very own. I want you to be free to give your heart and to live your life in any way you please."

"That's..." Layla couldn't find the words to describe what an immense and gracious gift this was. "What do you want in return?"

"I want you to be happy and make others happy," Isabel replied.

Tears were still such foreign things to Layla, but they slipped down her cheeks now. She didn't know that gratitude could make her cry, too. Isabel had done her a great kindness, but Layla had already given her heart to Ray and feared she might now have to live a long life without him.

Ray liked his chances. The Scorpion Group facility in Arlington was off the main road. A chain-link fence surrounded the large parking lot, and a set of stone stairs marked the entryway. Somewhere in this building he might find Missy. And if he didn't find her, there might be a file that would prove his innocence. Whatever strength Ray still had as a minotaur, he planned on using to get inside.

The two armed guards by the gate were easy enough to dispatch with his powers. He told them to take a walk and forget they'd seen him. Security was notably less lax inside the building where he forced the guy with a radio to pull the fire alarm. As soon as people started evacuating, Ray took the stairs up a floor and slipped into an empty office.

It was then that he felt the hard muzzle of a gun on the back of his neck.

Ray didn't panic. He just slowly raised his hands in mock surrender. Eventually whoever it was on the other end of the gun would let him turn around. And when that happened he'd catch their eyes and… *Shit.* The guy was wearing mirrored sunglasses, and a malicious smile, like he knew just what Ray had been thinking.

"So sorry to disappoint you, Rayhan, but you'd only hurt yourself in the labyrinth of my mind. My memories are as old as the world."

Seth. There was no question about it. Ray had never thought he'd lay eyes on a god until he died, and maybe not even then. Seeing one in the flesh was both humbling…and disappointing. Seth wasn't shining with light or wielding thunderbolts in each hand. In fact, the war god was of modest stature; Ray towered above him. But even in his mortal guise, when Seth removed his sunglasses, his burning amber eyes made Ray wilt under their intensity. Incredible power frayed the edges of Seth's mortal image and if everything Layla had told Ray was true, he was standing face-to-face with her creator as well as his own.

"Your abilities are coming along nicely," Seth said, tracing the barrel of the gun across Ray's skin. He was close. Too close. It was always safer to keep your distance when you were holding a gun on somebody. Ray tightened, waiting for the moment he could grab the firearm. "Oh, don't bother trying to disarm me, Rayhan. I can kill you without shooting you. It's just easier to explain bullet holes to the police than it is to explain a pile of human ash and bones."

Ray believed him. "You went to a lot of trouble to fashion me into a minotaur just to kill me now."

"Ah, so you know what you are." Seth smiled without showing his teeth. "I suppose it was good of Layla to save me the tedious explanations. Just where is my little domestic house cat? I felt certain that she'd be with you."

Ray silently seethed. Ever since he'd left Layla he'd been thinking he'd made the worst mistake of his life. Now he was glad that he had no idea where she was, because that meant he couldn't tell Seth anything even under torture. "Layla and I parted company."

"That's inconvenient," Seth said.

"For you, maybe. Now where the hell is Missy? Where are you keeping her?"

"Missy?"

Something inside of Ray shriveled and died when he saw the look of confusion on Seth's face. Ray wouldn't have been surprised to find that Seth was an expert liar, but he had a sinking feeling that Layla had been right all along. Somebody else had snatched Missy.

"Who is this Missy? A lover?" Seth asked. "You seem like a virile man...."

Ray clamped his jaw. He wasn't going to say anything else about Missy or about Layla or about anyone he cared about. But Seth's attention seemed to have wandered. "You've bulked up, I see. Good. I like a strong ox to pull my plow." Seth circled Ray, examining him as if he were a slave upon the auction block. He wouldn't have been surprised if Seth insisted on inspecting Ray's teeth. "But you look overtired. Did your mind games with the guards tire you that much?"

Ray ground his teeth, determined not to answer.

"Did Layla tell you that it'll kill you one day? Minotaurs get lost inside the minds of their victims and eventually turn into drooling simpletons. They waste away. But I think you might last a good deal longer than most. I let you escape from your Syrian prison to see how you'd survive. Thus far you've proved yourself capable, but from now on, you'll reserve your strength for me."

Oh. That wouldn't be a problem. Ray was all about saving his strength to crush Seth. "What the hell do you want from me?"

"Hell." Seth let the word roll off his tongue as if he were tasting it. "Hell is such an interesting concept, don't you think? In my time, dying men worried that their hearts would be found unworthy and fed to the crocodiles. We too had our lakes of fire. Now you fear Satan and his eternal flames. Yet, your living world is already burning with war. You've seen it."

There was an egomaniacal gleam in Seth's eyes that burned like all the roadside explosions Ray had witnessed—sudden, forceful and deadly. It wasn't cowardice that forced Ray to flinch away. It was the certainty that he could be drawn into Seth's magnetic pull if he wasn't careful. Ray burned with enough rage at what'd been done to him that he already had to fight his urge to smash and destroy. It would be something too easy for Seth to exploit.

"Yeah. I've seen war," Ray said. "I'm done with it."

"That's because it was terribly frustrating, I know," Seth said. "That was before. Now with me, you'll have so much more control over the outcome."

"You think I'm gonna help you start wars?"

"Mortal men don't need my help in starting wars. Your kind has been killing each other since you first crawled onto land. All I've done is feed off the bloody harvest of violence you mortal men sow. But chaos, lawlessness—now *that* is sometimes my doing. I've waited a long time for the whole world's focus to turn to the desert, and even longer for a war like the one in Afghanistan, where the desert itself is starting to swallow a whole nation."

Ray knew that thirty years of warfare had stripped Afghanistan of her forests and fertile valleys. War had made it a different place—where the only thing anybody would grow was poppy flowers, and drug lords ruled it all. The ecological and economic disaster there was plain for all to see, vegetation disappearing at an alarming rate. Is that what Seth was after? "What's it got to do with me?"

"You have the power to make sane men mad, Ray. You're a useful creature that I can unleash when and where I see fit. You see, I like this war very much. I like how mortal men think that it changes everything, and that none of the rules apply. You know a thing or two about that, don't you, Rayhan?"

Ray turned his head, closing his eyes against the memories.

"You're going to serve me well until the end of your days, Rayhan."

As a prisoner in the dungeon, Ray had been stripped of his freedom and of any power to defend himself. He'd been degraded. Humiliated. But the humiliation of being on some evil bastard's leash was more than Ray could bear. "I'd rather die."

"That can be arranged, but killing *you* for your disobedience would be so boring. Any true student of humanity would know that there are better ways to punish you. From now on, when you disobey me, I'll simply kill someone that you love. You have a family, don't you? Two little nephews… Two innocent children. The mere illusion that you'd eaten their flesh helped turn you into a minotaur. Imagine how you'll feel this time, when I make you watch as I peel the skin off their bones and force their flesh down your throat."

Ray would never, ever, forget the taste, the horror, the bile as he vomited. The violent wish for revenge had turned him from a man into an animal. Even remembering it now, Ray quaked. Seth could get to his family and use them against him, over and over. At least until Ray could find a way to hide them.

Layla had said that Seth didn't know everything; he could be fooled. Maybe what Ray needed was to buy time. "I'll tell you what, Captain Sandman. You tell me who it was that got me arrested—who it was that accused me of treason—and I'll do whatever you want."

Seth's smile widened so that his predatory teeth showed. "You'll do what I want anyway. Here. Let me demonstrate. A wolf must be trained, a lion must be tamed, and a bull must be broken."

With that, Ray felt the crushing pain of a blow to the skull. Then nothing.

Ray woke up in darkness. Fabric brushed his nostrils when he inhaled and he realized he'd been hooded. In spite of the agonizing pain in his body, he jerked his head up sharply, only to find that he couldn't move. His head was stuck between two bars with the rest of his body free. Ray tried to feel the outlines of the contraption and his hands encountered cold, hard steel.

That's when he heard Seth's voice. "It's a headgate,"

the god said. "I wouldn't want you to shift into your bovine form and harm any of my other playthings."

Ray banged against the metal, struggling to get free as anxiety welled up inside him. He couldn't get enough air.

"Is everything closing in on you, Rayhan?" Seth asked. "Do you feel the walls shrinking? Do you wonder if this is going to be how you die? If this is your tomb?"

Ray's heartbeat galloped, slamming against his rib cage painfully. "Stop," he gasped. He was going to have a heart attack. The crushing weight of it was coming down on his chest. He'd gone cold and felt the sweat drip from his body. He slammed violently against the metal, but the strength was going out of him. He was going to die. He was going to die right here in this headgate if he couldn't calm down.

He thought of Layla. Her calming presence and the coolness of her fingers on his fevered skin. He started to count his breaths, imagining the scent of her hair, the silken feel of her skin. He should never have left her. She'd trusted him with the whole truth; she'd trusted him when no one else would, and he'd abandoned her. The only blessing in all this was that she wasn't here to see him caged like a beast.

"Are you wondering what justice there is in the world?" Seth asked. "None, if I can help it. But you shouldn't be so offended, Ray. You don't care much about justice, do you? I wonder—does Layla know? Did you tell her you were an innocent man?"

"I am!" Ray roared.

"You're only innocent of what the government accused you." Seth chuckled. "We both know what you're really guilty of."

Ray thrashed in the headgate, tasting the blood in his nostrils.

"That's right, Rayhan. Let go of the parts of you that are human. Give yourself to me."

Ray had never known why his brother committed suicide. He'd never thought it mattered. He'd always believed that nothing—no misery—could justify leaving behind two little kids. He'd thought his brother was a coward, but maybe he'd just been in so much pain that suicide was the only way to make it stop. Now Ray was starting to think that death might be his only escape, too.

In more glorious times, no one would have ever interrupted Seth. Pharaoh would have sent priests to entreat with him in the desert. Lesser mortals would have whispered a prayer or made an offering. Blood would be spilled in his name. But such was the miserable, modern state of the world that Seth suffered the indignity of this silly little electronic box in his pocket. As irritating as it was to have his cell phone ring like a summons from Ra, Seth actually smiled at the name on the display.

ISABEL FLORES.

She would be thinking better of the wager they'd made, but he had no plans of releasing her from it. He had the minotaur, soon he'd have his sphinx, and then he'd have Isabel, too. *Xochiquetzal.* He wondered if, like the petals of a rose, she would smell more sweetly when bruised.

Leaving the minotaur locked in the headgate, Seth

walked to the hallway and answered the phone on the fifth ring, a smile of smug satisfaction upon his lips. “It’s too late to back out of our bargain, my little jungle flower.”

“Qué lástima,” Isabel replied. “This is a shame for you, because I’ve already won. I found Layla.”

Seth actually laughed. It wasn’t possible that a little goddess like her—of no importance to anyone—could have bested him. “If you think to distract me with a lie—”

“She’s right here,” Isabel said. “Do you need to hear her voice to know I’m telling the truth?”

The anger started in Seth’s belly, mixing with other emotions, deeper and darker by far. “How did you find her? I want to know!”

“That hardly matters,” Isabel said. “I’m going to put you on speakerphone now so that Layla can hear the words as you release her.”

“Never!” Seth’s shout reverberated throughout the corridor.

“Have you fallen so low, then?” Isabel asked. “I *thought* you were a great god of Egypt. Has the Scorpion King turned into a lowly government contractor in truth? After all, only mortals think they have the freedom to break an oath.”

Outside, thunder began to shake the sky over the nation’s capital, drawn there by Seth’s rage. He couldn’t deny the truth of Isabel’s words. He was bound by oath. Kings and pharaohs had called upon him to swear witness to their pacts. History had been carved from promises in his name. He would have to let Layla go. This time for good. The realization sank to the hollow pit of his stomach.

He'd never wanted Layla as much as he did now—when he must let her go. Two years ago, it'd given him immense satisfaction to rob her of the knowledge of her immortality and leave her wandering the world, wounded and incomplete. But now he wanted her back. She *belonged* to him. That he'd so cavalierly bargained with her for the young and foreign goddess filled him with regret.

"Layla?" he finally said into the phone.

She didn't answer. She didn't need to. He knew her by the sound of her breath alone, and why shouldn't he? Every breath she took was one that he'd given her.

Layla couldn't speak. Hearing her god's voice again filled her with paralyzing dread. She'd been afraid of Seth before she even remembered who he was. Now she quaked where she stood.

"Layla," Seth said again, his voice controlled and calm, as if he were talking to a child. "I must release you."

He sounded almost as if he were sorry. He paused for her response, but none was forthcoming. Words froze in her throat. After thousands of years, Seth was finally going to release her. She'd be free. It was what she wanted more than anything, so why did it frighten her so much?

Seth seemed to sense her fears. "Even after I release you, you don't have to serve *Xochiquetzal.* You can come back to me of your own free will. If you don't, you'll be as lost without me as you've felt for the past two years."

Seth *was* the only family Layla had ever known. He'd created her. Did she even know who she was without him? She'd been so desperate to run from Seth before, but now she was confused. Isabel must have noticed it, too, because she put a reassuring hand upon Layla's arm.

"I've captured my minotaur," Seth continued. "So he won't be a distraction any longer. I'll have the time to focus my attention on you, as you used to beg me to do. You'll be punished, of course, but I'll forgive you. It'll be better between us this time."

Sudden tears scalded Layla's cheeks. *Seth had Ray.* The knowledge of it burned like acid. There was no greater injustice she could think of than Ray having taken her place as Seth's minion. His mortal life would be made shorter every time he used his powers. That the rest of his life should be spent as a leashed monster was the most unbearable thing Layla could imagine.

She couldn't let it happen.

Chapter 17

Live without me,
You'll be queasy.
Give me to others,
They'll sleep easy.

Squeezing the little phone in his hand, Seth was certain that Layla would ask his forgiveness. She'd beg him to let her return to him. She might even promise never to challenge his authority again. Seth savored the tremor he heard in her breath. "Do you have something to say to me, Layla?"

"Yes," she replied. "Let him go."

It took Seth a moment to even guess at who she might mean. "The *minotaur?* He's mine. I created him, Layla." Seth pulled open his tie, irritated at the way modern clothing restrained and constricted him. In the desert he'd worn nothing but a loincloth, and nothing to smother his rage. "Just like I created you."

"It's not the same," Layla replied. "You made me from nothing but Ray had a life before you. He has family. He has dreams and ambitions. He has values that run counter to everything you stand for, and you won't break him."

"Then I'll kill him." It would be disappointing to have gone to so much effort to create a minotaur only to have to put him down, but Seth wouldn't shy away from it if need be.

"Why don't you just let him go? Give him what he needs to clear his name and live a normal life."

Ah. So she had feelings for the man. Seth's earlier tenderness for Layla started to melt away, and he felt his heart harden. He'd suspected the little trollop had debased herself with the minotaur. Now he was sure that Ray had plowed fields that belonged to him… Seth would make him pay for that.

"I have my memories," Layla was saying. "If you don't let him go, know that I have evidence of Scorpion Group's illegal activities. How you torture prisoners, how you take them to foreign countries to get around the law…."

"So what?" Seth barked. "Do you think the government doesn't know?"

"I'm sure a media outlet might be interested."

"Do you really think I care so much about this little corporation? There's no jail that could hold me and no riches I couldn't claim as my own if I wanted them. If you destroy Scorpion Group, I'll start a new company somewhere else. And all the while, I'll have the minotaur at my side."

She was breaking, Seth thought, and then she did. "If you let Ray go, I'll come back to you."

It stoked the last flicker of affection he had for his creation. Perhaps he hadn't lost Layla after all, but he couldn't allow her to hear the relief in his voice. "You'll return to me anyway, Layla. I'll live for eternity and so will you. No one knows you as I do. I know your thoughts before you think them. I know your nature. Time will erode everything in your life, including this mortal man whose freedom you're bargaining for. In the last sands of time there will only be you and me."

"No," Layla said. "Because if you don't let him go, I'll get pregnant."

Blasphemy! That she'd threaten to take the breath of life that he'd given to her, and give it to a child… Unthinkable. He'd given her immortality. She had no right to cast it away. "What nonsense is this? Have you posed yourself a guilty riddle? Have you sent so many to take their own lives that now you wish to embrace suicide?"

"It's not suicide," she said, her tone withering. "Yes, I'll grow old. I'll return to the sands from whence I came, but at least I'll have a child to love. A life that I created. And you won't be able to do a thing to stop it. I'll take the first man on the street that will have me and bear him a child."

"Is that how you chose Dr. Jaffe as a lover?" he asked, infuriated. "I made sure he paid the ultimate price for laying his unworthy hands on something that belonged to me. I strung him up in his tiny closet and watched him gasp his last. I brought my mouth close to his face, telling him that he was going to die for your sake, then inhaled his final breath. Is that what you want me to do to all the men who touch you?"

Layla gave a choked sob and it startled him. When had she learned to cry? For that matter, when had she learned to threaten him as if he weren't her lord and master? This was all Isabel's fault, and he ached to make the young goddess pay.

"All you have to do is release Ray and I'll come back to you, Seth. I'll say goodbye to him and then I'll stay forever by your side. I'll serve you—"

"As you were created to do," Seth reminded her.

"I'll remember my place," Layla said, a defeated whisper that was like a siren song to him.

Could he part with the minotaur? Why not? Made of rage and vengeance, the creature would either return to him eventually or burn out the candle of his life with his powers. It was a hollow bargain Layla was proposing and Seth felt as if he couldn't lose either way. "You'll have this one thing your way, Layla," he said. "Then nothing ever again."

After she hung up the phone, Layla stared at the ground as if she couldn't believe that it hadn't actually swept out from beneath her feet. Isabel shook her head from side to side, one hand on Layla's. "Oh, *mija*. I give you your freedom, and this is what you do with it?"

"You told me to love who I wanted and make people happy," Layla said, letting Isabel wrap her in a hug. "This is the only way that I can do it."

The last thing Ray remembered was being in the headgate. Now he was…where? Ray blinked several times before the words on the sign by the door made any sense to him. *Gallery Place—Chinatown.* He blinked again. Was he in the D.C. Metro system? Had Seth seriously just let him go?

Ray knew all about how guards sometimes invited prisoners to escape so that they could shoot them dead, but this seemed like a bad place for that kind of setup, unless the war god wanted lots of witnesses. Ray quickly patted himself down for weapons, drugs, or suspicious gadgets that could be confused with detonators. If he was being set up, they hadn't planted anything on him.

At least not yet.

He decided that Seth's men were less likely to gun him down in a crowd, so Ray pushed through the door. That's when he saw *her* on the platform and staggered toward her two steps at a time. "Layla…?" He said her name like a question, as if she were some kind of mirage. He couldn't think of any other way that she could be here with him, but then she wrapped her arms around him and he knew she was real. He winced at the pain in his beaten ribs, but didn't care. It was worth it just to touch her again. To hold her again. "Layla, I'm sorry. I'm so sorry."

Flashing lights on the platform announced the train for the Red Line.

"We have to get out of here," she said, grabbing his hand.

Layla pulled Ray into an empty car at the end of the metro train, and nearly sobbed with relief when the doors slid shut.

Just as she'd hoped, the metro car was apparently

spacious enough not to trigger his claustrophobia, or maybe he was too dazed to notice the metal doors close tight. Though the bruises on his face told of beatings she'd rather not imagine, she could see that he was relatively unharmed. She took a grateful breath, laying her head on his shoulder, trying to memorize the outline of him with her hands. She wanted to remember always what he felt like, what he smelled like. Everything.

Confusion swirled in his dark eyes. "Layla, what the hell is going on?"

She'd meant to explain things to him calmly. Coolly. In a professional, detached tone. She'd even practiced it. But when the moment came to tell him, her lower lip quivered and she had to fight to get the words over the lump in her throat. "Seth is setting you free as a gift to me."

Ray reared back, his brow furrowing as he held her at arm's length. "Layla—"

"I'm going back to Seth. I belong to him."

Ray's bloodshot eyes narrowed. "The hell you do!"

She'd feared he'd never let her trade her freedom for his, and now she could see she'd been right. That's why she had to lie. "I have my memories back. Now my feelings for him are coming back, too. I told you before that I loved him."

Ray's features twisted with incredulous anger. "He betrayed every feeling you ever had for him and he scares the shit out of you!"

All these years she'd never been able to cry, and now she couldn't seem to stop. Tears welled in her eyes as she said, "I guess love is complicated."

"No," Ray said. "Love is *simple*. Like what we have between you and me."

He was wrong. There was nothing simple about her feelings for him. Her love for Ray was deep and complex and tortured. She had to lie to him for his own sake, but it was agony to do it. "We don't have anything between us, Ray. I belong to Seth."

"Stop saying that," Ray growled, grabbing her by the arms so hard it made her teeth rattle. "I know how it must have felt when I left you by the side of the road, but I swore I'd find you later and I meant it."

"It's too late, Ray." She didn't know how something could hurt so badly without killing her, but it wouldn't. Nothing would ever kill her. Ray would die, but she'd be without him forever. Living every day with a hole in herself deeper than the one in which her memories had been buried. "I just wanted to see you this one last time to say goodbye."

She saw the air leave his lungs as if he'd been punched in the gut. "Do you think I'm stupid? I'm not letting you go back to him for my sake."

"I'm not doing this for you," Layla said as the world outside the train windows passed by in a blur. "I'm doing it for me. You're just a mortal man. Seth is a god. He's an immortal like me. We'll be together long after you're dead."

"He doesn't love you, damn it!" She tried to pry his fingers off her arms, but Ray held on and shook her. "He doesn't love you and I do."

"But I don't love *you,* Ray." She took a deep breath over the crushing weight of the lie. "At least, not in the way you want me to."

"You're lying," Ray said. "You're lying to yourself or you're lying to me or both. You don't want Seth. You want me."

Then he kissed her. The kiss was as tender as his grip was firm. This one was so different. It was as if he'd never kissed her before. A kiss filled with longing, his rough lips seared to hers as he breathed her in. His kiss was as salty as the ocean, as salty as the tears that welled in her eyes, as salty as the perspiration that beaded on the back of her neck with desperate want. She lifted her hands to push him away, but those traitorous arms wrapped around his neck instead. The train was pulling into a nearly empty station. She heard the rushing sound start to slow. When those doors opened, she'd leave him. Until then, for just this moment, she'd let him kiss her.

"You love *me,*" Ray whispered against her mouth, his breath warm on her cheeks. "I'm not letting you go."

The flashing lights of the station flickered and she steeled herself for this moment. The train screeched to a stop, its wheels sounding like a high-pitched keening wail. She'd chosen the subway system because of Ray's nature. The metro tunnels were a twisted warren, but they were spacious and wide. Hopefully, they wouldn't trigger his anxiety. Yes, it'd been a good plan as long as she could disentangle herself from his arms and leave him now.

The doors slid open and Layla felt the wall of warmer air buffet her as a few passengers jostled toward them. Ray caught the eye of a man about to step into the train, pulling away from Layla only long enough to growl, "Find another car, buddy."

The man staggered back, pushing several other passengers as he did so.

"Stop it," she whispered as he used his power to

force passengers to step back, leaving the car empty but for them. She should leave him here and now, but Ray held her fast by the wrist, and when she looked up at him in surprise he caught her in the snare of his gaze. She should've known better than to look Ray in the eye because now he'd captured her, using all the force of his control.

"Stay with me," Ray said, compelling her with his powers. A distinctive tone signaled that that the train doors were about to close and Layla couldn't move. She saw Ray grimace with the effort, but he was pushing through the pain, pinning her in place. She couldn't move her arms, couldn't move her legs, couldn't take a single step.

"Let me go, Ray. You're only hurting yourself. You're going to kill yourself."

He all but gnashed his teeth. "I don't care. Stay with me."

She couldn't stay with him. Going back to the god who created her was the only way to make up for everything she'd done. It was the only way to give Ray back what was left of his life. "Ray—" Whatever explanation she was going to give was drowned out by the sound of the car doors sliding shut.

She told herself she'd just get off at the next stop. Eventually, Ray would have to let her go. He was weakening; she could feel it as he closed his eyes to kiss her. The break in eye contact was dizzying. It released her from his control, like someone abruptly let go of a leash she'd been pulling against. She staggered and he grabbed her under the arms before she fell, his hand at her waist, his lips murmuring soft words against her neck that she couldn't hear. Then he captured her lips again and kissed her so passionately that she thought her lips might bruise.

He pulled her into a seat with him as the train churned beneath them. His lips parted from hers only long enough to say, "I was a goddamned fool to leave you before. It won't happen again."

His hands were like liquid fire on her body. She burned everywhere he touched. His hand slid beneath her shirt to caress her belly and her blood turned to lava. Before she knew it, her knees went to either side of his hips. She straddled him, holding herself upright by grabbing the metal rail behind his head. She felt unleashed, untamed, uncivilized. So this was lust in all its splendor. This was what it was like to be controlled by instinct and cravings of the flesh. To be pushed by desire beyond reason.

It wasn't only lust. She loved him and he loved her. She could see it in his eyes just before his lips drifted across her collarbone. He tasted her skin, the salt, the sweat of her, as his big hands cupped her breasts and her nipples pulled taut beneath her shirt. There was no hiding her reaction to him, and she could tell that he was just as excited. Kneeling over him as she was, she could feel him hard between her legs. Her skin was so hot. Her brow, her cheeks, her belly, her thighs. They all burned. There was nothing she could do to find relief against her fevered need but rub against him.

He groaned, taking her grinding hips as a signal that she wanted more. He wasn't wrong, but as he reached between them to unzip his pants, she finally found her voice. Her last shred of sanity. "No, Ray…"

He drew her head down so that her forehead touched his. Their noses touched as he stroked her hair and said,

"Layla, you want me. Not Seth. I'm going to show you that right now."

The tears spilled over her lashes and down her cheeks. "I'm not like this, don't you understand?" she asked. "I don't do things like this. I don't kiss for the pleasure of it. I don't cry with sadness or joy. I don't make love on trains. I'm not that kind of woman."

"You are with me."

"Yes," she said, her voice a sob. She didn't know what she'd become, what they'd begun. When she was with Ray, she felt like some naked creature trying to spread wings she hadn't known she had. The train sped up, the lights flashing by in the dark, and Layla knew only one thing.

Just once, she wanted to fly.

"You want *me,* Layla. You love *me,*" he murmured.

"Yes," she said. "And I want to touch you. I want…I want to taste you."

That made Ray groan. She slid down his body until she was on her knees. As she settled herself, the tunnel lights flashed through the window and put her in shadow. The motion of the train forced her to sway side to side, as if she were in prayer, but if she were, this was a cathedral of stainless steel, Plexiglas, and the magnetic buzz of the rails beneath them.

It didn't matter. The closeness of her face to Ray's groin actually dizzied him. "Layla…"

"Is this what you fantasized about?" she whispered, pressing her cheek against his thigh.

Her face had all the innocence of an ingénue, as if she didn't realize what she was doing to him with her eyes so wide and her lips so near. Ray nodded his head, bracing himself as she unfastened his pants and her lips brushed his erection. He growled low in his throat when her lips encircled the head of his shaft. If he hadn't already been seated, her delicate, experimental suction would have brought him to his knees.

Reflexively, his hips jerked against her face, but she didn't pull back. She made a startled sound at the deeper penetration, then dug her nails into his thighs to keep him still. With excruciating slowness, her tongue teased him and she sighed with something that sounded like contentment. When her eyelashes fluttered open, he could swear he saw a self-satisfied and smoldering seductress in those green eyes.

She worked her lips up his shaft, and a pleasurable jolt of electricity arced between them. The sight of her lips stretched in this most intimate kiss made him throb in her mouth. Her teeth grazed the underside of his cock, and her cheeks bulged with the size of him. He wanted to put his hand in her hair, but he didn't trust himself not to grab a fistful of it. And he didn't want to do anything that might scare her or make her stop. He just had to sit here and let her do this amazing thing with her warm, wet mouth even if it killed him. And it might.

The velvet of her tongue drove him absolutely insane. Every muscle in his body tightened and he had the brief but crazed thought that she'd come up with an entirely new way to torture him. Afraid that he'd spill in her mouth with embarrassing haste if this went on for even one more moment, he plucked her up from the floor by both arms and settled her back over his lap. That didn't seem to stop her from wanting to be in control. Her hands trembled as she hitched her skirt up over her hips, but she still found the courage to do it.

He responded to her urgency with a scorching kiss. In the rush, their teeth clashed, and they both gave a shy but heated smile. The steel bars seemed to glitter with conspiratorial winks, goading them to do more. To risk it. To give in to the reckless yearnings of their bodies.

"I'm going to make love to you," Layla said, trying out the words to see how they sounded falling from her lips. It made her blush to say it, but then she boldly pulled her underwear to the side in invitation.

He was ready and eager, still wet from the ministrations of her tongue. He pressed between her legs and pushed up. The broad head of his erection nudged at her entrance, swollen, and she wanted the thickness to fill her, to stretch her to the limit. The elastic of her panties cut into her skin and he must have sensed it, because he tore them. She didn't care. She just wanted him inside her. She lowered herself onto him, until she could get no closer. His pants were only open, and the zipper scraped her skin, but now all she felt was where she and Ray joined.

He panted and his hands cupped her, drawing her down in a slow and steady pace, but Layla didn't want slow and steady aboard a speeding train. The beams of light cut across her thighs as she rode astride him, and she strained, pushing faster than the train, grinding against him in the way that gave expression to the most primal part of her.

"Layla." He whispered her name as if to stop her or make her go slow, but she was heedless of anything but her own pleasure. Her hair flew wild behind her as she moved, their combined scent like an animal musk. Her breasts bounced against him and she felt herself clenching, convulsing, locking him inside her as if she could keep him there forever.

Her climax took her by surprise, fast and sharp, and her knuckles went white on the seat behind Ray's head as she came. She cried out once, twice, then again, then wilted against him. That's when she realized he was watching her, his lips parted in silent reverence. She thought that he'd come too, rapid fire, but now there was a flash of embarrassment as she realized what she'd done. She'd used her own body—and his—to bring only herself pleasure.

But if he minded, it didn't show in Ray's wolfish eyes. "You don't think we're done, do you?" What happened next was like a beautiful dance. He hefted her off him, the separation a momentary agony. But soon, he was lifting her, and she felt she was spiraling toward the sky. He turned her to the window, stretching her arms to the side and pressing her palms to the glass. She faced her reflection again, but this time she didn't see a whore in the mirror. She saw herself in all her facets. She also saw the night outside. She saw the whole world.

And she saw Ray too, behind her, his big body bolstering her. His teeth were on the back of her neck, catching the flesh just behind her ear. It felt so good that she was afraid she might fly apart, but Ray's solidness held her together. With someone so strong behind her, was there anything she couldn't do or feel?

He entered her from behind this time, his mouth on her nape. She could feel his thrusts speeding up. Faster, faster. He whispered her name as the lights started blinking. The next station was approaching. If they didn't finish now, they'd be exposed to anyone, everyone, but at this moment she didn't give a damn.

He loved her body. He loved how he felt when he was inside her. For Ray, all the pain and struggle went away when he was inside her like this. Even half-sated and pliant, Layla still moved with a feline grace that tugged at his deepest core. Her arms spread like the wings of an angel, and Ray's fingers tangled with hers against the window, her back arched to take him deeply. He had her like a bull mates. Like a lion takes his lioness. Only *she* could make something so animalistic into something that was also filled with meaning. Layers upon layers. The riddle of his feelings for her.

He was close—so close to climax that a single word could have made him explode. But he held back. He buried his face in her black satin hair, straining against his own pleasure, drawing it out even as time ran short, because he wanted her to climax again before the train pulled into the station.

She wanted it, too, pushing back against him to take him deeper, racing against the train. They passed into the tunnel and everything went black. He heard her murmured cry and everything in him released. His arms, his legs, his whole body. He spent himself inside her with three bursts, each one wringing him out.

He wasn't sure he could stand. He had to press his cheek against the glass, the chill of it steadying him, before the two of them collapsed into the nearby seat just before the train pulled into the station.

He realized how much trust it had taken for her to show him this side of her, and it moved him. He didn't just want her, didn't just love her. He needed her. Needed her breath. Needed her near him. Needed to have her like this, again, in the raw. She'd been so brave, and now he was going to have to tell her everything, because he couldn't bear to have anything stand as a barrier between them.

Not even a secret. Never a secret between them again.

Layla lay quietly nestled in Ray's arm, her head tucked under his chin as the train shot past another station and into another tunnel. She had no idea where they were anymore or where they were going. She wanted to savor this memory. She saw that his eyes were half-lidded and realized how tired he was; he'd been through so much, and his face was heavy in shadow. He'd start to bleed soon, from having used his power.

"I have to tell you something," he whispered. "Something that I did…"

"Shhh," she said, putting her finger over his lips. Nothing mattered now but the solace she found in his arms, for soon it would all be gone.

He kissed her finger, then put it aside. "I have to tell you what happened in Afghanistan. You deserve to know."

How many times had she tried to get him to tell her before? How terrible that he wanted to confide the truth in her now, when she was so close to betraying him.

"You have to understand how it was for us, Layla. We were walking around carrying guns with no idea who to trust. It starts to wear you down. It breaks people."

"And it broke you?" she whispered.

"No. It broke my buddy Jack." He looked slightly nauseated, but swallowed, and forced himself to go on. "There was this Afghani farmer. Always screaming at us. Pissing and moaning about the poppy crops our soldiers burned. Didn't matter that we were trying to curtail the drug trade. They've got hungry kids and few options, and here we are with our guns trying to tell them not to grow something the junkies in our country are buying. So this farmer, he's riding over to us on his bicycle cussing Jack out. I guess Jack thought he saw a weapon."

Layla could imagine the dust. The confusion. The fear.

"Jack thought the guy drew on him, and he shot him. When the other villagers came out of their houses, he just kept shooting. I tried to stop him. I screamed at him to stop. I'm the one who knocked him to the ground and wrestled the gun away from him, but when it was all over..."

"You lied for him," Layla finished.

Ray nodded, his eyes red and glassy. "Layla, out there, in the field, if your buddy screws up, you have to have his back. If a soldier shoots an unarmed civilian, every other soldier around is gonna swear it was an ambush."

Layla trod carefully. "Do you think that honors the hundreds of thousands of soldiers who do their duty every day *without* cracking under the pressure? All the fighting men and women who *protect* civilians from the enemy? Do you think covering up what Jack did is right?"

"No," he rasped, his head drooping. "But Jack was

the one person in that situation I could help. There wasn't anything I could do for the dead."

It broke her heart to see the anguish on his face, but she couldn't tell him another lie. "You're wrong, Ray. There was something you could've done for the dead villagers. You could've given them justice. The same kind of justice you want for yourself. You could've told the truth."

"It wouldn't bring them back," Ray said. "Besides, I wouldn't sell out my friends. I'm a good friend. A good soldier. I'm loyal."

After a few moments of silence, she said, "I was loyal to Seth for thousands of years and I learned that sometimes loyalty is misplaced. You're not ever going to be free of this until you set the record straight about Jack. You can't just see the things you want to see."

The loudspeaker boomed into the silence. *Last stop.* The train was coming to the end of the line. They were somewhere in Maryland. It was night.

"It's time to go," Ray said. Telling her his secret seemed to have sobered him. Wrung him out.

It'd wrung her out, too. Layla stood up on wobbly legs, straightening her skirt. She fought tears as Ray steadied her, helping her step off the train onto the platform. In a few moments, the train would reverse direction and go back into the city, and Layla would have to be on it. Alone.

"We'll have to take a bus from here," Ray was saying, wearily, starting toward the escalator.

He obviously thought he'd convinced her to stay with him; she didn't want to give him any indication otherwise. "You look so tired," she said, stopping him to kiss the corner of his mouth.

"I'll be fine," he said. "As long as I have you."

"You'll always have me, even if we're apart." She'd tell him the truth, and he'd have that much to hold on to when she was gone. "I love you."

"I know," he said, with just the hint of a cocky smile.

The lights were blinking. The train was getting ready to close its doors. She waited for the last possible moment. The last bell. The last warning. "Goodbye, Ray."

He wasn't expecting it—didn't even seem to comprehend what she was doing. Breaking away, Layla turned and ran, cutting it so close that the train door clipped her heel before slamming shut like a solid wall between them.

Chapter 18

I end conversations and accompany waves. I live in heartbreak and at the side of graves.

Goodbye? It took Ray a second to even realize what was happening. Then his sluggish mind roared to attention. "Layla!"

He ran after her, too late. Layla's palm was on the window in farewell. Ray pounded on the door to no avail as the metro train pulled forward, the metal sliding beneath his hands. *Damn it!* This couldn't be happening. He ran a few steps, contemplating smashing the glass to get to her, but finding no purchase for his grip. He couldn't even *make* her stop; she'd squeezed her eyes shut. She was shutting him down. Locking him out. "Layla!" he shouted again as the metro whisked her away.

He stood there on the platform of the tunnel in stunned shock.

Where the hell would she go? Back to Seth? The idea made him sick. Ray ambled up the empty escalator in a haze, wondering how to find her. He was bruised and battered, inside and out. He couldn't think straight. To make matters worse, a pay phone was ringing. Its shrill cry split the night air and reverberated through Ray's aching head.

The phone was housed in a silver stand, open on three sides. It had to be a crank call. A wrong number. There was no one else on the platform and who else could know he was here? *Unless it was Layla.* With that thought, Ray snatched up the receiver.

"Rayhan?" The war god's malevolent voice was unmistakable.

"How the hell did you find me, Seth?"

"I put a microchip under your skin when you were unconscious. It's something all responsible pet owners do. After having lost Layla once, I wasn't going to make the same mistake with you. I'm letting you go, as a favor to her, but I want to give you a parting gift."

"The only thing I want is Layla."

The god laughed heartily. "I have something else you want."

What Ray wanted was to hammer the receiver down onto the stainless steel until it broke into pieces. Then Seth said, "Don't you want to know who is responsible for taking everything away from you? Don't you want to know the name of the anonymous informant who named you a traitor?"

Ray had to know. "Who was it?"

"Jack Bouchier."

Ray burst into outraged laughter. *"Bullshit."*

"Who else needed to get rid of you? You witnessed his crimes."

Ray's jaw worked by the receiver. No, it didn't make sense. Jack couldn't have been that desperate. Couldn't have been that evil.

"Ray, even with your damaged mind, if you think it through, all the pieces fall into place. When you're ready to accept it, you know where to find him. Jack lives in Virginia, doesn't he? Not so very far, given how long you've come to exact vengeance...."

Layla stepped into Seth's office in Arlington, her feet whispering reluctantly over the rug until she stood in front of his desk. She didn't look at him. Didn't say anything. Just stood there, trembling, resolved to remember Ray's face no matter what Seth did to her.

The blow Seth landed across Layla's cheek was sharp enough to send her face to the side, and it stung afterward, needles of pain. It was only a warning strike; she knew Seth and how much more violence he was capable of. She also knew that he'd want to humble her, so she wasn't surprised when he hit her again with such force that one of her earrings came loose and skittered across the floor of his office. She lifted one hand in a pitiful effort to defend herself, but he wrenched it back just short of the breaking point. "Have you learned your lesson, Layla? What has all this taught you?"

It had taught her that there were better men in the world than Seth. Men who could master her without touch and hold her without chains. She'd learned that she was more than a minion. She was capable of love, happiness and more. She could feel things that had nothing to do with her creator and that she could stand on her own. But she could tell Seth none of that, so she said, "I've learned that you can take away everything that matters to me, and so I must submit myself to you."

Seth struck her again then shoved her into a chair. Even over the ringing in her ears, she heard him say, "Show me where the minotaur touched you."

Layla's chest rose and fell with her fear and indignation. She didn't want to tell him, much less show him, but the war god wouldn't be denied, so she put her hand over her heart. "Here."

Seth seemed confused. His thumb traced Layla's lower lip, which had split open from the blows and was now bleeding and throbbing painfully. "Did the minotaur touch you here?"

"Yes," Layla whispered.

Rough hands cupped both breasts, and squeezed with angry force. "And here?"

"Yes."

Seth grasped her by the nape of the neck, arching her head back as he forced her knees apart with his thigh. "And here?"

"He touched me *everywhere!* And I let him because he loves me and I love him."

Seth's brow creased, as if he'd never heard something so vexing. "You *love* him? Why?"

"Because he's a good man."

"Is he?" Seth caught her fingers in a crushing grasp. "Do you know why I chose him? I chose him because he was already the kind of man who could witness murder and look the other way. I knew that he was the kind of man I could shape into a monster. Why do you think I agreed to release him, Layla? Did you really think I'd trade his freedom for yours? I let him go because he'll return to me eventually—when he realizes that there's no other place for him."

Seth sleeked her hair back, like she was his house cat. It disgusted her. "Ray would never willingly serve you."

"Oh?" Seth let her go, walking around to the side of his desk to turn his computer screen so she could see it. "What do you think Ray is going to do with the freedom you've given him? I predict that he is, at this very moment, about to become exactly the vengeful monster I want him to be. Do you see that red dot? That's your minotaur."

"You're tracking him?" Layla staggered to her feet, the sour taste of betrayal in her throat. "You promised—"

"I promised I'd let the minotaur go. I've done that. I didn't promise to unleash a monster into the world without any notion of where he might roam. I'm not the only god who might want to use him and I'm not about to allow someone else the benefit of my work."

Layla's mouth was dry as she watched the little red spot move on the screen.

Seth's lips curled in amusement. "You're wondering where he's going, aren't you? I'll tell you. He's on his way to commit murder."

Layla's hands balled at her sides. "If only it were yours!"

Seth smirked. "You don't believe me."

No. She didn't. She'd never believe anything that Seth had to say. "Ray isn't a murderer."

"Tell me, what do you think Ray would do if he

found out that his best friend is the one who set him up to look like a terrorist?"

Layla actually felt the room spin. She didn't even have to wonder what Ray would do. After everything Ray had been through—after all the betrayals he'd endured—this final piece of the puzzle would push him over the edge. Ray's inner monster would take utter possession of him and he'd kill Jack. Probably with his own bare hands. "I've got to stop him…."

Seth shoved her so hard that she fell, landing on her hands and knees, the burn of industrial carpet beneath her palms. Seth hovered over her, saying, "See the truth, Layla. Rayhan Stavrakis is a rampaging monster. Not you or anybody else can stop him."

Prostrate at Seth's feet, Layla remembered that the god liked begging and she was too desperate now to let her pride get in the way. It disgusted her to use a transparently sexual appeal, sliding her hands up his thighs. But there was nothing else to do. "I could stop him. Just let me try," she beseeched and he allowed her to draw close. He even allowed her to slip her hands teasingly into his pockets. "Please let me try."

He'd only let her touch him so that he could hurt her. She didn't see the needle until it was jabbed halfway into her arm. "You and the minotaur already said your goodbyes," Seth said, shoving her away. She landed on her back, heat flowing up her arm even as her puncture wound closed over, hiding all evidence of the injection.

For a moment, she was afraid that Seth was going to descend upon her, kick her knees apart and reclaim her as he used to do. Instead, he stepped over her and she watched his black polished shoes retreat across the carpet to the door. "Now, my pet, it's time for you to get some sleep." With that, he closed the door and locked it behind him.

Sleep. Her eyelashes were fluttering closed, and she fought against the coming darkness. Layla opened her hand slowly, revealing the cell phone she'd stolen from Seth's pocket. She didn't know who she'd call for help until she saw the name in his call log. *Isabel Flores.*

Layla fumbled over the keys and hit the recall button. Struggling to bring the phone to her lips, Layla whispered, "Isabel, please find Ray. You've got to stop him...."

Then everything went black.

Outside Jack Bouchier's suburban McMansion in Virginia, Ray stayed in the shadows, watching his friend through the glass. Ray kept rewinding every conversation he'd had with Jack since his escape. All the times that Jack had tried to set up a meeting... Had those been earnest offers of help, or had it all been part of a plan to lure Ray into a trap? Had the authorities *really* followed and arrested Missy or had Jack called them? The pieces of betrayal started falling into place, and the sick certainty that Jack was the son-of-a-bitch that stole his life from him crowded out every other thought.

Ray used to think of Jack as a brother. When they got leave to come stateside, Ray had even been a guest in this home. Now he just wanted to smash it all to pieces. Ray forgot his family, he forgot Missy, he even forgot Layla... Because if Jack was the anonymous informant, the only way to clear his name for treason would be to tell the truth about what Jack did—which Ray couldn't do without implicating himself in the cover-up. If Jack had set him up, then Ray's whole life had become a maze with no exit. He'd be going to jail, one way or another. And that left only one option: revenge.

His shoulders heaving and fists raised, Ray crashed through the sliding glass door. Jack jumped up out of his chair, dropping the bottle of beer which shattered and mixed with the rest of the glass on the floor. Ray trampled it, heedless of being cut. His footfalls were hard and his face was elongated into a menacing snout.

A strangled cry escaped Jack's lips before he leaped back. He was going for the gun cabinet. Ray had been a guest in this house enough times to know where it was, and blocked his path. Trapped, Jack grabbed up the nearest thing he could find to use as a weapon—which happened to be a lamp. He swung it and it crashed into Ray's shoulder, popping and blinking out. Ray didn't even feel the pain.

"Who in the hell are you?" Jack asked. "What are you?"

So Jack didn't recognize him. Whatever Jack saw when he looked at Ray wasn't entirely human. Maybe Ray shouldn't have been surprised, because that's what had happened to Jack in Afghanistan. He'd forgotten how to recognize human beings; when he'd looked at those civilians, all he'd seen was an enemy bent on killing him. Now Ray didn't see human beings either. All he saw in front of him was the lowest kind of scum on earth. Grabbing Jack and throwing him down, Ray snarled, "We're both monsters now, Jack, but I'm a minotaur."

Chapter 19

Fragile enough to shatter, in happiness I soared.
Defeat brings me low but with love I am restored.

Seth had crushed Layla's petty rebellion and broken her spirit. He should've enjoyed his victory over his sphinx, but it left him cold. Why should that be? He looked over to where Layla lay upon the stainless steel table. He'd had his doctors examine her—more a function of his desire to humiliate her than for any true practical purpose—and he could sense her delicious misery.

Even in sadness and pain, Layla was still as beautiful as ever. So why didn't he desire her? Perhaps Layla wasn't truly worthy of him. What powers did the sphinx have except to riddle mortal minds? Layla couldn't make butterflies and hummingbirds appear from the air. She had no dominion over plants or flowers. She couldn't seduce a man merely by looking at him....

The war god frowned, trying to shake off whatever madness had him thinking about the Aztec deity. After all, he'd had enough of goddesses. More than enough. His first wife, Nephthys, was as forceful a goddess as ever lived. Seth still sometimes thought about her sharp talons and hawkish features, but their shared ferocity hadn't been enough to keep them together. His second wife, Taweret, was a savage demonic fighter who could take the shape of a hippo, a crocodile or a lion. But that relationship ended when she tried to chain him to a wall. His third and fourth wives, Anat and Astarte, were both war goddesses in their own right.... Yes, *all* of his wives had been goddesses, too powerful to tame. And each had betrayed or abandoned him in turn, which was why he'd created his sphinx in the first place.

The shape of Layla's face was precisely to his liking. Her breasts the exact size that he preferred in his hands. He'd molded her from sand to be his perfect companion and he should enjoy having her back under his power. So why wasn't he happier about it? What magic spell had Isabel—that painted whore goddess—cast over him that he couldn't get her out of his mind?

It must simply be that he hadn't truly reclaimed Layla yet. He could still sense the fingerprints of another man on her body and didn't feel as if she belonged to him in the way she once had. She'd given herself to the minotaur. He'd just have to ensure that such a thing could never happen again.

Ray duct-taped Jack to an old rocker by the fireplace. Jack writhed beneath his hood. "Ray?"

"You don't get to call me that anymore. You don't get to say my name like I'm a friend."

"Just take the bag off my head and we'll talk." Ray recognized the plaintive tone, the one they'd both used to calm down hostiles in the field, and it made him furious. Jack just kept talking. "Whatever kinda trouble yer in—"

Ray didn't let him finish. Instead, he punched Jack in the face, not sure if he hit nose or chin or mouth, and not caring. Jack made a choking sound, as if tasting his own blood. "I'm your friend, Ray. Whatever you done, we can find a way out of it."

"Like I helped you out of a court-martial? Or like you helped me when you told the government I was a traitor?" Ray slammed his fist down hard on Jack's hand, the crack of bones reverberating under Jack's howl of pain. It should've been deeply satisfying, but it wasn't. Maybe Ray just hadn't caused enough pain yet.

"I'm sorry," Jack whimpered.

Red fury danced before Ray's vision. "You're fucking *sorry?*"

"I thought you were gonna tell the truth about what happened in Afghanistan. I panicked. I just thought that if I cast a little doubt on you, then nothing you said about me would ever stick. I just thought they'd question you but wouldn't have enough evidence to do anything about it, so I spun one lie, and it became another..."

There it was, then. All the confirmation Ray needed. It really *had* been Jack who had betrayed him. Jack who had murdered civilians and condemned Ray to a dungeon. He could still taste the flesh that they'd told him had been cut from his own nephew. Remembering it, Ray yanked off Jack's hood, tape and all, taking some hair and skin with it. Then he stooped down to pull off Jack's socks.

"What are you doin', Ray?"

"I'm gonna show you a little trick I learned in a Syrian dungeon," Ray answered, his boots crunching on broken glass as he readied the jumper cables that he'd taken from the trunk of Jack's car. "I bet you don't know how sensitive the bottoms of your feet are..."

Jack's voice rose an octave. "You're gonna torture me? Make me scream like a stuck hog? That's what you want?"

"Isn't it the least you deserve?"

Jack's chest actually stuttered, his fists opening and closing, then he went still. Looking past Ray he said, "Maybe I do deserve it. Just don't do it in front of the girl."

The girl? Ray whirled around to see Missy standing at the top of the staircase. What the hell was she doing here? So, no one had grabbed her. Not Scorpion Group or the cops. That'd just been a lie Jack had told to get him to run. Just another lie like a thousand others. It killed him to watch Missy run down the stairs and put her body between him and Jack, as if to shield the fucker.

"Don't hurt him," Missy whispered, staring at Ray, her shoulders hunched in fear. She'd seen him beat her pimp half to death; she knew what he was capable of. "Jack's been great to me, Ray. He already got me a job working in a coffee shop and told me I could stay here until I get on my feet. Isn't that what you asked him to do?"

Ray shook his head, trying to understand, then decided he didn't want to. "Missy, just walk out that door and keep going. This doesn't have anything to do with you."

"Yes, it does," Missy said stubbornly, yanking the duct tape off one of Jack's wrists. She was setting the bastard free. "I'm not going to let you hurt him. Jack's your friend. You just have to remember that."

"Jack's the anonymous informant. Now get the hell out of here before you get hurt."

That was when they both heard the click of a pistol, cocked and ready. Jack had managed to reach into his desk and pull out his old service weapon with an unsteady hand. Ray wasn't about to let Missy stand between him and a gun, so he spun her away and shouted, "Run!"

But she didn't run, and Jack didn't shoot. "I'm not gonna hurt her," Jack said, his hand shaking. "You gotta understand, I never wanted to hurt anybody…."

So this was how it was going to end, Ray thought, staring down the barrel of Jack's gun. His best friend was going to shoot him dead. Visions of Layla passed before him, as if she were standing in the room telling him to breathe. As if her cool hands were soothing his face, as if her lips were open and inviting beneath his. If he was going to die, he was glad his last thoughts were of her.

"I'm sorry, Ray," Jack was saying, his face red and twisted with pain.

"So what are you waiting for?" Ray asked. "Pull the damned trigger."

Instead, the barrel of the gun slowly swiveled as Jack turned the gun on himself. Suddenly, everything Ray knew—or thought he knew—changed. He hadn't been able to stop his brother from killing himself, and now another man he'd called brother was about to do the same. "Don't you fucking do it, Jack!"

"Why not? You want me dead. That's why you're here, ain't it?"

No. Ray was here because he'd been blind with a killing fury that he couldn't control. He'd wanted Jack to hurt the way he'd been hurt. He'd wanted justice, and when he realized he couldn't have that, he decided upon revenge. But he didn't want this. "Listen, you country-fried douche bag, do you think killing yourself is going to erase the shit you've done? Because it won't."

Jack's pupils were wide and eerie, like maybe he wasn't listening. "There's no way to erase what I did to those people. Don't you think I've tried? There's no way I can ever make up for what I did to you, either, Ray."

That much was true. There was no apology that would ever return the past two years of Ray's life to him. There was nothing that could ever compensate him for the pain. That didn't mean that Ray wasn't just going to stand here and watch Jack blow his brains out.

"Well, I've got an idea," Ray said, inching forward as Jack's finger hovered over the trigger. "Why don't you man up, Jack? Tell the truth instead of checking out and leaving everybody else with the mess to clean up."

Jack's throat bobbed with emotion. "You think anybody would believe me? Even if they did, what do ya think is gonna happen to you, Ray? They aren't gonna throw you a ticker-tape parade. Trust me, nobody in Washington is gonna risk jail time to clear your name. They're gonna bury this and bury you, too."

Ray took another step forward, aware of the ticking of the clock on the mantelpiece. Aware of Missy's bated breath as she watched the unfolding scene in silence. Aware of every beat of his heart.

"I never meant to hurt anybody," Jack said again.

"Then don't," Ray said, summoning whatever was left of his powers. He tasted the blood in the back of his throat as he met Jack's gaze and held it, reaching for Jack's consciousness. "Don't hurt anybody. Hand it over."

Missy knew exactly what Ray was doing, and she broke in with, "Stop, Ray. You're going to fry your brain!"

She was probably right, but better that Ray burn out this way than doing Seth's bidding. "Give me the gun, Jack."

"I—I can't," Jack said, resisting Ray's weak influence. "Can't see a way out of this. No way, no how."

"But there is a way," Missy insisted, her sneakers crunching on the broken glass as she came close.

"Missy, get back," Ray barked. "What the hell are you doing?"

"My boyfriend's dad is some famous reporter, Jack. You can tell him your story." Then she looked at Ray. "Let him call Carson's dad."

"I need people to know that I never meant to hurt anyone," Jack said, shaking now like he might go into a seizure. That's when Ray was able to capture his mind. Blood flowed steadily from both Ray's nostrils, but he was able to hammer at Jack's will like hot metal in a forge.

"Give me the gun."

With a choked sound, halfway between a sob and relief, Jack shoved the handle toward Ray. The grip of the pistol slicked Ray's palm with sweat as he pulled it away and released the clip of ammunition, letting it fall harmlessly to the floor. Fighting down the urge to pistol-whip Jack, Ray pulled him free of the rest of the duct tape and said, "Go ahead. Make the call."

Jack crouched down, hands in his hair, sobbing. "If I tell 'em what really happened, Ray, we'll both go to jail. Me for what I did, and you—"

"For covering it up. I know." Ray leaned back on the arm of the couch, pinching his nose in a vain effort to staunch the bleeding. He just didn't care anymore. Without Layla, he didn't care about anything. Besides, Layla had been right. He'd told himself that everything he'd done so far had been in the name of justice, but the dead deserved justice, too.

A few minutes after Jack called the reporter, Ray thought he heard rhythmic footsteps clicking across the wooden deck. Someone breaking into the house? Ray grabbed the gun. He was still fuzzy-headed and near collapse, but through the bloody fog of Ray's mind, he thought he saw Isabel Flores gingerly lift one designer shoe over the broken glass door to step inside.

"*¡Ay, caramba!* This better be worth ruining my espadrilles..." she said. "Rayhan, the first time I saw you, I said you were trouble in a tight black T-shirt. How right I was."

It was all pretty surreal, and Ray didn't even know

where Jack had gone with the phone at this point, but what confused Ray most was the way Missy jumped to her feet and ran toward Isabel, throwing herself in her arms. "It's okay! He didn't kill anyone," Missy cried.

"You did well, my little butterfly," Isabel said, hugging Missy into an embrace. *"¿Cómo estás?"*

Ray squinted at Missy, who looked as happy as he'd ever seen her. "Wait. You two know each other?"

"How else do you think I found you?" Isabel asked. "Every goddess has her minions."

Isabel? A goddess? Normally, Ray would have asked a million questions but nothing surprised him anymore. All he managed to get out was, "But…how?"

Isabel pressed a kiss to Missy's forehead. "I wouldn't have found this little American Painted Lady if you hadn't sent her to follow Layla. You treated her well, so I'm willing to help you. Is that what you want to know?"

Ray was too exhausted to hold the gun and it wasn't loaded anyway, so he let his arm fall at his side, trying to make sense of the surreal scene unfolding before him. There was only one coherent thought he could cling to. "What I want to know is…where's Layla?"

Isabel shook her head. "Layla went back to Seth to buy you the rest of what looks to be your very short mortal life."

Ray braced himself, shaking the fog from his mind. There was no way in hell he was going to let Layla keep that bargain. Staggering to his feet, he forced the words through his raw throat. "Hey, Goddess Cha Cha or whoever you really are, will you help me make another trade?"

Chapter 20

I hold you tethered, I hold you still, and until you slip me, you have no free will.

Layla walked behind Seth like a beaten dog on a leash as he led her outside. Still groggy from whatever he'd injected her with, and confused, she squinted into the morning light as it lit up the grass and stone walkway at the entrance of the building.

"Get undressed," Seth said without even looking at her.

She'd known it was coming, but her stomach roiled and the breeze brought goose bumps to her arms. It was a weekend, so the parking lot was mostly empty but for some of the security personnel. Still, she looked up to the darkened windows. "Here?"

She knew from long experience the kind of room that Seth preferred for intimacy. Someplace like the one in which she'd awakened. A place that was white and steel that could be wiped down, all evidence of passion easily washed away afterward. She couldn't imagine why he'd want to reclaim her here unless it was to humiliate her.

"Stop stalling, Layla. You allowed other men to touch you, so I don't see why you shouldn't be eager to service me the same way."

Service him. It was a horrible thing to contemplate. It made her rebellious and defiant. "Just what is it that you want me to do? Do you want me to kneel before you and stroke your petty little…ego?"

Seth's eyes bored into hers, his power crackling in the air. "Did you kneel for the minotaur?"

She looked away.

"I think that's an obscene custom, but you probably enjoyed it." Seth removed his own jacket, folding it neatly and draping it over the stairway railing. "Now, don't make me tell you again. Get undressed."

Layla yanked her cotton shirt over her head and threw it on the ground. She kicked her shoes off next and felt the grass between her toes. She didn't do it for Seth, she told herself. She did it for herself. Better that she boldly bare herself before he took her hard-won love of her body and turned it against her.

"You should glance up at the windows to see if anyone is watching," Seth said. "I suspect they are. Security. Secretaries. Perhaps the janitorial staff… Isn't this what you want? All you whores, prancing about in your provocative clothing want the same thing. To be looked at. To be admired and idolized. Isn't that what you desire?"

When she didn't answer, Seth snatched her bra off

and let it fall. She was keenly aware of her exposed breasts, belly, shoulders and back, but lifted her chin to say, "Every desire I've ever had was something you created in me. You made me a woman and yet you want me to be ashamed of it."

This seemed not to have ever occurred to him before. His brow arched and he paused. "Then perhaps now is the time for me to honor you in all your natural splendor."

Seth yanked her skirt down, panties and all, until she was nearly tripping out of them, twisting to hide herself. "Oh, no need for shyness now. You really are quite lovely. You've always been a potent symbol. An ornamentation upon my arm. And you will be forever, Layla. Death will never find you and I'll ensure that you never give life to the child inside you."

Now Layla did stumble, falling naked onto the grass. She couldn't quite wrap her mind around all that Seth had just said. He laughed at her confusion. "Didn't you know that you were pregnant? You can't tell me that you hadn't planned it this way, just to spite me."

Pregnant.

The word hung in the air before her like some ripe pomegranate swaying in the breeze. Like forbidden fruit that she ached to pluck before it vanished. Instinctively, her fingers splayed over her belly then drifted lower, to the place that covered her womb. It was a spot that had been numb and barren before Ray came into her world. Now everything had changed. She was going to have a baby. Ray's baby. Even if she never saw him again, he'd given her this....

Seth may have created her, but she and Ray had created a child. She knew it was too soon for her to feel anything inside her, but just the idea of a child was precious to her. This was something beautiful and sacred. A little life that she'd die to defend. That she'd kill to keep safe. The hairs bristled at the nape of her neck as Layla understood just what Seth meant to do to her and to the baby inside her. "Stay away from me!"

Seth grabbed her and she would've screamed but everyone in the Scorpion Group compound worked for Seth. She knew that none of them would raise a finger to help her. None of them ever had. Instead of a scream, it was a roar she felt at the back of her throat. It carried over the wind and sent a flock of pigeons squawking into the air. She held up her hands to fend him off and saw her nails grow into claws. Layla's body grew sleek and heavy with the muscles of a huntress. She was a sphinx. Part riddler. Part woman. Part lion. And it was the lioness that came out of her now.

"Give your master one little kiss," Seth snarled, and she slashed at him, shredding open his dress shirt and tearing at his divine flesh. The war god howled in outrage as his blood spattered to the grass and turned to sand. Then he threw her as if she were a mere stone in his pocket, and she skipped hard on the ground, until she tumbled to a stop, her tail twitching as she gasped for breath. She hoped there'd be time for her nose to elongate into a muzzle, for her jaws to give her teeth sharp enough to rip him apart.

Once, she'd have tried to run, but she'd been running her whole life. Instead, Layla launched herself at Seth and they tumbled together as she raked him with her powerful back claws. Somehow the war god managed to climb on her back, dragging her down, his arm locked around her throat. She was trapped now. Half in lion form, half in woman form. It's how he wanted her, she realized. It's how all the other sphinxes had appeared throughout the world. His mouth was drawing closer and closer to hers. "Don't struggle, my pet. I'm finally going to give you everything you've always wanted. Imagine how all manner of men will admire you as they come into this building."

Layla thrashed against him, using her back claws to try to gouge out his intestines. But Seth was stronger. "Every breath you take is one that I gave you," he whispered, holding her shaking face still for his ruinous kiss. "Now I'm going to take some of it back and you'll breath no more."

In the distance, Layla thought she heard a crash, like some kind of truck hitting a barrier, but her world had narrowed to the air she could still breathe.

"Sand you were and sandstone you'll become," Seth whispered, taking his lips away just long enough to inhale. "Think how you'll enjoy it when strangers touch you. How they'll take pictures of you. Think of all the photos the sphinx in Giza poses for...."

Seth found her mouth again and his lips tasted like ash. Desperate to wound him, Layla gnashed with her teeth. Bit him. Seth's divine ichor spilled over her tongue, but it didn't stop him.

"Bitch," Seth said, wiping his mouth, but the damage was done. He was inhaling, taking the breath from her. Sucking it from her lungs. She was never going to see the face of her baby. She was never going to wrap her arms around Ray. Never spend the night cradled in his arms. Never feel safe, or whole, ever again. Crushing pain pinned her to the ground. Her bones were calcifying. She felt her tail go rigid. Layla could scarcely believe that even Seth could be this cruel. He would turn her to stone and her baby with her, so that it could never be born. He meant to trap her here for eternity.

Layla fought for breath and could find none. She tried to get up, but couldn't. Her hindquarters were already stone. Soon the rest of her would be, too. And her mind was already spinning away, caught up in a sandstorm of its own.

Ray saw Layla on the ground at Seth's feet and he didn't think; he just reacted. Crashing Jack's truck through the security gate, braving the hail of bullets that followed, he pressed the gas pedal to the floor. The thump of the god's corporeal form against the bumper wasn't as loud as the resulting crash. The impact sent Seth's body rolling up the hood of the car and his flying limbs punched through the windshield, forcing a spray of safety glass into Ray's face.

"Basta!" Isabel shouted, and though Ray didn't speak much Spanish, he slammed the brakes. He flung himself out of the truck, shaking off bits of glass as he ran to Layla. When he reached her side, his blood turned to ice. She was half herself, half lioness, all sphinx. Still as stone.

Behind him, Scorpion Group security guards came running. Ray heard the zip and ping of bullets ricocheting somewhere near him and returned fire as Isabel climbed out of the wreckage of the car and went to her knees in front of Layla. The goddess knelt beside Layla, caressing her.

"What's he done to her?" Ray shouted, eyeing the security team closing in on them.

Isabel raised her hands and held off the men by

entangling them in a thick net of jungle vines. Ray had never seen anything like it, but right now he didn't have time to be amazed. All he could think of was Layla, who was murmuring, "Baby…save the baby…"

The *baby?* Surely he misheard.

"She needs your breath," Isabel said, standing up. "Breathe for her."

He'd given mouth-to-mouth resuscitation to enough wounded soldiers. He knew what to do, and yet his hands were shaking as he took Layla's face and exhaled into her mouth. He was horrified by the chill of her skin. How had he let this happen? She'd always said there were worse things Seth could do to her than kill her, but Ray wouldn't have believed it if he wasn't seeing it with his own eyes. Her tail and hindquarters were already carved like a statue. Stone was creeping up her spine. Seth wasn't killing her—he was entombing her.

And Ray was losing her.

The dark god of Egypt rose from the steaming wreckage of the truck that had plowed into him. Shouts came from all directions as his security team tried to figure out who to shoot at. The Scorpion King slid off the hood, his mind black with fury. The war god's suit was a ruin. Shredded rags. So much the better. Seth tore off his shirt, and the remainder of his pants, revealing himself as in battles of old. Thunder announced his towering rage, and he knew that storm clouds would roll in soon after.

That's when he saw her. *Isabel.* She was here, close enough to crush, and the possibilities of how he'd vanquish her danced before his eyes. He forgot the minotaur; he forgot the sphinx. He stalked the young goddess until a wall of jungle plants rose up in front of him, blocking his path.

"Xochiquetzel!" Seth shouted, easily withering her plants away. But no sooner had he done so than another wall of greenery rose up before him, this time surrounding them both.

"I come with a proposal," she said.

"No more trades," Seth growled. "No more deals. No more pacts or bargains. Nothing as civilized as that ever again. I'll honor none of them. You could've gone your foolish way, but you've stepped back into the quicksand of my world now and you'll all be sorry for it."

"But it's *my* realm you're trespassing in," Isabel said, her hair damp from the rain that leaked through her wilderness roof. "You may have dominion over the industry of war, but I have dominion over pregnant mothers. I wouldn't have let Layla go back to you if I'd known she was with child."

"She's *mine,*" Seth said, heedless of the petulance that he heard in his own voice. "The sphinx is mine!"

"You don't even want her," the sex goddess said, coming so near to him that the dampness evaporated from her skin. "*I'm* your match. Not her."

"Is that so?" Seth asked as he summoned the storm to blow her jungle canopy to dust. Rain turned to scorching wind. His rage was hot, so hot that her vines withered and burst into flames. The fire engulfed her. Her clothes charred and fell away from her body. He smelled the burning magic in the air and heard her shriek. Yet, even writhing in pain, the young goddess was strong. He reached for her smoldering form, but she broke free and ran for the building as terrified mortals scattered.

His employees were just ants now. He paid no attention to any of them. Not his workers, not his minions, not anyone. He'd trod them underfoot without another thought. His quarry was Isabel and he'd need to focus all his power to capture her. He chased her into the building, up the stairs and into the atrium where a massive tree burst from the floor, shooting up into the skylight and sending glass crashing down to litter his path. It annoyed him that she was causing such damage to the Scorpion Group building, but he had her trapped now. She must have known it, because her ivy grew so swiftly over the walls and windows that it soon blocked out all light, forcing Seth to hunt her in the darkness.

"You should have never toyed with me, Isabel. Don't you know what I do to other gods? Haven't you heard of my battles?" She didn't answer, but he heard the young goddess panting. He liked that. Let her be afraid of him and of the dark. "Are you trembling, Isabel? You should be. I caught another nature god once. His name was Osiris. I drowned him in the Nile, then cut him to pieces."

"That was in Egypt," Isabel said when he was close enough to see the faint illumination of her eyes. She was shrouded in nothing but leaves, peering between vines like a jaguar. "I don't think you'll be able to conquer me here."

He lunged for her, but just as he grasped hold of her, two vines dropped from the ceiling and caught him by the arms. The force of it threw him to the ground where leaves grew thick over his body. He gave a mocking laugh at her pitiful attempts to restrain him. It was only a matter of summoning enough power to break these bonds.

And yet…he couldn't.

This wasn't possible, Seth thought, his own breath coming out in ragged gasps. Of all the old gods, the war gods were the strongest. Everyone knew that.

"You're farther from home than I am," the young Aztec goddess explained, her silhouette all curves. "My powers are stronger here than yours."

"War is stronger than peace," Seth said, pulling frantically on his bindings. "Hate is stronger than love."

"Maybe," Isabel said, kneeling over him. "But creation is as strong as destruction."

He felt the heat of her as she straddled his hips and it filled him with frustrated need. She leaned forward, her hair in his face. Her eyes were a chaotic storm that called to him like a siren's song. "Forget about the sphinx and the minotaur," Isabel said, her lips brushing against his like a whisper. "Let them go and I'll let you go."

Seth thrashed again, enraged that he should be under a woman's power. When his second wife had tried to chain him, he'd hated her for it. Now Isabel was reminding him of those epic battles, those glorious days when he'd been at his prime. When the power had flowed through him, and he was a potent force. And in spite of everything, she was making him feel that way now. Potent. "You can't hold me here forever, Isabel. You'll lose your strength, day by day."

"Yes," she admitted. "But by the time I'm drained, I'll have swallowed up your Scorpion Group compound in the earth, and think how the other immortals will laugh at you."

Pride. It already stung and she was picking at the wound. Still, it was hard to pay attention to anything but the insistent throb between his legs. She was throbbing too, shifting her weight subtly back and forth, to drive his lust. The wide expanse of her hips glistened bare and tantalizing below her belly button. Her hands splayed across his chest and electricity seemed to tingle in every line of her hands. "Oh, Seth, if you'd won your bargain with me—if you'd taken me as a lover—you'd have been the envy of other immortals."

"Why would they envy me?" he said. "You're just a whore. Anyone could have you for a price."

"Then why don't you pay me? I have a price. I've told you what it is. Leave the sphinx and the minotaur free to live their lives."

The scent of her, the warmth of her skin, the sheer power of her being drove him mad. He'd pay any price to thrust inside her, but when it was over, what if he wanted her to stay? "Why should you go to all this trouble on behalf of two mortals? You realize if Layla has her child, that's what she'll become. Just another worthless mortal, no use to you either."

"I didn't come for Layla," Isabel said, the tender skin of her inner thighs clinging to his hips. If she shifted only an inch, he could be inside her. "I came for you."

Hearing that did something to him; he searched her eyes for the lie, but found none. "Should that flatter me?"

"Ay, Papi," she said with a little tinkling laugh. "I knew the first moment I laid eyes upon you. You're a match for me. You're not the only one with pride, you see. I'm a young goddess. I yearned to taste the lips of a god older and more fearsome than any in the new

world. Mortal men all fall at my feet, but you're the Scorpion King, and almost immune to my charms."

"Almost," Seth said wryly, because he couldn't hide his body's response to her.

"I think we were always looking for each other," she said.

He didn't want to admit it, but he knew it was true.

"Even if there weren't any sphinx or any minotaur," she continued, "you'd have found me, wouldn't you have?"

"Yes," Seth said. It was more than agreement, and they both knew it. It was an acceptance of terms. All of them. Spoken and unspoken. She moved over him, lowering herself onto the solid length of his erection. He closed his eyes and groaned as Isabel shamelessly undulated over him, her lips parted in obvious pleasure. She didn't move in the way he would've anticipated. Her skin wasn't the color he most favored, and her breasts were more ample than he would've desired. And yet, these unexpected things about her—womanly qualities outside of his control—ensorcelled him.

She seemed to know it. She loosened his restraints, and he snapped them, turning Isabel onto her back. She didn't fight him, but wrapped herself around him like a python. She gave herself to him even though she wasn't something of his creation. She owed him nothing, and yet, she was here with him. It was a mystery that might take centuries to unravel, but they both had time....

Chapter 21

Opened up, surprise!
Bitten gently, coquettish lies.
Gently together, beckoning.
Together hard, time for reckoning.

Ray's lips were on hers when he felt Layla take the first ragged breath on her own. She was coming back to him. Ray couldn't be sure if it was the gulps of air he forced into her lungs, or the fact that Seth seemed to have forgotten about his diabolical punishment the moment he saw Isabel. Whatever had happened, color rushed to Layla's face and her body became flesh again. She transformed before his eyes. First stone, then tawny lion hide, then the smooth skin of the woman he'd made love to. The woman he loved. The woman he'd nearly lost. "Ray?" Layla gasped, her eyelashes fluttering against the rainstorm. Her teeth chattered against the cold.

Ray wrapped his massive arms around her, willing the heat from his body into hers. "I'm here," Ray said, though he wasn't exactly sure where *here* was anymore. Isabel's plants had all but swallowed the Scorpion Group facility, transforming the grounds and parking lot into a veritable jungle. Even if Ray could've found the wreckage of the truck, he wasn't sure he could have started its engine. Meanwhile, the storm overhead was ugly, the winds more savage by the minute.

Layla took another shuddering gasp, her fingers clawing at the earth as she did so. He would've liked to let her take a few moments to recover, but there was no telling when Seth would be back for her, and Ray would die before he let Layla fall into Seth's clutches again.

Hefting her up into his arms, Ray started off on foot. Rain lashed at him as he navigated the maze of plants, some of which appeared to be orchids and banana trees. Layla murmured against his chest, "Is Jack…dead?"

"I didn't kill him," Ray grunted. "I didn't even hurt him. Not much, anyway."

"I'm so glad," she sobbed against his chest, with what sounded like relief. "I love you."

"I know," Ray said, though it helped to hear her say it. "I told you that over and over again. Do you believe me now?"

"I believe you," she whispered as he held her, using his body to shield her from the wind. "I believe *in* you…"

It had made all the difference before, and it still did. The trees swayed overhead, but the wind was dying down and the road wasn't far. A few more minutes and he found an underpass to shelter her from the rain. It was only then, in the shadows of the concrete that he finally said, "Layla, when you were turning into a stone sphinx, you said something about a baby."

That was when she told him, in hushed and reverent tones. It took him a few moments before he could work his mouth. "We're having a *kid?* You and me?"

She actually smiled. "Yes."

Some warm feeling started to bubble its way up inside him. "I'm going to be a…"

"Father," she whispered. "If you want to be."

But he remembered what she'd told him. "Not if it's going to kill you!" He cursed himself for every selfish time he'd touched her. She'd told him that having a child would take away her immortality, but he hadn't given birth control a thought.

"Our baby isn't going to kill me, Ray. I just won't have the power to riddle anymore…and I won't be deathless anymore."

He felt his mouth draw into a thin, grim line. "I'm sorry, Layla. I don't know what else to say. I'm so damned sorry…."

"Don't you understand that you've given me the greatest gift?" she asked, pushing her rain-soaked hair out of her eyes. "It's what I wanted. Seth could never give me a child. He convinced me that it was blasphemy, but this is *my* body and you gave it back to me."

Ray watched the pounding rain beat against the pavement of the empty road. "But I took forever from you."

"No," Layla said, touching his cheek. "You gave me a different kind of immortality. We live on forever in the memories of our children, don't we? You gave me the rest of my life and I want to spend it with you. The baby and I belong with you. If you want us."

If he *wanted* them? Was she crazy? "There's nothing I've ever wanted more in my life, but I'm going to jail, Layla." Even if Jack's story broke on the front page of every newspaper in the country, Ray still had things to atone for. Besides, what the hell kind of father would he be? Sure, he was good with his nephews. He loved kids. But he was a monster.

Layla seemed to read his thoughts. "You can't use your powers anymore, Ray. Never again. Not even for my sake. If you're going to be a father—"

"I've got to be a normal man," he finished. "A better man." Down the road, he saw flashing lights of police cars, and decided it wasn't too soon to start. He moved to get up, but she clutched his arm. "I've got to turn myself in, Layla."

"I know," she said tearfully, pressing a kiss to his lips.

It buoyed him. He stood up, even though the force of the wind pushed him back. As the sirens got closer, Ray lifted his hands in surrender and felt stronger than he ever had, as a man or a minotaur.

A congressional inquiry had been opened into Ray's torture and extraordinary rendition to Syria, but Layla held out little hope of justice being served on that account. And then, of course, there was Ray's trial. She wished she could be inside the courtroom, but the government demanded secrecy on the grounds of national security.

All she could do was wait. Outside the gate, Layla

found a seat on a bench, heedless of the reporters that crowded in around her. Whether Ray emerged as a prisoner or a free man, she wanted her face to be the first he saw. He hadn't wanted his family here. Didn't want his parents or his nephews to be caught up in the media circus, so Carson and Missy waited with her, the two teenagers holding hands like it was the most innocent and natural thing in the world to do.

"It's going to be okay, Dr. Bahset," Carson said with a shy shrug of his shoulders.

"It's sweet of you to try to reassure me," Layla said. "Especially because none of this would be happening without you or your father's newspaper."

"I guess I've got a better appreciation of what my dad does," Carson said. "I'm feeling a lot steadier these days."

"I wish I could've done more to help you," Layla said.

"You did plenty. I'm still in therapy, but I'm getting better," he said, smiling at the girl on his arm. Meanwhile, Missy shifted from foot to foot as if trying to make peace with the long white sundress that covered just about everything but her arms.

The former call girl winked at him. "He just had to learn that nothing is perfect, everything is flawed. He just has to let himself see things how they really are."

Layla smiled at Missy. "I think you'll make a good therapist one day."

Missy beamed at the praise. "What's taking the judge so long anyway? *¡Ay, caramba!*"

If Layla weren't so nervous, she'd have laughed at Missy's spot-on imitation of Isabel. Since the day she was almost turned into a statue, Layla hadn't seen the goddess. Then again, she hadn't seen or heard from Seth either, and she hoped that would last for the rest of her mortal life. Maybe Seth would find some measure of happiness and the world would be better off for it.

When the trial was over, Layla rose awkwardly from the bench, and squinted into the sun as Ray emerged, looking uncomfortable in his dress uniform. In spite of her very pregnant belly, she found the energy to run to meet him.

Their eyes met and locked.

The crowd rushed forward, reporters jostling them. "Specialist Stavrakis," one called to him by rank. "Do you have anything to say about your sentence?"

"Time served," Ray said, his voice low and stunned and just for her.

Layla had been preparing for this moment, practicing how she'd tell him that she'd wait for him, no matter how long it took. "It doesn't matter. I'll come see you every opportunity—"

"Layla, I'm not going to be locked up," Ray said, a slow smile crossing his lips. "They considered my time in the dungeon as time served."

She grasped his wrists and realized he wasn't in manacles. "You're not going to prison?"

"No," he said, as if just realizing it himself. "Jack's going in for psychiatric evaluation, but I'm free, Layla."

"Free?" A burst of happiness made her tremble. Ray had given her this feeling, too, and the joy of it made her laugh. He laughed, too, sweeping her up, pregnant belly and all, into his arms.

The reporters jostled them. "C'mon, Ray! Give us something for the news."

Ray's eyes were for her, and only her. "So, Doc, what the hell are we gonna do now?"

"Whatever we want," Layla said.

A thousand flashbulbs went off as she kissed him, and she didn't care.

There had been moments when Ray thought he'd never live to see this day. Never thought he'd ever hear the creak of the porch step under his boot. Now, here he was, slowly climbing the stairs of his childhood home.

"Are you sure you don't want to do this by yourself?" Layla asked, cradling their baby girl in the nook of her arm.

Ray chuckled. "We got into this mess together, didn't we?"

The petunias were in bloom, petals unfolding in hanging pots by the railing, and the front door opened before Ray even had the chance to ring the bell. His nephews came shrieking toward him and both boys were up into his arms, leaping at him like overeager puppies. "Uncle Ray!"

They smelled like milk and grass and he gloried in their wholeness and the way their big brown eyes lit up. They weren't afraid of him and they wouldn't have to grow up thinking that they lived in a country where people could simply be *disappeared* without consequence. That was something that he'd done for them; something for which he could be proud.

He swept the boys around, settling them down only when he saw his mother and father. He tried to say something, but whatever it was caught in his throat.

"Rayhan," his mother wept, coming to him, her tears wet on his cheek. "Oh, Rayhan. Rayhan...Rayhan."

It was as if she couldn't say his name enough. Ray's father was more stoic, looming in the doorway, but his hands were trembling. It was so hard for Ray to face them, knowing what he'd done. Not just the things he'd confessed to in court, but the things he'd done as a minotaur, too.

"I didn't think you were ever coming home," his father choked out. "I didn't have faith. I didn't believe."

"I'm here now, Dad," Ray whispered, his voice thick with emotion, his chest tight with regret. "But I've done some things I'm not proud of."

"You're our son and we love you," his mother said, her arms around his neck. "We don't care. It doesn't matter...."

"No, it *does* matter," Ray's father said, putting his hand on Ray's shoulder. "Maybe if we'd admitted something was wrong with your brother, we could've helped him before it was too late. It *does* matter what you've done, Ray, but you've paid for it more than any man should have."

Ray swallowed, hoping he'd be that kind of father for his own kid. He wouldn't close his eyes to his child's faults, but would lovingly guide his daughter to do better. Ray reached for Layla's hand, their fingers twining. "I know you've talked on the phone, but this is my wife, Layla, and our daughter. Your granddaughter. Isabel."

As Ray said this, he swelled with pride, but Layla wilted beside him. "Mr. and Mrs. Stavrakis..." she began, but couldn't finish.

Ray's mother tried to smooth over the awkwardness with a tight smile. "Come in, Layla. Bring my beautiful grandbaby and we'll talk over tea and baklava!"

"I need you to know that I'm sorry." Layla's voice wobbled on the last word and her eyes filled with tears. "I'm sorry for my part in what happened to your son."

"Ray wouldn't be a free man today if it weren't for you," Ray's father said. "So if he forgives you, so do we. That's what family does."

Tears slipped over Layla's long dark lashes. "I've never had a family…."

"Now you do," Ray said, kissing her until her hard-won tears turned to joy. "Now you do."

* * * * *

Lucy Flemming and Ross Mitchell shared a magical, sexy Christmas weekend together six years ago. This Christmas, history may repeat itself when they find themselves stranded in a major snowstorm... and alone at last.

Read on for a sneak peek from IT HAPPENED ONE CHRISTMAS by Leslie Kelly.

Available December 2011, only from Harlequin® Blaze™.

EYEING THE GRAY, THICK SKY through the expansive wall of windows, Lucy began to pack up her photography gear. The Christmas party was winding down, only a dozen or so people remaining on this floor, which had been transformed from cubicles and meeting rooms to a holiday funland. She smiled at those nearest to her, then, seeing the glances at her silly elf hat, she reached up to tug it off her head.

Before she could do it, however, she heard a voice. A deep, male voice—smooth and sexy, and so not Santa's.

"I appreciate you filling in on such short notice. I've heard you do a terrific job."

Lucy didn't turn around, letting her brain process what she was hearing. Her whole body had stiffened, the hairs on the back of her neck standing up, her skin tightening into tiny goose bumps. Because that voice sounded so familiar. *Impossibly* familiar.

It can't be.

"It sounds like the kids had a great time."

Unable to stop herself, Lucy began to turn around, wondering if her ears—and all her other senses—were deceiving her. After all, six years was a long time, the mind

HBEXP1211

could play tricks. What were the odds that she'd bump into *him*, here? And today of all days. December 23.

Six years exactly. Was that really possible?

One look—and the accompanying frantic thudding of her heart—and she knew her ears and brain were working just fine. Because it was *him.*

"Oh, my God," he whispered, shocked, frozen, staring as thoroughly as she was. "Lucy?"

She nodded slowly, not taking her eyes off him, wondering why the years had made him even more attractive than ever. It didn't seem fair. Not when she'd spent the past six years thinking he must have started losing that thick, golden-brown hair, or added a spare tire to that trim, muscular form.

No.

The man was gorgeous. Truly, without-a-doubt, mouth-wateringly handsome, every bit as hot as he'd been the first time she'd laid eyes on him. She'd been twenty-two, he one year older.

They'd shared an amazing holiday season.

And had never seen one another again.

Until now.

Find out what happens in
IT HAPPENED ONE CHRISTMAS
by Leslie Kelly.
Available December 2011, only from Harlequin® Blaze™

HBEXP1211